The Bayeux Embroidery

Also by Howard of Warwick

The First Chronicles of Brother Hermitage
The Heretics of De'Ath
The Garderobe of Death
The Tapestry of Death

Continuing Chronicles of Brother Hermitage
Hermitage, Wat and Some Murder or Other
Hermitage, Wat and Some Druids
Hermitage, Wat and Some Nuns

Yet More Chronicles of Brother Hermitage
The Case of the Clerical Cadaver
The Case of the Curious Corpse
The Case of the Cantankerous Carcass

Interminable Chronicles of Brother Hermitage
A Murder for Mistress Cwen
A Murder for Master Wat
A Murder for Brother Hermitage

The Umpteenth Chronicles of Brother Hermitage
The Bayeux Embroidery
The Chester Chasuble
The Hermes Parchment

Brother Hermitage Diversions
Brother Hermitage in Shorts (Free!)
Brother Hermitage's Christmas Gift

Howard of Warwick's Middle Ages crisis: (History-ish.)
The Domesday Book (No, Not That One.)
The Domesday book (Still Not That One.)
The Magna Carta (Or Is It?)

Explore the whole sorry business and join the mailing list at
howardofwarwick.com

Another funny book from The Funny Book Company:
Greedy by Ainsworth Pennington

The Chronicles of Brother Hermitage

The Bayeux Embroidery

Howard of Warwick

your obedient servant

First published in 2019 by
The Funny Book Company
Dalton House
60 Windsor Ave
London SW19 2RR
United Kingdom
funnybookcompany.com

A catalogue card for this book
is available from the British Library.

ISBN 978-1-9998959-9-0

Cover design by Double Dagger
Typeset by Wynne Editorial
Printed in the UK by Clays Ltd

CONTENTS

Stupendous thanks are due to:

Mary

Susan Fanning

Karen Nevard Downs

Lydia Reed

Claire Ward

Caput I

Your Mission, and You're Going to Accept It

Brother Hermitage, Wat the Weaver and Cwen stood waiting outside the tent of King William of England, Duke of Normandy. This expanse of canvas was pitched on a field just off the northern road from Derby, and the place was busy with Normans going about their business. What that business was, was none of their business, and so they just stood and did their waiting in silence.

Of all the accommodations that had sprung up when the great caravan came to a halt, they knew this was William's tent because the guard, who was standing not five feet away, had yelled the king's title at them at the top of his voice. He had screamed with pride that this was William's tent and that they were now standing outside it.

'You have been summoned to the tent of King William of England, Duke of Normandy,' the guard added at full volume for the world to hear. Being summoned was obviously a great honour and the people before him would probably be grateful that he was letting everyone know.

'Yes, thank you.' Brother Hermitage nodded his polite acknowledgement and gave a little smile.

The guard scowled back. He was clearly happy that he had imparted the necessary information but was worried that these three people did not seem to be taking their privilege seriously. A young monk, a very well-dressed looking merchant with an impudent look under his unkempt black hair, and a slip of girl who kept glaring at him. These were not the sort of people who deserved to be summoned to the king's tent. Perhaps there was a mistake and his scowl would uncover it.

He stood tall and proud, but these three were almost slouching. It was a disgrace. The greatest achievement of his life was to be shouting at people outside the tent of the king. Of course, it was his duty and he had been ordered to be here. Perhaps one day he'd be summoned, but he knew in his heart that this was a dream too far.

Still, they were Saxons, so what could you expect? As far as he had been able to tell, the whole country was full of savages. It was highly likely that the king had summoned them here so he could kill them. What a wonderful way to go.

'Can we go in?' Wat asked, nodding towards the tent flap.

'Can you what?' The guard's voice had been loud before, now it was almost shaking the ground and had risen towards a shriek.

'Go in,' Wat repeated, nonchalantly. 'You know, into the tent we've been summoned to go into. This one.' He pointed to confirm they were all talking about the same tent.

'Into the king's tent?' The guard's response was that of a man whose outrage had discovered appalling new heights.

'That's the one,' Wat confirmed.

'No, you may not.' The man almost bounced on his feet and the urge to hit someone was oozing from him. 'What you may do is wait here. Right here.'

Wat shrugged that they could do that. 'Shall we shout at the king then?'

The guard obviously couldn't comprehend this statement.

'He won't be able to hear us from here unless we shout,' Cwen said. 'Him having summoned us and all. He probably wants to speak to us. Like he usually does.'

This was simply too much for the guard who just looked repeatedly from left to right, desperately seeking some escape from this nonsense.

Relief came as the tent flap was thrown aside and the shape of William's chief doer of horrible things, Le Pedvin, emerged.

There was really no need for the tent to flap much at all to let this figure through, as it had all the substance of a slight breeze that passed by last week. How the cadaverous shape managed to kill people so frequently was a mystery, but not one that any of the Saxons wanted to test.

Le Pedvin's sole, despairing eye considered the small gathering before him, the patch across his other showing no interest at all. 'What are you waiting for?' he asked the idiots who stood outside a tent when they'd been summoned to attend the king.

'Yes,' the guard barked. 'What are you waiting for? Get in the tent this minute.' He waved his pikestaff in the required direction.

Hermitage, Wat and Cwen all gave the guard their own looks. Hermitage's was of puzzlement that he'd only just been saying that they couldn't go in. He did wish people would make their minds up. Wat's was contemptuous for a fool who would bite his own ear off if he was told to. Cwen's look was the one that made the guard shiver.

'I don't know,' the guard muttered to Le Pedvin as the three entered the tent. 'Bloody Saxons, eh?'

Inside the king's tent, all was as it should be for a monarch whose chief occupation was conquering people. It was more military than regal, with weapons and armour scattered about. A large table towards the back did have a significant quantity of parchment on it, as well as a scribe who sat behind it, reading things, putting them down and making notes with a quill as the matter demanded. Every now and again the scribe looked up, as if hoping that he could have the king's attention - at last. He saw that he couldn't and went back to his work.

Hermitage was fascinated by the sheer volume of parchment, and slightly horrified by the way it was thrown hither and thither with careless abandon. He longed to read the words that flashed by but suspected they would be very mundane. He was quietly confident that King William would not have a commentary on the lexicography of the post-Exodus prophets amongst his urgent business.

The king was sitting in an ordinary camp chair, considering a map that he held in his hands. Doubtless, it showed the world split into the two bits that mattered; what he had already conquered, and the bits he hadn't done yet.

'They're here.' It was clear that Le Pedvin couldn't see why the king wanted the Saxons at all.

William looked up from his map and considered the three of them. There was nothing particular about his face, no marks or disfigurements that would warrant the trickle of fear that ran down three Saxon backs. Even Cwen, who thought that fear was what other people did, found her breathing had sharpened. The face was simply that of a conqueror. A man of middle age who went round conquering things; people, mainly. And he did his conquering by killing; a lot of killing. The face simply said that he was ready to do some more at any moment now. An enquiring glance from William was usually enquiring if you'd like to be killed now or later.

'Ah, the monk,' William said, recognition coming to him. The look of impending doom lifted from his face and the Saxons breathed again.

'Your Majesty.' Hermitage bowed.

'And the other two.'

Wat bowed while Cwen tried hard not to but found her head had gone down against her will.

'A weaver.' William gestured towards Wat and made the word half a question, half a statement.

'Indeed, Your Majesty.' Hermitage agreed. He could feel Cwen's eyes burning into him, instructing him to point out that she was a weaver as well.

King William's eyes were right in front of him though and he felt they took priority.

The king just shook his head slightly, confused why a Saxon

monk had a weaver with him. Perhaps it was just what they did around here. 'Could be useful, I suppose.' He moved on from the question.

Hermitage gave Wat and Cwen a worried look. He knew perfectly well what the reason for his summoning would be: murder. It was always murder. He was the King's Investigator, after all. It was a position he didn't want and one he suspected the king didn't even understand, but there wasn't much he could do about it. King William was the conqueror and it was generally advisable to do whatever he wanted.

Having been made Investigator under Harold, he supposed that he should be grateful that the role continued. Many of those who had served under Harold were now under the ground, so it could be worse.

But weavers? How on earth could weavers be useful in a murder? Was there a King's Weaver perhaps? Or had there been? Had he been called to investigate the murder of a weaver? The weavers' grand moot he attended with Wat had ended up with him investigating murder, but he put that down to the fact that everywhere he went someone ended up being killed.[*] If it was bad enough being the King's Investigator; being an innocent bystander while he was around was positively life threatening.

'What do you know about nuns?' the king asked.

It never took much to confuse Hermitage. People who said things that appeared to be completely disconnected usually did the trick.

'Nuns, Majesty?'

'Yes, nuns. I assume you have them here.'

Hermitage quickly understood that the king meant England. 'Oh, yes, Majesty. We do have nuns.' He knew they had nuns. Nuns scared the life out of him. In fact, they scared the life out of most people; it was probably part of their training. He'd had

---

[*] *A Murder for Master Wat* makes a whole book out of this sentence.

to deal with nuns as well as weavers in his role as investigator.*
Could it be he was working his way through the murder of every
role in the kingdom? He'd be Investigator for years at this rate.

'Are you all right?'

Hermitage was brought back to his senses as he realised he
had drifted off a bit.

'Of course, he isn't,' Le Pedvin coughed.

'Nuns, Majesty, and weavers,' Hermitage nodded. 'Yes, we
have them both.'

'Good. There are a lot of dead ones I want you to look at.'

Hermitage didn't have any words that worked in response to
that. A lot of dead nuns? Who on earth would have a lot of dead
nuns that needed looking at? He knew that William did kill a lot
of people, but they were generally soldiers or nobles. Nuns were
hardly likely to take arms against the invader; certainly not in
great numbers. He was sure he would have heard of the slaughter of an army of nuns if it had taken place.

And what was he supposed to do if he did look at a lot of
dead nuns? Confirm that they were dead? Surely anyone could
do that. 'Dead nuns, Majesty?' It was always worth checking,
perhaps he'd misheard.

'Dead weaving nuns,' the king said.

No, it wasn't worth checking at all. The king had simply gone
mad. Or madder.

'I see,' Hermitage nodded cautiously. If the king wanted him
to go away and investigate some dead weaving nuns, he would
just smile politely and go off to do so. If he couldn't actually find
any, that was hardly his fault. He didn't dare look directly at Wat
and Cwen but could tell that their understanding of what was
going on here was no better than his.

'I'm not mad,' the king said. Hermitage nodded at that as
well.

'My brother has them.'

Hermitage took his time replying, just to make sure he was following this. 'Your brother has some dead weaving nuns.'

'Well, half brother, Odo.'

'Aha.'

'And obviously the nuns aren't weaving any more, not now that they're dead.'

'Of course.' Hermitage agreed with this. Everyone knew that weaving nuns stopped weaving when they died.

The king sighed. That was never a good sign. 'What's so difficult about this?' he grumbled. 'My half-brother, Odo, has gathered some nuns to make a great tapestry of recent events. I made him Bishop of Bayeux and he's going to hang the thing in the church there, so that everyone can see what a great success the conquest of England has been.'

That did make some sense, of a sort; at least it didn't seem completely insane. Hermitage had only heard rumours of this tapestry and it sounded most peculiar. Still, kings were laws unto themselves and so he supposed their brothers were as well. If this Odo wanted a tapestry, he could have one. If he wanted it made by nuns, why not? Hermitage felt that he didn't really want to pry into this too much. He also felt he wasn't going to get much choice.

He chanced a glance at Wat, whose face said that he too knew of this tapestry. Why it had to be made by nuns was a question that could wait until later. Preferably much later.

'A Bayeux tapestry,' Hermitage said.

The king thought about this for a moment. 'Yes, if you like. Don't think it needs a name though; it's only a tapestry.'

Hermitage could feel Wat stiffen slightly at this.

'And the nuns,' Hermitage pressed on, reluctantly. 'They're sort of, erm..,'

'Dead. Yes. The nuns are dead. Odo sent word that they were all working on the tapestry and now they're dead.'

Hermitage really didn't like the sound of them all being dead. 'How many are there, I mean were there? Nuns, that is?'

'I don't know, do I?' The king's anger started to seep out; seep out like a waterfall from a very high place. A waterfall full of fallen logs, most likely; with points on. 'You'll have to ask Odo, won't you?'

'Naturally,' Hermitage agreed, although he couldn't see that there was anything natural in any of this.

'Off you go then,' the king waved that they could leave now that they had all the information they needed. 'I told him I have just the monk for a job like this. I want this tapestry finished and up on display, so you'd better sort this dead nun business out.'

'Excellent,' Hermitage said; another word he wasn't at all happy about. There was one question remaining though. 'We'll erm, just set off to, erm, Bayeux then. Somehow.' He didn't like to ask the king to provide transport. It seemed a bit rude, somehow.

'Bayeux? What on earth are you going there for?'

Hermitage had been lost so often in such a short space of time that he really didn't have any sort of answer. 'Odo. Bishop. Bayeux. Tapestry?' It made sense to him.

'Yes, but he's the Earl of Kent, isn't he?'

'Is he?'

'Of course, he is, you idiot.'

'Told you,' Le Pedvin drawled.

'So that's where the dead nuns are.' Wat helped Hermitage out.

'Exactly.'

'Kent?' Hermitage said.

'You have heard of it?' William sounded as if he was losing confidence in his investigator.

Hermitage would be quite happy about that, but people probably died from William's lack of confidence.

'Of course, of course. Kent, yes, quite. Canterbury, the archbishop and such.'

The king was frowning at them all now. 'You did deal with the murder of Umair, the Saracen? That was you?'

'Oh, yes, Majesty.' Hermitage confirmed.[*]

'And de Turold's little accident?'

'Absolutely.'[†]

'As well as the business in Normandy?'

'That too.'[‡]

King William just shook his head as if he was finding this hard to believe.

'This is going to end badly,' Le Pedvin said to himself, loudly enough that everyone else could hear.

Hermitage thought that it hadn't started that well.

'Well, get off and see what you can do. But be warned.' The king raised a finger.

Hermitage didn't know what else there could be to be warned about.

'Odo is not the reasonable man I am.' William smiled.

Hermitage couldn't stop his mouth dropping open.

'When things don't go his way, he tends to take it out on people. You'd better sort out these dead nuns of his or you'll be joining them.'

For the very briefest of moments Hermitage had thought that this mission might not be too bad. It had raised the opportunity for travel to Kent and the shrine of Canterbury. He would be in the same town as the archbishop himself; what a treasure.

He had also reasoned that William, being the king of the Normans, must be the worst of the lot. Surely, Normans would make the most Norman person their leader? To hear that he was nicer than his brother was a real shock. King William terrified him; Le Pedvin wormed inside his head and worried him from

---

[*] *The Case of The Curious Corpse* for reference.

[†] *The Garderobe of Death* for reference as well.

[‡] *Hermitage, Wat and Some Murder or Other*; what a lot of references.

the inside out. What this brother was capable of, he dreaded to think.

The glare from King William said that he was going to find out very soon.

South by Further South

As expected, the time allowed for them to prepare for this mission was none at all. The king had given them their instructions, and he wasn't going to understand if they said they had something else to do first, or that they needed to go home and pack.

Even though he had summoned them to resolve a horrible and potentially dangerous issue, his only help was to point in the rough direction of Kent and grunt that they should be on their way by now. As they left, the shouting guard waved his pike for added encouragement.

The road to Kent would be a long one, doubtless full of its own challenges and dangers, never mind what waited for them when they got there.

'It's disgusting,' Wat said, once they were safely out of range of any Norman ears.

Hermitage was relieved to hear that his own thoughts were shared. 'I'm not sure I'd use exactly that word, but I agree.' He nodded as they walked along. 'I really thought that King William would be the epitome of the Norman,' he said. 'To think that there could be worse behaviour than we have already witnessed is most disturbing.'

Wat gave him a very odd look. 'What are you talking about?'

'The Normans, of course. "Disgusting" seems a bit rude, but I agree that there is something very worrying in the prospect of this brother of William.'

'I'm not talking about the Normans.' Wat sounded quite exasperated. 'I mean the nuns.'

'The nuns?'

'Of course. We know the Normans are disgusting; how could you be more disgusted by more of them?'

Hermitage did feel a pang of guilt as he recalled the reason for their journey. 'You are right. The death of these nuns is a truly awful event. It must take precedence over any other concerns.'

'I do wish you'd concentrate on the problem in hand,' Wat complained. He rolled his eyes at Cwen, as if failing to understand how Hermitage could be so stupid.

Hermitage was lost and looked it.

'The weaving,' Wat prompted.

'The weaving?'

'The nuns are weaving.' Wat said this very plainly.

'Well, they were,' Cwen clarified.

'That's something, I suppose.' Wat still didn't sound happy. He laid the very serious issue out for Hermitage's consideration. 'You can't have nuns weaving.'

'Erm,' Hermitage said.

'Weaving must be done by proper professional weavers; people who've learned their skills over years. They've been approved by masters and they're known to the trade. If some nun can pick up a loom and call herself a weaver, where will it end? I mean, I don't go around nunning, do I?'

'Nunning?'

'Or whatever it is nuns do. I'm a weaver, I stick to my trade. It's only reasonable I should expect nuns to do the same. What's going to happen to my craft if a bunch of old nuns start doing it?'

'We don't know that they were old.'

'Doesn't matter. Young nuns, old nuns, they're all nuns.'

Hermitage had to agree with that.

'What's disgusting is nuns doing weaving at all. If this Odo wants some weaving done, he goes to a weaver. Not a nun. They haven't been properly trained, they won't be in the guild and the standard of work will be shoddy in the extreme.' He seemed to be saving the worst for last. 'And they'll doubtless be cheaper than anyone else.'

'If William's description of Odo is anything to go by, the nuns may not have had a choice,' Cwen said.

'Everyone's heard of Wat the Weaver,' Wat went on. 'If Odo wants a tapestry done for Bayeux, he's only got to ask. Doesn't take much effort, does it?'

Hermitage couldn't help but gape at both of them.

'And pay, of course.' Wat's face said that a truly horrible thought had arrived. 'I bet he's getting these nuns to weave for free; how outrageous is that? They won't be doing a decent job anyway and he's taking money from the mouths of starving weavers.'

'You don't know any starving weavers,' Hermitage pointed out with a rare frisson of sarcasm. 'We have a Norman who may be worse than William and a number of nuns who have been murdered. Your chief concern is that they shouldn't have been weaving in the first place because you want the money?'

'Well,' Wat back-tracked slightly. 'You're making it sound worse than it is. But it is a concern.'

'But not the primary one, perhaps?'

'We'll see.' Wat wasn't giving up. 'What if he wanted some monk-things done and asked the nearest nun instead? How would you feel?'

'Quite relieved, I think.'

Wat ignored this. 'When we get there, we'll need to find out just what is going on. If these Normans are going to use nuns for their weaving, well, I don't know what we'll do.'

'Probably have to put up with it?' Hermitage suggested. 'The Normans being in charge now?'

Wat didn't seem to have an answer to this. 'It's not right,' was all he could come up with.

'I'm not sure this Odo is the sort of fellow to enquire carefully about who should be doing his weaving anyway.' Hermitage tried to soothe his friend's concerns, even if he thought they were totally unjustified. 'He sounds the demanding type, and if the nuns were close at hand, it's no surprise he turned to them.'

Wat just shook his head at such nonsense. 'You don't turn to a nun for a tapestry. It's not natural.'

Hermitage sighed. 'You don't turn to a monk to get your murders investigated, but that didn't stop William.'

'Bloody Normans,' Wat said.

That was something upon which they could all agree.

◆　　◆　　◆

Their journey south towards Kent was remarkably uneventful. The most disturbing aspect of it was how well it went. This was not what they had been expecting at all. The Normans they met on the way seemed positively anxious to help. A Norman anxious to help was a whole new experience and one that worried the habit off Hermitage. One or two even offered to organise lodging for them or refresh their supplies.

'This Odo even scares the armour off the other Normans,' Cwen observed helpfully. 'He must be really horrible.'

'I'm sure it's nothing like that,' Hermitage said, sincerely hoping that it was nothing like that.

'We've never been given this much help before, even when we were investigating the murder in William's own camp.'

'It's like pass the flaming log,' Wat said.

'I beg your pardon?'

'Pass the flaming log. It's a game we used to play as apprentices. You get a flaming log out of the fire and throw it to one another. You have to get rid of it quick or it burns your hand.' Wat smiled at the recollection. 'The one who burns their hand loses,' he explained.

'That sounds like an extremely stupid thing to do, if I may say so,' Hermitage said. 'Especially for weaving apprentices who need their hands for their trade.'

'Boys,' Cwen coughed.

'It was fun. And now we're the flaming log. These Normans are passing us along quickly so Odo can't blame them when we go missing.'

'Go missing? Why would we go missing?' Hermitage was pretty sure that they knew the way.

'Robbers, accidents, bears; it's a dangerous country.'

'Bears? I don't think there are any bears in Kent.' Cwen dismissed that problem.

'Snakes then. Whatever stops us getting to Odo will be someone's fault. Each Norman wants to make sure it's not theirs.'

'They can't know that we're going to see Odo,' Hermitage reasoned. 'The king only just sent us himself, how can word have got ahead of us?'

'You'd be surprised how quickly word can travel when it wants to,' Wat said.

'And these dead nuns have probably been the main topic of conversation for weeks,' Cwen speculated. 'I mean, it's not every day you get a bunch of dead nuns.'

'Dead weaving nuns,' Wat added sourly.

'Quite right, dead weaving nuns. Most people don't have anything to talk about at all most of the time. It's the weather or the crops or the animals. Dead nuns must be quite exciting. And we don't know how long ago they got killed.'

Wat was nodding at this exploration of the issue. Hermitage was trying to ignore it and think about something else completely.

'The people of Kent could have been going on about their dead nuns for weeks now. Odo's told them he's sent for the King's Investigator and so the whole place is on the lookout for us.'

'But.' Hermitage very much wanted there to be a but here, quite a big one.

'A monk and two weavers?' Cwen said. 'Pretty easy to spot. And that's why we're being hurried along. This Odo will want his dead nuns looked at. He's probably taking it out on everyone now. You know what Normans are like at taking it out on people. And at taking it out of people.'

'He is a bishop.' Hermitage tried to cling to a straw of hope.

'And they're better, are they?' Wat asked.

Hermitage was about to say that of course they were, when he recalled most of the bishops he'd ever met. He said nothing.

'A mad Norman with dead nuns who's also a bishop. It's an interesting combination.'

'And he's sitting in Kent waiting for us to sort it all out for him.' Cwen sounded horribly gleeful about this.

◆   ◆   ◆

Such was the encouragement that the Normans gave them that they arrived in London before they knew it. Even Hermitage was starting to understand that people wanted them to get in front of Odo as quickly as possible. There was palpable relief as they passed by; relief that someone was going to deal with Odo, which meant they didn't have to.

Hermitage had always been very good at worrying and was now getting a lot of practice. He was even able to reason that the prospect of an awful experience was more intensely worrying than the event itself. He had been in the middle of some horrible events and had managed them pretty well, he thought.

Being told that he was going to a horrible event in a few days' time really gave his mind time to ponder. The pondering usually took the worst that could possibly happen and then festered. He had already concluded that this Odo would want to know what had happened to his nuns the moment they arrived. There would be no invitation to consider events carefully, or even be told what the events were, most likely. It would be straight in with "right, you're the investigator, are you? Who killed my nuns then?"

William was bad enough, but he did give some time for investigation. Never enough, of course, and he was always very demanding. He folded his arms a lot and grumbled and complained, but then waited until Hermitage had something helpful to say. He never said thank you, or anything like that, of course. That would be completely unreasonable from a Norman and a king.

All Hermitage knew was that Odo was worse. William had said so. Hermitage had simply extrapolated that Odo would be worse in every conceivable way.

By the time they arrived at the River Thames, Odo had become ten feet tall with the teeth of a lion, the temper of a demon and the power to pull monks apart with his bare hands; which he did quite frequently.

'Ferry sir?' a voice rang out in the early morning mist as they stood by the great bridge over the river.

Their lodgings in London had been comfortable enough, but it felt as if they were within striking distance of Odo now. Everyone wanted them to move on as fast as possible and get on with their mission. The sooner they did so, the less risk there would be of Odo deciding a visit to London would solve his problems.

'Ferry?' Wat called back. 'We're standing by the bridge.'

'I know,' the voice called back, getting louder as it approached. 'That's why you'll want the ferry.'

Hermitage felt recognition of that voice swim through his head, recognition and an overwhelming sense of dread resignation.

Out of the swirling fog of the river a figure appeared, walking decisively up the beach from the waters that lay below, his appearance doing nothing to counter the thought that the river had thrown some spirit from its depths at this early hour; a spirit it didn't want any more as it was making the river bed messy.

'Oh, hello,' the figure said on arrival.

A long grey beard bobbed on a chin that seemed to have a life of its own, twitching, as it did, without any coordination with the body that supported it. That body could have been thrown together from drift wood; the leftover bits that scavengers didn't want. A single tooth hovered towards the back of the beard, standing sentinel to a mouth that no decent person would even think about.

In the midst of this picture of hopeless decay, bright, lively eyes, jumped about as they considered the potential passengers before them. Those eyes were plainly as mad as a man who ran a ferry under a bridge.

'More?' Cwen asked in disbelief.

'You're them people,' More the boatman concluded with his usual, rather insane happiness.

'Oh God,' Wat muttered as he ran a hand over his face.

'What are you doing here?' Cwen asked. 'We left you in Wales.'*

'I run a ferry now,' More said excitedly, giving no explanation of how he had got here. An observer might conclude that was because he didn't know.

'Someone's got to ask.' Wat sounded very resigned. 'Why are you running a ferry under a bridge?'

'Best place,' More nodded at his own cleverness.

'And why's that?'

'It's where all the people come.' More was hugely enthusiastic about this, but then he was hugely enthusiastic most of the time, usually without good reason.

'I'm sure they do.' Wat held an arm out to draw More's attention to the magnificence of London Bridge that stretched out before them, disappearing into the mist. 'They come because there's a bridge here. A bridge they use to get across the river. A bridge that means they don't need a ferry.'

---

*   *Hermitage, Wat and Some Druids* saw More the boatman at his best. He pops up quite regularly, best or not. *The Domesday Book (No, Not That One)* is another one and *The Case of the Cantankerous Carcass* - although that might have just been a relative.

More just looked very puzzled by this, but he did consider the bridge. 'That thing's not safe.'

'Not safe? It's been there for hundreds of years. The Romans had a bridge here.'

'Falling down.' More shook his head with a worried look. His beard followed the movement, but it looked as if it was doing so because it wanted to, not because it was joined on. 'Everyone knows that.'

'Knows what?' Cwen asked, looking from bridge to ferryman.

'London Bridge is falling down.'

'Falling down?'

'Falling down. The new king's said he's going to repair it, but you know what kings are like. You get half way across that thing and you'll be in the river, mark my words.'

'And it's safer on a ferry with you, is it?' Cwen enquired, with heavy doubt.

'Oh, yis. Nice solid boat get you across no trouble. No risk of the bridge falling down under you. Or the spirits pushing you in.'

'The spirits?'

'Spirits of the river. They don't like the bridge. Well, what river spirit would want a great thing like that going over the top of them? They're always up there they are, pushing people in.'

'It's not you then?' Wat asked. 'Up there pushing people in to make sure they use the ferry? Perhaps you go and rescue them, for a fee?'

More looked horrified at the very idea. 'I can't help it if they're grateful, can I?'

Hermitage considered the scene before him and the options they had. 'Can we just board the boat and get it over with?'

'Why on earth would we get on the boat?' Cwen asked, sounding positively annoyed by the idea.

'We know we're going to,' Hermitage explained. 'It's only a matter of time.'

'There's a perfectly good bridge that we can just walk over.'

'I know, but there's More as well. He's unavoidable. It's fate.'
Hermitage felt as powerless as he ever had.

'Fate?' I didn't think you believed in that sort of thing.'

'God's will then.' Hermitage shrugged. 'There's no avoiding More. Whenever he's here we end up doing what he wants. Why don't we just surrender straight away? It'll save us all a lot of time.'

'That's ridiculous.'

'He's right,' Wat's voice sounded bereft of hope.

'What?'

'We do always end up in one of his boats.'

'Just take a step onto the bridge.' Cwen's anger at their idiocy was becoming clear.

'We can't,' Hermitage was almost in a daze. He knew the story of the river Hades and the ferryman, and that it was all complete nonsense, of course. He'd also bumped into More too many times for it to be coincidence. Despite his best efforts, and most worthy thoughts, there was something in his head that said he needed to stay on the right side of More; he'd be meeting him again in very different circumstances.

'Of course, we can.' Cwen took a pace towards the bridge. Once on the threshold, she turned to them. 'Coming?'

'It's only tuppence,' Wat said.

'How do you know that?'

'It always is.'

'Please yourself.' Cwen waved them away and strode off on to the bridge.

Hermitage, Wat and More stood silent in the mist, waiting.

Cwen's steps faded as she walked away, the intensity of the sound betraying the annoyance they were going to face on the other side.

Hermitage was waiting for the invitation to get in whatever contraption More was calling a boat these days, but the ferryman made no move, and was clearly waiting for something himself.

Very rapid steps approached them now and Cwen reappeared, not looking very happy at all.

'It's sixpence,' she complained.

More held a hand out to invite them all on to his ferry.

'Why didn't you just say the ferry was cheaper, you idiot.' Cwen marched ahead of them, clearly anxious to get on the boat, and off it again, as quickly as possible.

Caput III

More of More

I could take you to Kent,' More sounded very enthusiastic about this as he rowed them into the middle of the river.

'Not bloody likely,' Cwen snapped back.

The boat turned out to be quite solid and serviceable, a bit of a surprise considering the condition of its owner; if he was its owner of course. More had a bit of history when it came to using other people's boats for his ferry services. Services the owners of the boats only came to discover after they sank.

Cwen was sitting comfortably in the back of the boat with Hermitage, who was adopting his normal procedure when travelling on water; he was gripping the sides of the vessel until his hands turned white, he had his eyes shut and was praying silently not to be snatched to the depths by the monsters that everyone knew lurked below; monsters that particularly liked monks.

Wat was in front of More, shifting his gaze from the direction they were going to the back of More as he pulled away on the oars. Despite the old man's meagre frame, his pull was strong and regular, and the outflowing tide helped speed them along the river.

More's endless stream of inane chatter had extricated the fact that they were going to Kent. Hermitage had managed not to tell him why they were going, or what horrors they were facing, but it was hard not to tell a ferryman why you were using his ferry.

'Look,' More explained, taking his hands off the oars. 'I wouldn't even have to row; the river will take us there. It goes to Kent.'

'Could you row please,' Cwen shouted.

'Be quicker than you walking all the way round,' More went on. 'And it's a nice day for a boat trip.'

'Nice day!' Cwen just pointed towards the other bank, which was now visible through the steam and damp of the river.

'I took those Normans from Kent.' More nodded to himself. 'They're still alive.' He clearly recognised the source of Cwen's worry.*

'Another tuppence?' Wat asked, wearily.

'Oh, no,' More comforted them. 'Sixpence. It's a long way to Kent.'

'Perhaps we'll walk,' Cwen bit the words out.

'We'll take the boat.' Hermitage said this as if he had no choice in the matter, which he felt that he didn't anyway. It was a statement of fact rather than any independent decision.

More grinned to expose his tooth once more and hauled on the left-hand oar to swing them downstream towards Kent. 'You going to see the bishop?' he asked. It was obvious that he had very little idea what a bishop was, he just knew there was one in Kent.

'That would be marvellous,' Hermitage said, still in his stupor as he felt he was being driven along by an unknown hand. 'But no, we have other business.'

'I could come with you,' More enthused. 'I came to Wales, didn't I?'

'Yes,' Cwen said. 'But you didn't stay there, did you?'

'There was some trouble,' More excused himself. He sounded as if he didn't want to talk about the trouble; and wasn't actually quite sure what it had been.

'Why am I not surprised?' Cwen asked.

'I don't know,' More replied, genuinely.

'I'd stick to your ferry, if I were you,' Hermitage said.

---

* *The Domesday Book (No, Not That One)*: More's place in the history of Britain.

'I'd like to see a bishop.' More nodded happily to himself that he might do that anyway.

'We're not going to see the bishop.' Cwen spelled it out.

'Be a shame to miss him, as you're passing by.'

'He's not on display.' Cwen's irritation still burned.

'We're going to see Odo,' Hermitage said, blankly. 'King William's brother.'

There was a silence on the river. 'I'll just drop you off then.' More was suddenly a lot less interested in joining the company. 'Lots of ferrying to do.'

'You've heard about him, have you?' Wat asked.

'Oh, just this and that,' More replied in an offhand manner.

'What's worse?' Hermitage asked. 'This, or that?'

More took a moment to look around them, just to make sure no one was within ear shot. The others looked around the open expanse of river as well, wondering why on earth he would think anyone could be listening at all, unless it was a mermaid; and any mermaid that ventured into the filth of the Thames was most likely to be floating on the surface not doing anything much anymore.

He beckoned them close with a bony finger. 'Horrors,' he said.

Hermitage surprised himself by not being totally paralysed by this news. He supposed it was because that was exactly what he had expected.

'Any horrors in particular, or just general horrors?' Cwen enquired.

'And him a man of the church.' More gave no help on the horrors.

'So, there's horrors then?' Cwen checked. 'Lot of them, I expect.'

'Oh, yes,' More confirmed with a sorrowful shake of the head.

'And all over the place.'

'And all down to Odo the 'Orrible.'

'Odo the 'Orrible?' Wat snorted a laugh. 'Who made that up?'

More thought for a moment. 'I think he did. They talk funny, these Normans; can't say aitch. If they could I suppose he'd be called Hodo. Hodo the Horrible, that'd be better.'

'Not much,' Hermitage grumbled.

'But you've never met him, or been anywhere near?' Cwen said.

'Me? Lord no. Wouldn't catch me going down there.'

'Unless someone was paying you sixpence,' Wat pointed out.

'Ah, well, there's Kent and then there's Kent.'

'Is there?'

'That's it.' More bubbled with his fascinating knowledge of the county. 'This bit's all right.' More waved over to his left where the land was low and marshy. 'Of course, you've got your Archybishop up this bit, that keeps things nice.'

'Archybishop?' Hermitage had to ask.

'Yis. His church has lots of arches, that's why he's the Archybishop and in charge of everyone else. I thought you'd know that, being a monk and all.'

'You'd think I would.' Hermitage really didn't want to try and explain anything to More.

'The Archybishop's in Cantyburh, so it's all right round there. It's down Dover way you don't want to go.'

'We'll bear that in mind.' Cwen shook her head.

'So, you can take us as far as Canytburh; I mean Canterbury,' Wat said.

'Oh, that'd be extra,' More nodded happily.

'Extra? How can it be extra? You said you'd take us to Kent.'

'And I will. The River Darent's the border, I'll take you there.'

'Very generous. That's barely out of London,' Wat complained. 'You could at least take us to Chatham.'

'Chatham?' More was appalled. 'That's miles away.'

'Not really.'

'And there's a bit of a problem with Chatham.' More said this more to his boat than to them. 'They don't like me in Chatham.'

'Only Chatham?' Cwen asked.

'Told me not to go back.' More sounded as if this action was entirely unjustified.

'And that's our problem why, exactly?' Wat asked.

'I could do Gravesend,' More offered. 'I did a lot of work in Gravesend. Took them Normans from Gravesend.'

'And they like you in Gravesend?' Cwen checked.

'Well, no one's said I can't go back.' More seemed to think that this was as good as it got.

'All right,' Wat relented. 'Gravesend it is.'

'Good,' More grinned. 'That's sixpence.'

◆　　◆　　◆

Arrival and disembarkation at Gravesend couldn't come quick enough for the passengers. Hermitage simply wanted to get out of the boat as soon as he could. Wat and Cwen looked ready to throw More over the side of his own ferry by the time they arrived. The man's senseless ramblings had plumbed such depths that Cwen had resorted to calling for quiet as she thought she heard Odo the 'Orrible's boat coming up stream. More was content to accept this, rather than raise the host of obvious questions.

They hurried quickly up the muddy shoreline, while More started to bother the locals with his latest ferry offering: Gravesend to anywhere in the known world; sixpence.

The town was a haphazard collection of hovels and homes that had gathered at this spot with very little obvious rhyme or reason. Rich merchant homes stood aloof from the shelters of the working men and women, and the three wound their way between all of these until they could get to a track.

'Up here for a bit and we'll be on Watling Street,' Wat said. 'Turn left and we're off to Odo land.'

'How do we know exactly where he is?' Hermitage asked. 'All

William told us was that he was Earl of Kent.'

'I think the locals could tell us,' Cwen said. 'If the man's reputation is anything to go by, they'll all know where he is, mainly so they can avoid him.'

'Probably Dover,' Wat suggested. 'It's the port and there's bound to be one of William's castles there. If this Odo is as horrible as More said, he'll stay indoors at night, with big walls and guards all around him.'

Hermitage nodded that this seemed reasonable, even though he had no idea where Dover was. There was one burning question now that they were in Kent though. He knew it was selfish and entirely outside of their current task, but as he was here, he had to know. As nonchalantly as he could manage, he said, 'Does the road to Dover happen to go anywhere near, erm, Canterbury at all? By chance? Maybe?'

Wat smiled at him. 'Yes, Hermitage. The road goes through Canterbury itself.'

'Ah,' Hermitage managed to contain his excitement, or so he thought.

'But Odo's expecting us,' Cwen pointed out.

'Oh, yes, of course.' Hermitage was crestfallen.

'Don't tease the monk,' Wat reprimanded. 'We shall go to Canterbury, Hermitage, and you can see if the archbishop is in.'

'Oh, heavens, I don't want to see him, I mean, I couldn't, I wouldn't. Just to see the abbey established by the blessed Augustine would be a wonder.'

'Have you never been then?' Cwen asked. 'I thought all monks and church types went there.'

'It is a great place of pilgrimage,' Hermitage said. 'But all of the abbots I served said that I couldn't go.'

'Even your great friend, Abbo the Abbot.' Wat smirked at the name.*

---

*	Another regular visitor. See *The Case of the Cantankerous Carcass* and *A Murder for Brother Hermitage*

'He was going to arrange for a journey, but it never came about. He was happy for me to go alone but thought the dangers of the road too great.'

'In your case, he was probably right,' Cwen said.

'We haven't got there ourselves yet,' Wat observed, rather grimly. 'It's still a good thirty miles to Canterbury, a lot of ground to cover in dangerous country.'

Hermitage couldn't see why this road would be any worse than the others they'd trod. 'But, if we tell people we are journeying to Odo, they will doubtless help us as they have so far.'

'We're in Kent now, Odo country. Where most of the locals probably hate him. If they know we're Odo's men, they could think that dealing with us pretty harshly might be for the best. Show their resistance to the tyrant, that sort of thing.'

'Oh, Lord.'

'Anyway, we'll have to stop overnight somewhere. Let's get up to Watling Street and see what we can find. We certainly won't be in Canterbury until tomorrow. As far as anyone we meet is concerned, you're a monk on the way to Canterbury, Cwen and I are weavers who just shared the ferry. No mention of King's Investigators, dead nuns or Odo at all.'

Hermitage could see the sense of this, but also knew that he would not find it easy to lie.

'And it's true.' Cwen could see Hermitage's doubts, wandering all over his face. 'You are a monk on the way to Canterbury and we are weavers who shared the ferry. Right?'

'Ah, yes, right.' Hermitage was happy with that. In his time with Wat and Cwen he had come to accept that leaving things out wasn't quite as bad as a bald lie. If no one asked him a direct question, he should be all right.

'Here we are.' Wat pointed ahead to where the ground rose a good ten feet up to the surface of Watling Street.

Once again, Hermitage marvelled at the achievements of the Romans who had built this thoroughfare a thousand years ago. And here it was, still in regular use. Yes, large portions of the road had fallen away over the years to be patched and repaired quite poorly by the local people. True, those local people had also removed sections completely, so that they could build houses with the stone. But none of that was the Romans' fault.

He also pondered his own insignificance as he reasoned that this road had been here for six hundred years before St Augustine even set foot in England and became the first Archbishop of Canterbury. Would it be here in another thousand years? Judging from the current state of it, he thought not.

It was dawn when they had embarked on More's ferry and even with the tide pushing them along, the day had been taken up with the river journey. Evening was approaching as they climbed to the road and continued eastwards. Traffic was light, a few travellers making for their shelter for the night, and the occasional cart travelling empty on its way back from market.

'Next best place will be Rochester, if we can make it that far before towns lock up for the night.' Wat said. 'Otherwise it'll have to be some small place where we can get lodging.'

'And how far is Rochester?' Hermitage asked.

'About six miles I'd say. A good couple of hours if we get a move on.'

Hermitage looked to the sky and thought that full darkness would be with them long before that. Still, he thought, with some minor shame, Wat's purse usually managed to find them something.

'Perhaps there's a monastery nearby we can stay at.' Wat clearly had the same thought about the call on his purse.

'Aha, yes,' Hermitage said, with little enthusiasm, which he also felt ashamed of.

'Or perhaps we can ask this lot.' Cwen pointed down the road to the east, where clear movement was visible. It was fast movement as well, not the ambling passage of someone who really didn't mind when they arrived. This was a group of men of intent; men of intent on horses. This was either good news or bad. But then what other sort was there?

'Odo's men?' Hermitage wondered. 'He is expecting us. Maybe he's sent people to greet us.'

'For one thing, how would he know we were here? Who in their right mind would take a ferry with More? For another, a lone man on the shore would be a greeting, this looks like a small army.' Wat seemed resigned to whatever fate was now going to throw at them.

'It could be they don't want us at all,' Hermitage offered. 'As you say, who knows we're here? They are doubtless on their way somewhere else completely and will merely pass us by, ignoring us all together.' He nodded to them that this was the only reasonable conclusion.

'There they are,' the lead horseman called, putting all thought of a chance encounter straight out of Hermitage's head.

The three of them could do nothing but stand on the road and await the arrival of the horsemen.

There were six of them in total; not many, really, but as they were all a good five feet higher as they sat on their beasts, and they bore arms of significant quality and quantity, Hermitage rapidly concluded that the new arrivals were in charge. 'Hello,' he said.

'Hello?' Wat muttered under his breath.

'Just as we were told,' the leading horseman announced. 'A monk and two weavers.'

Hermitage longed to explore how this man had concluded that Wat and Cwen were weavers when there was no external sign. He sensibly thought that a man with a sword, high up on a horse was free to conclude whatever he wanted. He just nodded this time.

'You're coming with us,' the horseman said.

"Why? Who are you? Where are we going?" and "We'd rather not", were all reasonable statements in this situation. Hermitage kept his reason to himself.

The man leaned down from his horse and held his hand out towards Hermitage. As he looked on and thought that shaking hands was a nice gesture, he saw that Wat and Cwen had been hauled up to sit behind two of the other riders. He nearly collapsed at the thought of riding on a horse at all, let alone when it was already occupied.

With no invitation for discussion, Hermitage held out a weak hand of his own and was instantly launched into the air before finding himself on the back of the horse. This rider had done this sort of thing before.

Without a word, they were off. The horses could be trusted to navigate the poor roadway and they were quickly making rapid progress.

Every now and then, with a quick backward glance, the rider would check that Hermitage was still there.

'Erm,' Hermitage shouted, over the noise of their passage. 'You knew we were coming, then?'

'Of course,' the rider shouted back. 'Our master told us to look out for you on the road and bring you to him straight away.'

'Excellent,' Hermitage congratulated the horseman.

'Didn't expect you so soon, or as far east.'

'We took the river.'

'Really?' The man sounded surprised.

'We know a ferryman, name of More,' Hermitage made conversation.

The rider turned his head right round and looked at Hermitage with what appeared to be admiration. 'And you got off still dry? Amazing.'

'Are we going to erm, Dover then?' Hermitage enquired politely.

'What?' The man didn't seem happy with that suggestion, which was odd.

'Dover? To see Odo?'

'No, we are not going to see that stinking puss-pile of greed and sin.'

Oh dear, thought Hermitage; they'd been captured by rebels. This was not going to go down well with William.

'Stigand wants a word,' the rider said. He said it with an alarming tenor of threat, for someone who only wanted a word.

'Stigand?' Hermitage repeated. Doubtless this was the leader of the Kent rebellion and would be a fearsome Saxon warrior, fighting the Norman invasion, even though it was pretty much over now.

'Absolutely. No one passes through this part of the world without Stigand having a word. And you're not going anywhere near Odo until Stigand says so.'

'Good, good,' Hermitage said, thinking it was best. 'And this Stigand is where, exactly?' He had a vision of them being taken to some dank camp in the woods where rough men would be living in the wild. Stigand would be the one biting a chunk off a whole venison leg and spitting quite a lot.

The rider turned again and gave him a very odd look. 'Canterbury, of course.'

'Ah, Canterbury, I see.'

'Where else would the Archbishop of Canterbury be?'

The Old Archbishop Ploy

here you are, Hermitage,' Cwen smiled as they dismounted the horses in Canterbury. 'You do get to see the Archbishop of Canterbury. In a personal audience, no less.'

It was now full dark, and this had all been too much for Hermitage. His mind had simply not kept up with events. He knew that the archbishop was called Stigand, of course he did. He just didn't associate the name with bands of powerful horsemen who literally swept people up off the road.

In his mind, the archbishop was the most pious individual imaginable. Of course, he had to run the church and manage all the other bishops, which must be a bit of a handful, but he would spend most of his time in prayer, surely. He had the abbey and cathedral at Canterbury to pray in, after all.

The archbishop wouldn't have anything to do with bands of armed men roaming the country, whisking people to meetings in the middle of the night. That was all too, what was the word? Earthly, yes earthly. The Archbishop of Canterbury would not be an earthly fellow.

The three stood, largely helpless, in a small courtyard as the horses were led away by their riders. Riders who left no guidance as to what they should do now. Would Stigand come out to meet them? Surely not.

The courtyard was in the centre of a conclave of buildings that huddled together as if keeping secrets from the outside world. Here and there, lighted windows looked out on them like eyes, peering at the new arrivals to see if they could be trusted.

They had come through an arch into the yard, and to the left of this a small door opened, allowing a friendlier light to spill onto the ground.

A figure appeared in the doorway, holding a lamp and beckoning to them with some urgency. 'This way,' the lamp holder called. 'Make haste.'

With no better invitations this evening, the three of them moved towards the door.

Once inside, Hermitage saw that these were quite lavish apartments. A long corridor stretched out to their left, turning within a few yards, doubtless following the line of the courtyard buildings. Tapestries hung on the walls, sconces burned, and small tables and chairs sat along the walls as if they were spare, and had just been put out of the way.

Without further introduction, the man with the lamp, who was obviously a cleric of some sort, bustled along the corridor, beckoning occasionally to make sure they were following. He led them around the first bend and then stopped at a large and ornate door, set into the middle of the corridor on their right. He waited to make sure they were all present and correct before knocking.

'Enter,' a voice replied from behind the thick wood of the door.

Hermitage swallowed, hard. This door was about to open and reveal the Archbishop of Canterbury. He didn't even know anyone who had even seen the man, let alone been in the same room with him. He knew that he was going to be spoken to as well and would have to speak. That was going to be real trouble, but he would just have to face the problem when it arrived. He cleared his throat in preparation. His throat didn't feel terribly cooperative.

The cleric put down his lamp on one of the spare tables and pushed the door open.

The room revealed was a wonder. It was warmed by no less

than two fireplaces, one at either end. There were tapestries on the floor and the walls, and the straw was neatly arranged around the edges of the room. People would have to go over to the walls to relieve themselves, instead of doing it in the middle of the floor; how very civilised.

In the centre of the room sat a desk. Well, more of a table, really. Actually, more like the foundations for a decent sized house that had been polished to a shine that could reflect the glory of God himself.

Hermitage gaped for a moment, and then remembered himself. 'My Lord,' he said, bowing low. He was quite pleased he managed to get two words out.

An unimposing man in very fine clerical garb stood from behind the desk.

Hermitage was slightly disappointed to see that he wasn't holding his crozier and didn't have all the archbishop's regalia on. He knew that no one could go round wearing that all day; still, it was a shame.

The man even bowed to them. Such humility. 'Welcome,' he said, in a calm and quiet voice. 'Come with me; His Grace the archbishop awaits.'

If this wasn't the archbishop, Hermitage's imagination had run out of ideas. Of course, his imagination ran out of ideas quite quickly anyway, but he just looked around the room again, wondering what could be more magnificent than this.

The man behind the desk came out and nodded that they should follow him to the door they now saw was behind him, on the far side of the room. 'I am Aethelmaer, His Grace's amanuensis,' the man explained.

Hermitage couldn't stop himself thinking that this was a very nice room for an amanuensis.

Aethelmaer stopped at the door and gave the very lightest of knocks. Without waiting for a response, as if the knock had only been a formality, he pushed the door open and entered.

This next chamber was more modest than the first. Of course, it was lavish and comfortable, but was more workman-like, somehow. The desk here was large and imposing, but more of a normal size.

Hermitage's first impression was of the books that lined the walls. From floor to ceiling and wall to wall, volumes sat on shelves, their spines outwards, somehow turning their backs on the mundane and short-lived world of men. Those spines were the outer wall of knowledge, and Hermitage's overwhelming urge was to climb a ladder and have a peek over the wall.

It was only a moment before he remembered that there was an archbishop in the room with them.

Standing by the single fireplace to their right was a short man, with short cropped grey hair, dressed very simply. He was studying a parchment he held in his hand and turned to face the arrivals.

He was probably well over sixty years old but looked fit and well and healthy. But then, being archbishop probably meant that you got the best of everything anyway and so staying alive would be less of a problem than for normal people.

Hermitage had never seen the archbishop, nor had any description of him, so he had no idea if this was really the man, or yet another official. It would be hard to find a cleric who looked less like an archbishop, or at least Hermitage's idea of one.

'Ah.' The man put down his parchment and held his arms out wide. 'You have come, I am glad.'

Hermitage wanted to point out that they'd been snatched from the road and brought here, but he noticed the Episcopal ring on the man's finger and rapidly concluded that this really was Archbishop Stigand.

'Your Grace,' he said. He quickly stepped over to Stigand and knelt, head bowed.

Stigand smiled broadly and held out the ringed finger. More

by instinct than intention, Hermitage kissed the ring and then lowered his head.

He almost froze when he felt the archbishop's hands on his shoulders.

'Rise, Brother, rise. You are most welcome.'

Hermitage did so but was frozen to inaction.

Stigand patted his shoulders and then turned to face the others.

'Master Wat the Weaver; well I never,' he said, still smiling. 'Who would have thought that the chambers of the Archbishop of Canterbury would see the great Wat the Weaver just standing there. And invited in, no less.'

Wat said nothing but did look rather nonplussed, for once.

'I know that several of my colleagues take rather more of an interest in your works than they should.' And the Archbishop of Canterbury winked. At Wat the Weaver. 'Not that you do that sort of thing anymore, thanks to the attentions of Brother Hermitage, here.'

Now Wat was looking surprised and a little worried that this archbishop seemed to know a lot.

'And Mistress Cwen,' Stigand turned to Cwen with another smile.

Cwen just looked back.

'A very fine weaver yourself, if I may say so.'

Now it was Cwen's turn to be confused.

'We shan't tell the guilds, of course, but your skill is unmatched. I have heard tell of the Saint Patrick you produced and if the reports are true, I must see this work for myself.'

Hermitage looked on and couldn't believe that he saw Cwen blush. He had seen her turn red quite often, but never blush.

'Oh, erm, yes,' was the best she could manage.

The door opened again, and they realised that they hadn't noticed Aethelmaer leave. He returned now, bearing a large tray of wine and food.

'Sit, friends, sit,' Stigand beckoned. 'There is business we must discuss, and we must be quick about it, I fear.'

More like people in a daze than those following deliberate actions, Hermitage, Wat and Cwen sat at the chairs drawn up for them and faced the feast now laid out on Stigand's desk.

There was no way Hermitage was going to be able to put food and drink in his mouth while he was sat with the Archbishop of Canterbury.

Stigand was very relaxed and took a goblet and tore a chunk of bread from a loaf. 'You had a good journey thus far?' he asked.

'Erm,' Hermitage said.

'I do apologise for the manner of your arrival here, of course, but it was most urgent that I saw you before you reach Odo.'

'Ah,' Hermitage added.

'And I only got word of William's instructions to you very late in the day.'

'Hm,' Hermitage continued his valuable contribution.

'King's Investigator then?' Stigand smiled warmly at Hermitage. 'A tiresome role, I imagine.'

Hermitage couldn't make any sound now but tried to nod. He felt that his head went in the right direction, but he wasn't sure.

'First by Harold, then by William. You do seem to have been effective though.'

Hermitage tried a humble and insouciant shrug, but thought it came out as more of a twitch.

'And thank you for sorting out dear Abbot Abbo,' Stigand smiled some more and incredibly, gave Hermitage a short bow of the head. 'He is a fine fellow and deserved better.'*

'It was nothing,' Hermitage mumbled, incoherently.

'You are very well informed,' Wat said, more in awe than accusation.

---

*   *The Case of The Cantankerous Carcass* again

'Ah, well,' Stigand leaned back in his chair. 'You don't stay in royal circles for as long as I have without making sure you know as much as possible. And these are very difficult times.'

Hermitage couldn't help but relax. This archbishop was friendly, disarming, humble and interested. His expectations, of some remote and saintly figure of ultimate authority, who would have as little time for them as he did for the fleas in his bed, was being dismantled.

'I even remember old Cnut. I was his chaplain, you know.'

Now that really did confuse Hermitage. That the archbishop had once been a chaplain? Like a normal person? He knew that archbishops didn't simply spring into existence, ready made, but he'd thought it must be something like that.

'Of course, I was a young man then, barely twenty, about your age, I should think, Brother.' Stigand nodded and smiled at the recollection. 'Simpler times.'

That was it. Hermitage was now in total thrall to the archbishop. If the man told him to walk into the fireplace, he would get up and do it straight away.

'And then there was Harold Harefoot, and Harthacanute. And Edward, of course. Followed by Harold, for a very brief time, and now William. What times I have lived through.'

'And Odo as well,' Wat added.

'Ah, Odo, yes. The man in question.'

'You obviously know why Hermitage is sent,' Wat said.

'Of course. The poor nuns.' Stigand bowed his head for a moment. 'We heard the report from Odo's camp and wanted to take action ourselves. Such deaths are unconscionable.' There was a first sign of strength emerging from Stigand. This was clearly a man who could charm the birds from the trees and then shoot them if he had to. 'But William seems in thrall to Odo for some reason. I know they are brothers and Odo supports William in everything he does, but he seems to think that gives him leeway to do whatever he likes in his own demesne. And William lets him get away with it. The death of nuns while producing this wretched tapestry of his should be dealt with most severely.'

'But William has sent Hermitage to find out.' Wat's implication being that this would avoid William having to deal with it himself.

'He has indeed. And I think he expects a simple solution. Either show that this was nothing to do with Odo or vanish yourself into the long list of people who get near the man, never to appear again.'

'Do you think it could be Odo himself?' The worry of this possibility had brought Hermitage to his senses and enabled him to talk to Stigand as if he was human.

'For the sake of posterity, I have recorded my consideration of Odo of Bayeux.'

Hermitage couldn't immediately see what this had to do with anything.

'Mayhap it will pass into history. One can only hope so.' Stigand looked to the ceiling and recalled his words. 'Ambitious, rapacious, greedy, ruthless, arrogant, tyrannical and destitute of virtue. I think that about sums him up.'

Hermitage did his swallowing again. 'So it could be that the death of the nuns making Odo's tapestry is Odo's own doing.'

'I wouldn't doubt it for a moment,' Stigand said. 'If they weren't doing what he wanted, or were showing any signs of disobedience, he wouldn't hesitate. There is still resistance in Kent. Not so much to William any more, but Odo has not won the people over. He is cruel and dangerous. If these nuns gave any sign that they were rebelling against him, he wouldn't hesitate.'

'Rebelling nuns?' Hermitage couldn't immediately think how nuns would rebel.

'Perhaps they put some secret sign of their opposition in their work.' Stigand looked to Wat and Cwen.

'It could be done,' Wat confirmed. 'Show Odo in a poor light, or as fool, that sort of thing.'

Stigand nodded at the idea. 'Just the sort of thing to send him into a frenzy. He kills the nuns, or has them killed, it makes no difference. Then he gets William to send the King's Investigator as a pretence of doing something about it. And to divert the blame away from him.'

'How awful,' Hermitage breathed.

'Awful.' Stigand agreed.

'But,' Hermitage had thought ahead a bit, and saw a problem. 'If I do go and investigate the death of the nuns, I mean when I do, I may find that it was indeed Odo. What then? The investigation will have done him no good at all.'

'In that case,' Wat spoke up. 'There will be a dead investigator and two weavers to go with his nuns.'

Stigand nodded solemnly at this.

'Oh, my.'

'You see why I had to speak to you before you got to Odo. Doubtless he will have some tale of explanation that will divert you from the truth.'

'Oh my, oh my.'

'But you have a suggestion,' Wat said, addressing Stigand quite directly.

Stigand put his hands together as if in prayer. 'There is a possibility.'

'I wondered if there was.' Wat was sounding positively impudent in front of the archbishop.

Stigand ignored him. 'As I say, there is still resistance to Odo in Kent, and I have my sources of information close to his court. If your investigations do reveal that Odo is responsible for these appalling deaths, you get word to me and I will send help.'

'That is most thoughtful.' Hermitage said.

'And don't tell me,' Wat put in. 'You'll have a word with William who will then have no choice but to deal with Odo, instead of letting him run Kent as he will.'

'You understand, Master Wat,' Stigand acknowledged. 'There

is no one who can deal with Odo but William.'

'And you have William's ear.'

'Just so.'

'As you did Canute and Harefoot and Harthacanute and Edward and Harold.'

'And if we find that it wasn't Odo? What if there really is some mad killer wandering the place doing nuns, and it's nothing to do with Odo?'

Hermitage didn't like the sound of that at all.

'Then so be it,' Stigand accepted the suggestion. 'I have every confidence that Odo is behind this though. Nuns did not start dying in Kent until he arrived and instructed them to make his tapestry. And I also have every confidence that your investigation will confirm this is the case.'

'Yes,' Wat said, sounding very knowing. 'I rather expect that you do.'

Odo Explains, so Pay Attention

O h, this is marvellous,' Wat almost howled as they set off next morning towards the depths of Kent.

'I know,' Hermitage agreed. 'Meeting the archbishop and staying in his own lodgings.' He still felt as if he was floating on the feather mattress the archbishop had provided. An experience he knew he would never have again in his lifetime.

'No,' Wat said, quite fiercely. 'What I actually mean is that it's not marvellous at all.'

'Oh?'

'We are now caught between the king, his archbishop and his brother. What did we do to deserve this?'

'Become weavers, obviously.' Cwen seemed to be in an equally bad mood. 'I mean it should be clear, shouldn't it, but no one tells you. Become a weaver my child and you'll end up murdered by a mad monarch's brother. All at the whim of the Archbishop of Canterbury.'

Hermitage couldn't understand the obvious anger. 'Archbishop Stigand knew you were a weaver,' he pointed out.

'Just to keep me sweet,' Cwen replied. 'He's just using us to get Odo. Just as William is using us to keep Odo out of his hair.'

Hermitage didn't even have to do his totally confused look, Wat and Cwen seemed positively keen to explain.

'Odo is terrorising Kent, yes?' Cwen asked.

'Erm, so it seems.'

'Seems, yes. We don't know that. For all we know, Odo could be a lovely man who's running the place under the beaming smiles of his subjects.'

'But the archbishop said..,'

'Yes, he did, didn't he? Can't be very nice, being Archbishop of Canterbury and then having some Norman turn up to run your county. A Norman who's only the brother of the king, not even the king himself. And he's probably interfering in all sorts of things that are really none of his business. Be much better for everyone if this Odo just went away.'

'Well,' Wat put in, 'better for Stigand.'

'Exactly. So, let's send the investigator to prove that Odo killed his nuns. Then we can set the king on Odo and everything's back to normal.'

'Stigand can even be sympathetic to the horrible decision the king has to make; execute his brother for nun killing.'

Hermitage couldn't help a short snort bursting out. 'I think you are both getting rather carried away.'

Wat held up a finger on his right hand. 'One, we find out that Odo really did kill these nuns or have them killed and so Odo kills us.' He held up the other hand. 'Two, we find out it wasn't Odo at all, and Stigand has us dealt with.'

'The Archbishop of Canterbury?' Hermitage didn't know whether to laugh or scream.

'The Archbishop of Canterbury who has been in the service of more monarchs than most people live through. I've never heard of any servant of the crown lasting more than a few years, never mind a few kings. He's obviously a master at manipulation.'

'He's lovely,' Hermitage protested.

'Of course, he is. He's lovely to everyone, all the time, on both sides, probably several times a day. He's the sort of man who tells you exactly what you want to hear and then goes out and does the opposite.'

Hermitage shook his head in despair at their cynicism.

'He did tell me what a wonderful weaver I was,' Cwen said. 'And if he ever meets the master of the weavers' guild, he'll probably say he once met that awful Cwen woman and he totally agrees that they should do something about me.'

'Now, now,' Hermitage had nothing he could say to this.

'We'll see.' Wat sounded ominous. 'We shall see. We could be in Dover in five or six hours, unless Odo has his own horsemen out looking for us.'

'And if we decided not to go,' Cwen said, 'I imagine we'd find the archbishop's men close behind, urging us on. Whether we like it or not.'

'If we do manage to get out of this one,' Wat said heavily. 'I suggest our route home does not include Canterbury.'

◆   ◆   ◆

They didn't have to go all the way to Dover, nor did they need Odo's men to come and get them. It was clear as the day went on that they were in Odo territory. The Saxons they saw gave them very cautious looks, as if expecting the worst to spring upon them at any moment. They even gave Hermitage a wide berth, perhaps thinking he had knives under his habit.

On the other hand, the local Normans looked very comfortable indeed. Most were soldiers, but there were also some ordinary people, judging from their dress. This close to the coast, Hermitage assumed that they had simply moved over here from Normandy. It hadn't really occurred to him until now that conquest meant someone else taking over your country, not just sending soldiers to patrol the place. Perhaps that day was not too far away when they'd all be dressed like Normans. At least a monk was a monk, and you knew where you stood. He wouldn't be changing his habit for some fancy Norman version.

They had only got to the outskirts of Patrixbourne, when they were stopped on the road by what could only be described as a reception party. Hermitage thought these people might even have been waiting for them to emerge from Canterbury before jumping out.

There was one well dressed and official looking fellow, who bowed before them. He wasn't a soldier but wasn't far off. He wore a brown leather jerkin and carried a sword at his side. He must be something to do with the Normans if he was carrying a weapon so openly. Gathered around him was a group of four men, all of whom beamed smiles of quite alarming breadth.

'I am Haimo,' the bowing one announced. 'Lord Odo's sheriff, and I have been sent to bid you welcome, master investigator.' He bowed again.

'Aha,' Hermitage said, giving a little bow back. Haimo bowed again in response to the bow and Hermitage felt Wat's hand on his shoulder, holding him back before this became a bowing contest.

'My Lord Odo bids you welcome, and I am to accompany you to Dover.'

Wat glanced over at the beaming ones behind Haimo's back.

'These are the good Burgesses of Dover, most anxious to see the great investigator as he comes to rid us of our evil.'

The only words that stuck in Hermitage's mind were "great" and "evil", and he didn't like either of them.

'Not safe then, the road to Dover?' Wat asked.

'The whole of Kent is safe.' Haimo smiled. 'Now that Lord Odo is our glorious earl.'

'I see.'

'Unless you're a nun, of course,' Cwen said. 'Doing tapestry. Not so safe then, it seems.'

This did not put Haimo out at all. 'Which is why the great master investigator is here. Good King William has sent the solution to our ills.'

'Well,' Cwen pointed out, 'the nuns' ills.'

'The ills of us all as we face this curse upon our land.'

Curse. That was another word that stuck in Hermitage's head.

Haimo bowed yet again and indicated with an outstretched

arm that they would move on down the road. Without anyone particularly taking the lead, the whole ensemble set off for the south at a gentle stroll.

'To Dover then?' Wat asked.

'Absolutely,' Haimo replied. 'Lord Odo awaits your arrival with great eagerness. The king speaks very highly of you all.' He smiled his smile at them one at a time, although he seemed a bit more confused about Cwen.

'I'm surprised he speaks of us at all,' Wat said. 'He certainly never has anything nice to say to our faces.'

'Aha, ha, ha,' Haimo made the sound of a laugh without the laughter.

'These nuns then,' Cwen got down to business. 'The dead ones. How many were there?'

'Lord Odo will have all the details,' Haimo said, clearly not interested in going into the matter.

'How did they die then? And when?'

'Lord Odo will be able to cover that.'

'Were they with Lord Odo when they died?'

Haimo did give his attention to Cwen now. 'Certainly not. They were doing their work at the abbey, and then word came that they had gone. Taken from us. In the middle of the tapestry.'

'Hm,' Cwen was clearly not happy with any of this but could see that she wasn't going to get any more out of Odo's sheriff. She would have to wait for the man himself.

It was another thirteen miles to Dover and the journey was made with no useful information of any sort emerging. There was lots about wonderful Lord Odo and the even more wonderful king, but none of that was much help when it came to considering the death of nuns.

Seagulls shrieked their warnings that the group was approaching the coast, and long before they came to Dover, they could see the sea shining the horizon to a blur. Up on the top of a high promontory to the left of the town, the presence of the

Normans was making itself known. A typical castle sat on the top of the hill, which at least meant the locals hadn't been forced to move huge amounts of earth, just so that the Normans could look down on them.

A wooden keep inside a timber palisade provided security for the Normans from attack, and loomed as the source of attack for the town of Dover. Each looked as if it was watching the other, just to see which would jump first. It was clear it would be the castle.

Haimo led the way up the hill to the gate of the place, which was thrown wide in a clear sign that the Normans were very much in charge. He continued inside the walls, although his walk did seem a little more nervous than it had been when he was miles away.

On the far side he pushed at the large doors of the keep and stepped through.

The outside had been a perfectly normal rough yard. Horses and their mess, jostled with people and their mess, the outcome being more mess than horses or people. Some of the people had the job of moving the mess around, while others delivered goods and supplies.

It was clear that the doors of the keep were not open to mess. The space inside, while not large or imposing, was spotlessly clean. There wasn't even any straw on the floor.

Haimo appeared to walk on tip toe, as if hoping not to sully the place as he led them on towards an inner door. This one he did not open but stood respectfully and waited until they were all together before he knocked.

'What?' boomed from the inside.

Haimo bowed to the three of them once more. 'Lord Odo will see you now.' He pushed the door open and beckoned that they could enter.

They did so, giving him puzzled looks as it was clear that he was not going to join them. In fact, the Burgesses of Dover had already started to retreat to the entrance of the keep before the investigator and his companions had crossed the threshold. As the doors were closed behind them, Hermitage could swear that he heard running feet; running away.

And there was Lord Odo. In a fine room, neat and well ordered, and as unnaturally clean as the rest of the keep, what could only be the Earl of Kent sat by his fire. He turned his head to look at the arrivals but didn't get up.

Hermitage nervously walked across the room so that he was in the Norman's line of sight. Wat and Cwen were at his side.

'My Lord,' Hermitage bowed.

Odo considered him with some surprise. 'Good God, there's a monk in here.'

Hermitage considered this to be an odd response as Odo himself was wearing clerical garb. The man looked about thirty or forty years of age, tall, strong and very purposeful. His skin had the tone of a man of the fields, rather than the pasty pallor of a true cleric. Knowing that this was the Bishop of Bayeux didn't help at all; the impression was still of a soldier who had stolen some clothes from a priest.

'We are sent from the king,' Hermitage said nervously.

'Ah.' Odo seemed happier about this. 'You're that monk.' He looked at Wat and Cwen. 'And the weaver.'

Cwen bit her lip.

'Just what we need.' Odo now rose to his feet. If the sitting man had been commanding, the standing one weakened Hermitage's knees. He had the look in his eyes that William carried. The vacant stare that said he was seeing you, but it mattered to him not one jot whether you lived or died.

'Come to sort out my nuns, then.'

Hermitage's voice was in danger of breaking and was so fragile it wouldn't let any words out.

'So we are told,' Wat said.

'I sent that sheriff to get you from Stigand's clutches. Don't want you corrupted by the so-called Archbishop of Canterbury.'

Hermitage thought that he was so called because that was what he was.

'I hope my man treated you right.' The implication was clear that if the sheriff had not treated them right there would be trouble for the sheriff.

'Of course,' Wat gave a short nod.

'Hm.' Odo seemed slightly disappointed that he wasn't going to be able to make some trouble.

'The nuns have died, we're told.' Wat moved on.

'They have. Useless bunch.'

'How?'

'How should I know?' Odo didn't seem happy answering questions. 'How do nuns normally die?'

'Like the rest of us, I imagine.'

'Not in the middle of doing my tapestry, they don't. Not if they know what's good for them.'

Hermitage could well imagine the dead being worried about what Odo might do to them. 'Could you erm,' he found his voice again, and was worried that Wat was not going to get on at all well with Odo. 'Could you tell us what happened?'

'That's what you find out, isn't it?' Odo looked a bit puzzled but also a bit angry. Despite his inability to pick up on things like that most of the time, Hermitage had already concluded that making Odo angry was not a good idea. He nodded as happily as he could manage.

'Oh, of course, yes, absolutely. But if we start with what you can tell us, we'll be able to do it more quickly.' He had absolutely no faith that any of this was going to come to pass, but the Earl of Kent didn't need to know that.

Odo scowled but grunted as he sat down again. 'The tapestry, yes?'

'The one that shows the history of King William and the conquest?' Wat asked.

'Oh, a lot more to it than that. Goes right back to Edward and has the treacherous Harold in it.'

No one said anything to that.

'Going to be quite big then?'

'Bloody huge. Biggest there's ever been.' Odo seemed to think that this was the most important aspect of the work. 'So, I got the nuns to start work on it.'

'Not weavers?' Wat asked.

'Certainly not. Nuns do what they're told. Weavers are a difficult bunch.' Odo didn't seem at all concerned that he was actually talking to one of the awkward bunch. 'And nuns are cheaper.'

'Cheaper.' Wat managed to get a weight of disdain into the one word.

'Next thing is, they're dead.'

'Just like that.'

'Just like that. I get word that they're working on it, all going well. Next thing is, work has stopped. They can't carry on because they're dead.'

'I can see it would be difficult to keep going.'

'Get some more nuns, I say.'

'Do you?'

'Oh, yes. If these nuns are no good, get some more. I mean, there's plenty of nuns in the world, aren't there?'

'I suppose there must be.' Wat looked to Hermitage as if he was going to be able to confirm how many nuns there were in the world.

'But can they all make tapestry?' Odo asked the question. 'Apparently not.' He answered it and clearly thought this was a real failing.

'Were they old nuns?' Hermitage asked.

'What's that got to do with anything?' Odo narrowed his gaze at Hermitage. 'You haven't got a thing about old nuns, have you?'

Hermitage had not a clue what the man was talking about. 'If they were old nuns, they'd be more likely to die. You see?'

Another grunt from Odo. 'All sorts. The abbess promised me the best weaving nuns she had, not ones that were going to drop dead at the sight of a needle.'

'Abbess?'

'The one at Lyminge.' Odo seemed impatient that they didn't know things he hadn't told them. 'That's where they all were, and that's where they're all dead.'

'But you don't know how many, or how they died.'

Odo just looked at Hermitage, making it clear that he was not going to do his work for him. 'Someone killed them to stop my tapestry. Now you're going to get in there, find out what's happening and put a stop to it.'

'Stop the people who stopped the nuns.' Hermitage nodded that he at least understood this.

'Rebels,' Odo said.

'Rebel nuns?'

'No, not rebel nuns, you idiot. Rebels must have killed the nuns to stop the truth of the tapestry coming out.'

'I see.'

'And when you find out who they were, you bring them to me and I'll deal with them. I can't have them still wandering about, can I? What if I get some new nuns? They could be killed as well.'

Hermitage was beyond saying anything now.

'And I wouldn't be at all surprised to find out that Stigand had something to do with it.'

'The Archbishop of Canterbury?' Hermitage simply couldn't comprehend the suggestion.

'That's him. He's always trouble. Doesn't like me and won't like my tapestry. Could be that he killed the nuns.'

'I'm not sure..,' Hermitage began.

'But you can show all that.' Odo looked very happy at the idea of Hermitage accusing the Archbishop of Canterbury of murdering his own nuns. 'Seems I'm not supposed to go into a nunnery and start sorting things out myself.' This was a personal complaint of Odo's. Perhaps the king had told him to keep out of nunneries. 'Not that I couldn't. Do it in no time, but oh, no. Don't cause trouble. Don't cause trouble? I've had my nuns murdered, and I mustn't cause trouble. I ask you.'

Hermitage nodded and shook his head in sympathy.

'So,' Odo reached a conclusion. 'Simple enough task. Go to Lyminge; it's just down the road. Find the rebels who killed my nuns and bring them to me.'

'Er, right.'

'Now.'

◆　　　◆　　　◆

'Great,' Wat said as they tramped yet another road of old England. And this time Hermitage could tell he didn't mean "great". 'Now we've got the king, the archbishop, the mad Earl of Kent and a bunch of Saxon rebels to deal with.'

'And one other,' Hermitage said as he felt the shiver at the prospect run down his back.

'Who's that?'

'An abbess.'

Do You Want Lyminge With That?

part from the nagging thoughts about all the people who were putting them in harm's way, the journey to Lyminge was very pleasant. The countryside was charming, the weather clear and the road safe. This was a stronghold of the Normans and it soon became clear that the new earl kept order very strictly.

The hints of this along the way were less than subtle. The way the local people cowered in their hovels whenever they heard a footstep; the way one or two came out and begged for mercy before the three of them had even done anything; and the way one young man proclaimed that he would kill them all before they took his mother. All of this gave the impression of a whole county under siege - from the inside.

The charm of the countryside and the pleasantness of the weather were not enough to lift the pall of dread that cloaked Hermitage like a second habit.

Those nagging thoughts were enough on their own, never mind adding the clear distress of the local folk.

Wat said that it must be ten miles to Lyminge and so would take them at least half a day. Odo had not been as hospitable as the Archbishop of Canterbury and had sent them on their way as soon as he'd finished talking. It was now getting late and they would need to stop for the night. Imposing themselves on any of these poor, downtrodden people seemed too much. Well, it seemed too much to Hermitage.

As they walked on, the forest grew around them, dark and unkempt. The sun vanished completely, and the murk and damp of the woodland swirled around them like a great cloak. This was ancient wood, no Norman hunting ground, this place. The trees that towered and twisted around them did so on the bodies of the trees that had fallen hundreds of years before. Although they were close to the Norman stronghold, the land hereabouts shrugged off such modern problems.

The path they followed grew thin and sparse and there was a real risk of getting lost completely if they carried on without daylight to lead the way.

Before the dark got too impenetrable, Wat spotted a small gathering of houses off the main road. It wasn't really a main road, barely even a track now, tunnelled by the overarching trees and buried under years of leaf fall. And they weren't really houses in the modern sense. The half dozen buildings gathered round a central clearing looked like real old Saxon dwellings. A low foundation dug into the ground had a timber frame built within it, on top of which a simple structure of four walls and a grass roof squatted.

Anyone entering would have to step down and duck to get in. And then they'd be in the one room that served every purpose.

The clearing had a fire gently burning in the middle, doubtless where the folk would gather of an evening.

The surprising feature of this place was that it was all in very good order. These did not look like the homes of the poorest folk whose highest ambition was to survive the day and perhaps eat half their fill from the provisions of the forest. These were well tended and maintained homes of people of some means. But people who chose to live in this fashion, rather than in a larger village or even town.

There was something ancient about the whole place, as if the three of them had stepped back in time, to some period long before Normans bothered the country. The surrounding forest and hills protected them from the outside world, which could be over the next ridge, or a hundred miles away.

Soft smoke also rose from the roofs of the houses, and the smells of cooking wafted about.

The appearance of the place even gave Wat some pause and stopped him striding up and just walking into someone's home, as he usually would.

The sound of their arrival had alerted the dwellers and one goat-skin door was thrown aside and a face peered out.

It was the face of the forest. Dark skinned from a life spent outdoors and worn from the weather of a significant number of years.

The owner of the face, a bearded man with bright blue eyes, stepped out of his home and looked down at them. If he fitted in his house, Hermitage thought that the foundations must go down quite a way. He was dressed for the woods as well. Leather and hide were everywhere, and it was hard to tell where the skin of an animal ended and the man's own began.

Instantly on his guard, although having no idea what he was going to do if there was trouble, Hermitage breathed as the man smiled broadly and held his arms wide.

'Wilcumaþ gúþwine,' he said.

'Oh,' Hermitage was taken aback to hear the old language spoken so naturally. 'Erm, þancie, I'm sure.'

'Aha,' the man of the forest laughed from his toes to his mouth. 'New folk, eh? Well, you're still welcome, even if you can't talk properly.'

The man's accent was so thick that it was clear he seldom spoke the language of modern England. The Normans had brought their French with them, the official language was Latin, and old English was still in common use. Anyone who wanted to do business had to have mastery of several languages.

Hermitage didn't like to admit that the whole language of the country was changing. Bits of Latin and French and English were being mixed up in the most awful way. It wasn't uncommon for one sentence to use all three languages, every one of them incorrectly. Every area of the country had developed its own dialect and language, but Hermitage had not heard such pure speech for many years. How long had these people been here?

'I am Ulf,' the man introduced himself. 'Travellers are always given welcome; sit ye.'

Hermitage now looked properly and saw that the clearing between the houses was laid out with logs and tree trunks for sitting around the central fire.

More heads now popped out of their homes, presumably to see what all the fuss was about. Several people came out and greeted the new arrivals with a smattering of old English, pats on backs and broad smiles. Anyone would think they hadn't seen a visitor for years.

They moved over to the fire and sat on the wooden seats, which proved to be very comfortable. It wasn't a few moments before wooden bowls of steaming stew were presented, along with flat bread, freshly made. They had obviously arrived at meal time, and all the dwellers came out to enjoy their food together. There must be at least a dozen people, men and women, all similarly dressed, and Hermitage quickly lost track of who was who, the names given to him having vanished from his head.

'So,' Ulf enquired, after everyone had had their first mouthfuls. 'What brings fine folk like you down our track? One a monk, and all.'

'We are travelling to Lyminge,' Hermitage said. He really didn't want to bother these simple people with the trials of the king and dead nuns.

'Lyminge eh?' Ulf nodded to himself. 'Where's that then?'

Hermitage was quickly confused. 'Er, just down the road a bit. To the west?' Surely these people weren't that local.

'Ah,' Ulf had it now. 'You mean Limegē.'

'Er, probably.'

'Oh, a fine place it is. Grand and with a great feasting hall.'

'Marvellous. It's actually the nuns we've come to see.'

Ulf did not look so happy at that. 'Nuns?' He obviously knew what they were and didn't like them. 'You are a monk, I suppose.' He seemed to think this was a bit of an excuse. 'But taking these two with you to see nuns?' he nodded towards Wat and Cwen.

'Wat,' Wat introduced himself. 'Wat the Weaver,' he added with a wink.

'Aha,' Ulf smiled some more, the name meaning nothing to him. 'A weaver, eh? A fine trade. And your daughter is a weaver too, is she?'

'Eh?' Wat didn't know what to say.

'Yes,' Cwen said happily. 'Yes, I am a weaver.'

'That's good to hear. Algar is our weaver.' Ulf nodded to one of the men on the opposite side of the fire, who raised his spoon in acknowledgement. 'Strange mix of folk off to see the nuns of Limegē? A monk and two weavers? What will the nuns want of you?'

Hermitage didn't know how far to go. All folk welcomed talk and conversation, it was what passed the hours and made life bearable, but troubled talk was seldom welcome. 'We have been given a mission.'

'A mission, eh? Good thing for a monk to have.'

'Just so. A mission to see the nuns as we think they have had troubles recently.'

'Troubles? The nuns? I seldom see trouble going towards the nuns. Coming from them, yes.'

Hermitage tried to look solemn. 'We have heard that some of them may have died recently.' As he said this, he thought that it was only reasonable to ask. These folk were local. If there was any gossip about the death of the nuns, it may be known here.

'Dead nuns, eh?'

'So we hear.'

'Not seen any in our woods. Just up and died, did they?'

'That's what we're going to find out.'

'Anyone know of dead nuns?' Ulf asked the gathering.

No one had anything useful to say about dead nuns.

Hermitage thought a little more information may help. 'Apparently, they were making a great tapestry for the Normans.'

'The Normans, you say?' Ulf asked.

'That's right.'

'And who are the Normans?'

Hermitage couldn't quite take that in. 'Who are the Normans?'

'That's it. Is it Norman someone or other? Wants a tapestry and asked a nun. A strange thing to ask a nun for. A weaver for a tapestry, that's the thing.'

'Quite right,' Wat agreed.

'No,' Hermitage said, looking to Wat and Cwen to see if they believed what they were hearing. 'The Normans. William. The King. The conquest.'

Ulf just looked mildly interested in what was obviously news to him.

'The Normans from Normandy, across the sea. They invaded the country, killed King Harold, and William was crowned at Westminster.' Hermitage was positive that some of this would trigger recognition and Ulf would say "oh, those Normans." But he didn't.

'Is that right?' he said instead.

'Have you not seen any?' Wat asked. 'Soldiers tramping about? They're all over the place.'

'We don't get many visitors,' Ulf explained. 'Not in the woods.'

'We're in Kent,' Wat pointed out. 'The invasion was only just down the road at Hastings.'

Ulf frowned. 'Hæstingas,' he concluded. 'Oh, we don't go down that way. Hæsta's people were always trouble.'

His fellows nodded their agreement at that.

'And we're only five miles from Dover,' Wat went on. 'Sorry, Dofras. That's a Norman town now.'

'There you are then,' Ulf said. 'We don't have no doings with towns. Bad places. Best stick to the woods. The woods'll look after you.'

'I think you may have been in the woods too long and are in for a surprise any day now.' Wat shook his head in disbelief.

'And who's this Harold?' Ulf asked.

'Oh, now you are joking,' Wat contained a laugh. 'Harold Godwinson, King of England. And before him Edward? Any of this ring a bell?'

Ulf did nod slowly at this. 'I heard tell of some such. We don't bother ourselves with the doings of people outside the woods.'

'I can tell.' Wat gave a little shudder.

'But you do know of the nuns?' Hermitage asked.

'Nuns.' Ulf let the word pass his lips with some distaste. 'They come into the woods now and again.'

'Really?'

'Going to convert us, they say.'

'Convert you?' Hermitage managed to contain the shock. 'Convert you to, erm, Christianity?'

'Ar, that's the one.'

'As opposed to what you do now?'

'Spirits of the woods.'

'Of course.'

'We care for the spirits of the woods and they care for us. That's as right as it can be.'

Hermitage did his best to ignore this, as well as the conviction that loomed in his head that these people probably sacrificed monks and ate them when the moon was in the right position. 'Have there been any nuns recently?' he got out as a sort of whimpering squeak.

'Not for a while.' Ulf looked to his fellows, who had nothing to add. 'They was all over us, once upon a time, but then they didn't come so often.'

'I wonder if the Archbishop of Canterbury knows that he's

got pagans in his woods,' Cwen laughed.

Hermitage thought there was nothing laughable about this. Let Cwen wait until she was tied to a tree, then she'd see.

'Course,' Ulf went on. 'If the nuns is dead, they wouldn't be coming round so much, would they?'

'I suppose not.'

Ulf peered rather alarmingly at Hermitage. 'Do you think they was done for?'

'Done for?'

'You know.' Ulf helpfully drew a finger across his throat and made a slicing noise. 'Is that why you been sent? Find out who did for the nuns?' He considered his own suggestion for a moment. 'It isn't right.'

Hermitage gulped.

'Doing for nuns. I mean, they're holy people, aren't they? Doesn't matter if they've got the wrong end of the stick, you still shouldn't go round doing for a nun. Same as a monk.' He nodded towards Hermitage.

Hermitage was grateful to hear this and didn't like to ask if weavers shouldn't be done for either.

'There has been a lot of coming and going,' a voice from the other side of the fire called out.

'What's that, Cafnoth?' Ulf called back.

'I say there's been a lot of coming and going, down by the nuns.'

'Cafnoth's our hunter,' Ulf explained. 'He gets all over the woods and sees things the rest of us wouldn't be interested in.'

'What sort of comings and goings?' Hermitage asked across the fire.

'Down in the marshes,' Cafnoth replied, sounding very wary of the marshes.

'The marshes,' Hermitage said. Up until now he'd been thinking that getting out of the wood full of pagans would be good. Now there were marshes to look forward to.

'That's right. Some of the nuns been going down to the marshes.'

Ulf just sat shaking his head at this sorry news.

'Why would they go to the marshes?' Hermitage asked.

'Why would anyone go to the marshes?' Ulf responded. 'They's funny folk down in the marshes.'

'They're funny folk?' Wat sounded as if he looked forward to meeting someone funnier than current company.

'Strange ways, they have. Not civilised like the rest of us.'

Hermitage found himself speculating what on earth the marsh people could be like. Being odd by the standard of people who worshipped the spirits of the trees must be very odd indeed. 'And the nuns have been going down there?'

'Perhaps they want to do some more conversion,' Cwen suggested.

'Yes, could be,' Hermitage agreed. 'How many nuns? Do you know?' he asked Cafnoth.

'Be plenty, I reckon,' was the helpful reply. Hermitage thought that Cafnoth probably counted anything more than one as being plenty.

He didn't know if this had anything to do with the matter in hand though. The nuns might go down to the marshes regularly. They could be different nuns. Whoever they were, they wouldn't be going down there if they were dead, obviously. All they could do was get to Lyminge and ask around. He still dreaded the thought of asking nuns anything at all.

'Cafnoth can take you the quickest way to Limegē in the morning,' Ulf announced. 'Easy for foreign folk to get lost in the woods.'

Hermitage saw straight away that Ulf considered a foreigner to be anyone not born within about half a mile of this spot.

'Thank you very much.'

'He won't take you to the marsh though,' Ulf warned in a voice heavy with mystery and dread.

'That's fine. Hopefully, we won't have to go anywhere near the marsh.'

'Aye,' Ulf said, his eyes widening to add to the slight air of insanity that hovered in this place. 'I hope you won't either.'

Caput VII

A Yawning Abbess

afnoth deposited them at the edge of the wood, within sight of the Abbey of Lyminge. Hermitage considered the stones, still some mile or so away, and could feel the presence of an abbess, oozing out of the mortar. The building displayed the common architectural eclecticism of the period: pillaged Roman stone abutted wobbly Saxon wattle and daub while fresh cut timber buttresses stopped the whole thing falling down. It was a depressing sight.

'Dead nuns,' was all he could say to the others.

'Can't see any,' Cwen peered out. 'Mind you, they might be piled up inside, just waiting for us.'

'Aha.' The image leapt into Hermitage's mind before he could do anything about it.

'I must say, Odo seemed genuinely concerned about his nuns,' Wat said. 'Well, not concerned in any human sort of way, just put out that they'd died before they could finish his tapestry. And he thought the archbishop might have done it.'

'Which is completely ridiculous,' Hermitage said. 'And this helps us how, exactly?'

'Could mean he didn't kill them himself.'

'Or he's so mad that he killed them and has forgotten all about it,' Cwen suggested.

'Ah yes.' Wat nodded. 'Could be.'

'Perhaps they produced something, he didn't like the look of it and got in a bit of a temper.'

'I've had a few customers like that,' Wat mused.

'Or he sent someone to do it for him. Like "who will rid me of these troublesome nuns?"'

'And then some Norman blood thinks "rid me of nuns" means kill the lot.'

'That's it.'

Hermitage was starting to think that meeting an abbess was not going to be the worst bit of his day after all. 'Shall we just go and find out?' He beckoned towards the abbey.

'Can't wait.' Wat led the way.

✦　　✦　　✦

All of Hermitage's fears concerning his encounter with the abbess, all his premonitions at the difficulties that faced him and the challenges waiting behind those walls faded to nothing as he finally met the woman who was the leader of this community.

The ghastly apparition he had conjured in his mind, combining all the worst aspects of every abbess, nun and even woman he had ever met, dissipated as Abbess Cartimandua introduced herself. One look from her intelligent and purposeful eyes told him that his nightmares had been completely wide of the mark. She was something far, far worse.

He almost felt urged to confess to the murder of her nuns himself, just to stop her looking at him like that. It felt that every moment of his life was open to her gaze and every single one of those moments was a huge disappointment, of which he should be deeply ashamed. And he was.

Even Wat and Cwen seemed stunned by the silent appraisal that reached into their souls and found them seriously wanting.

Hermitage dreaded to think what was going to happen when the abbess found out who Wat was.

'So.' It was only a single word, but it was the most hurtful, disparaging, contemptuous one Hermitage had ever heard.

The abbess stood with her arms folded, barring the entrance into the abbey compound as she considered the arrivals. She was only a short woman, somewhat stout and solid, and there was plenty of room to walk around her if anyone cared to try. No one cared to try. She was certainly a good age, probably quite incapable of chasing anyone any distance, but the stare stopped them all moving.

Her garb was the simple cloth of the nun. A long tunic hung from neck to floor, and the scapular was draped on top of this. Her head piece was a plain length of cloth that covered the hair and was tied tight at the back. The whole was the outward representation of her inner spirit: plain, forbidding, cold and daring anyone to so much as think about touching it.

'A monk.' Abbess Cartimandua said the word as if she knew of monks and had never met a good one.

Hermitage bowed his head, at least that meant he avoided her gaze for a moment.

'And others.' The gaze took in Wat and Cwen, who at least managed to keep still and return the look.

'What do you want?' This was a plain question and in normal circumstances its tone could range from the happy enquiry of the tavern keeper, to the threatening manner of the drunk. This tone was of the pointy finger variety; the finger that jabbed you in your chest until you answered properly. And left a bruise to remind you to be more prompt about it next time.

It also sounded as if she was getting impatient with people knocking on her door. With her on the other side, Hermitage found it hard to believe anyone would knock on the thing voluntarily.

'We are sent,' Hermitage got out, before he lifted his head once more and had to look at the abbess again.

'Sent? By whom?'

Hermitage quickly considered his options. He was confident that this abbess would not be impressed by either the king or Odo and would likely send them straight on their way. 'The Archbishop of Canterbury,' he said. 'Among others,' he mumbled.

'Pah,' Cartimandua dismissed the archbishop with a snort. 'And what does he want?' It was as plain as day that if Stigand himself turned up at the door dressed in all his regalia and offering the blessings of his divine position, Abbess Cartimandua wouldn't let him in.

'The, erm, death,' Hermitage began. 'Of the tapestry. I mean of the nuns, weaving the tapestry. That is.'

At least the abbess simply scowled at this and offered no vocal criticism. Mind you, her scowls could probably rust metal.

She considered them all again. 'I suppose you want to come in?'

'If we may?' Hermitage knew perfectly well that he wanted to do no such thing. But all hopes he had of her saying "what death" had gone.

With a heavy sigh that made it clear this was a great sacrifice on her behalf, for which they should be truly grateful, Abbess Cartimandua took half a step to one side and indicated with the slightest movement of the head that they could pass. Even then, there was no certainty that they would avoid a clip round the ear for their impudence.

Once they had negotiated the abbess herself, they stood in the courtyard of her abbey while she closed the great doors behind them. They all felt that any offer to help with this task would not be well received. The abbess had been built for heavy tasks and put them in their place with grim fortitude.

With the doors closed, she strode across the small space and they just assumed they should follow. Through a small door set in the far wall she led without any backward glance to check that they were with her. She strode on through winding and laborious paths to her study.

This was a study in which to study; and if the student had any sense, they'd get it over with as fast as possible. Cold grey stone on floor and walls only lent weight to the ceiling which glowered over them. One single book was resting on the lectern in the room, and there were no desks or chairs in which the idle could rest.

Abbess Cartimandua said nothing, but it was clear that they may speak.

'The, erm, archbishop said that some of your sisters had met with an untimely end while working on a tapestry for Lord Odo. I mean, the erm, Bishop of Bayeux.' Hermitage thought about a smile but didn't want to waste one.

Cartimandua's sniff said all that there was to be said about bishops and archbishops. 'The whole thing is a complete fuss over nothing.'

Even in the abbess's terrifying company, Hermitage felt some relief at hearing this. He should know by now that you could never believe what people told you. You had to find out for yourself. William hadn't been here, he'd only had word from Odo. And it seemed that Odo hadn't come either. All he knew was that his tapestry had stopped. There was doubtless some simple explanation, and everyone would be satisfied once they heard it.

'Fuss over nothing,' Cartimandua repeated. 'One simple nun dies and suddenly everyone's getting excited.'

'One?' Hermitage didn't mean to sound disappointed, but after the trouble and worry of being sent to look for a whole flock of murdered nuns, to find there was only one was a bit of a let-down. Perhaps there were more and this abbess didn't know about them. This feeling was quickly taken over by the disappointment that there was even one dead nun.

'One simple nun died?' Wat asked.

'Of course.' The abbess didn't look happy at being addressed by Wat. She didn't look happy the rest of the time either, but this had an extra shine to it.

'Simply?'

'Sisters die all the time. I don't know why this one is so interesting.'

'And was this sister making the tapestry by any chance? Before she died, that is?'

'That thing,' the abbess bit the words out. 'People are more interested in the wretched tapestry than they are in the well-being of the abbey.' She gave Wat a stare of exquisite scrutiny. 'Who are you, anyway?'

'Weaver,' Wat said. 'That's why I'm here, with Cwen. We're both weavers. The, erm, archbishop thought we'd be useful.'

Cartimandua looked on as if Wat had just babbled Frankish.

'With regards to the tapestry,' he tailed off.

The stare was dragged across to Cwen, who took it well. 'You weave, child?'

'I do.'

'Hm.'

Hermitage didn't like the sound of that "hm".

'Odo, erm, the Bishop of Bayeux gave us to understand that several nuns had died.' Hermitage said. 'Many, in fact. And we were to look into the deaths.'

'Deaths?' Cartimandua sounded as if the plural was beyond her understanding.

'Erm, that's what he said.'

'I'd be surprised if that man can count to more than one,' the abbess replied. 'The one sister in question died and because she was leading work on the tapestry, it stopped. Perfectly normal and nothing to worry about.'

'Unless you were the sister,' Cwen muttered to herself.

'No other sisters have died here.' Cartimandua made the count of dead nuns quite clear.

'Bit of a coincidence her dying in the middle of Odo's tapestry. Him being Earl of Kent and the king's brother.' Wat half enquired.

'Vanity,' the abbess declared.

'What is?'

'The tapestry. Pure vanity. A huge great thing just saying how wonderful the Normans are.'

'You do tapestry as a, erm,' Hermitage couldn't really think of the word. He wanted to say pastime, but thought these nuns, under this abbess probably didn't have pastimes.

'It is our work. Well, it was under our dear departed sister. She had a talent, you see. A gift, if you will. The bishop and his men came visiting one day and enquired of our function.'

'Just passing by?' Wat asked.

'Checking what they could rob and steal, more like.' The abbess was clearly under no illusions concerning the Normans. 'Rather than have him take every valuable piece we have, we said that we could make the tapestry he kept going on about.'

'Keep the wolves from the door, eh?' Wat nodded at the plan.

'Give the wolves a tapestry to play with, stop them stealing our land,' the abbess clarified.

'But then the bishop's idea turned out to be the tapestry of all tapestries.'

'Completely ridiculous. I said it would take years to make and he just said we'd better get on with it then. Ghastly man.'

Hermitage could see that anyone who managed to get Cartimandua to do what they wanted, must really be very ghastly indeed.

'So, when this sister died, the work stopped, and the bishop was not happy.' Wat concluded.

'The others can do what they're told, but without the sister to lead, there was no point.'

Hermitage knew that he had to question the abbess on the death. She had said it happened, but not how. Murder tended to result in death, in his experience, so that was still a possibility. He went nonchalantly over to look at the book on the lectern and asked as if it was only a passing interest. 'The bishop, and the archbishop, indeed, think that the sister was, erm, how can I put it? Murdered.'

'Ha.'

Hermitage looked quickly over to see if he had heard right. Had Cartimandua really laughed? There was certainly no sign of it on her face. 'Not murdered, then?'

'Of course not. The very idea is ridiculous. Nuns don't get murdered. What sort of world are you living in?'

Hermitage didn't like to explain.

'Was she old, then? This sister?' Cwen asked.

'She was neither young nor old.'

'But she still died.'

'As do we all.'

'Not usually when we're making tapestries for the Normans.' Wat made it sound as if this was his own thought, rather than any challenge to the abbess's version of events.

Hermitage had a most impertinent question to ask but had learned that when questioning potential killers, impertinence was sometimes necessary. He still wasn't very good at it. 'Were you, erm, with the poor sister when she passed?'

'I was not. She failed to attend the tapestry work in the morning and so I went to look for her.'

'Weaving,' Wat muttered.

'I beg your pardon?'

'Tapestry work. It's generally called weaving. Done by weavers.'

Cartimandua ignored him with great vigour. 'I found the sister on her cot, in her cell from where the Lord had clearly called her.' She gave them all a thorough frowning. 'I don't know what all this has to do with you, anyway.' She offered no further explanation of the death. 'Once we have a new weaver, we can begin the work again.'

Hermitage found that he had stepped between the abbess and Cwen without really thinking about it.

'This sister is respectfully interred, I imagine,' Wat said.

The abbess's eyebrows rose and vanished under her head dress. 'She most certainly is. What did you want to do, have a look at her?' Cartimandua had sounded appalled at very many things in the few minutes they had known her. She had obviously been keeping some appalled in reserve and now drained her stock.

'Good Lord, of course not. Perish the thought.' Wat said, sounding very sincere when Hermitage knew that they really would like to see the body. Investigation involved a lot of looking at dead bodies and he'd rather come to expect it. He should be relieved that this one had already gone, but instead, something nagged at him. He felt a whole piece of his investigation would be missing if he didn't have a body to look at.

'We just want to pay our respects,' Wat went on. 'If she was as talented as you say, it's the least two fellow weavers can do.'

Cartimandua's face pinched tight as she considered what Wat might be up to. 'You may pray in chapel. Just as any others who ask.' She clearly thought that they were special in no way whatsoever.

'Of course,' Wat nodded that he would really like to do that.

Hermitage marvelled once again at his friend's ability to lie through his teeth. Wat had never wanted to go in a chapel in all the time he'd known him. Paying respects to a dead nun was simply not in his nature.

Abbess Cartimandua reached to her waist and took out a small bell that had been tucked inside her cincture. She lifted this and shook it once, releasing a pleasing tinkle into the air, which quickly killed itself.

After moments of waiting in silence, which would normally be embarrassing, but which were now quite a relief, the door opened and a timid face peeped round.

'Sister, show these people to the chapel,' Cartimandua instructed. 'Then to the door.' She had nothing else to say to any of them and so they just followed her very explicit instructions.

With no farewell of any sort, the door shut behind them and left Cartimandua to whatever it was she did when there weren't other people to terrify.

The quiet sister led the way and said not a word. After several yards, and many turns through the dark corridors of the abbey, Wat did speak. 'Did you know the sister who died?'

If this nun replied, it was something so quiet that none of them caught it.

'We're going to the chapel to pay our respects to her,' Wat continued. 'We're weavers as well, you see.'

The sister did give a shy and nervous glance at this.

'Well, the ones who aren't monks are weavers.' Cwen even gave the young nun an encouraging smile.

They now approached one door that was at the end of the corridor, presumably the entrance to the chapel. Their escort stopped with her hand on the door and, with her head facing the floor, managed to lift her eyes and give them all a very nervous look. She made some whispering noises that could be speech.

'What was that?' Cwen asked, very gently.

They all leaned in to hear the words.

'Are you from outside?' the sister spoke without disturbing the air.

'Erm,' Hermitage felt very puzzled. 'Yes. We're not nuns.' He didn't know why he was explaining this.

The sister nodded and looked quite surprised at the news.

'Have you never been outside?' Cwen asked.

The nun shook her head in reply.

'How old were you when you came in?'

The sister gave this careful thought and then held up the right number of fingers.

'Two?' Cwen couldn't stop the word coming out much louder than intended. 'How can you become a nun when you're two?'

'She was probably left at the door,' Hermitage said. 'An orphan.'

The nun nodded confirmation.

'And did you know the nun who died?' Hermitage asked. He

thought it extremely unlikely that the death of nun in a nunnery would go unnoticed by the other nuns.

The cautious nun looked at the door of the chapel, then at the walls and then at the ceiling. Then she looked at her normal spot on floor just in front of her. There was the very slightest shake of the head.

'It must have been a sad occasion,' Hermitage sympathised.

Wat put his hand up in Hermitage's face, which was quite rude. 'Do you mean she didn't die?' he asked very quietly.

The nun shook her head very slightly once more and let more words seep into the quiet of the space. 'She escaped.'

Caput VIII

Nun The Wiser

In the quiet of the chapel, Hermitage's confusion crowded in on him, giving very little opportunity to reflect on anything.

Wat had bundled them into the austere space, the quiet sister included, and closed the door behind them. Hermitage looked around for a seat to rest his body on while his mind tried to organise itself.

There were no such luxuries in this chapel. The sisters clearly stood through the daily orders; either that or they brought their chairs with them. From his one meeting with Abbess Cartimandua, he concluded there was probably not a single seat in the whole abbey.

The chapel itself was only recognisable as such because it had an altar. The study had a lectern and the chapel had an altar. Apart from that, the rooms were identical.

Wat beckoned them to join him in a huddle in the middle of the space. 'This sister is not dead, she left?'

The quiet sister looked cautiously about the room.

'There's no one here, you're quite safe,' Cwen reassured her.

The sister nodded.

'What's your name?' Cwen asked, quietly.

An inaudible whisper fell from the nun's lips straight to the floor.

'Pardon?'

This time the whisper made it to about waist height.

'Come again?'

'I don't have one.' The sister eventually managed to raise her head and her voice to the level where she could be heard.

'You don't have one?' Cwen looked very puzzled, or very angry, or both, most likely. 'What do you mean, you don't have one?'

'I don't have a name.' The sister cast her eyes down again. 'And I may only speak when I am spoken to.'

Now it was clear; Cwen was angry. 'What about the other nuns?'

The sister replied as if reciting her lesson. 'Those who come late in life may bring their given names with them or choose a new one. Those born to the abbey have no names. God knows us all. God and the abbess.'

'You weren't born here,' Cwen said. 'You must have had a name when you arrived.'

The nameless nun just shrugged.

'And anyway, what does it mean, born to the abbey?'

'Mothers,' Hermitage explained. 'If there are soon to be mothers who have none to look after them, they may come to the abbey to seek its protection. It's fairly common.'

'They have their babies here and give them up to the abbess?' Cwen looked ready to have a very frank discussion with Abbess Cartimandua.

'Where little nuns come from is not really our concern now,' Wat interrupted. 'We need to know where they go. Or where one of them went.'

'Did the sister who escaped have a name?' Hermitage asked.

The nun shook her head.

'This is hopeless,' Wat complained. 'We've gone from having a whole county full of slaughtered nuns, to just one, who doesn't even have a name. And she jumped over the wall and ran away before being slaughtered at all.'

'Well, that's good,' Hermitage decided. 'No murder anywhere.' As he said it he felt the pall of investigation lift from him. 'No need to investigate anything. We can go back and say that there aren't any dead nuns, and no one needs to worry. It wasn't

Odo and it wasn't Stigand because it wasn't anyone.' He turned back to the timid sister.

'Are you sure she escaped? Cwen asked. 'How do you know?'

'She's gone,' the nun whispered, with some awe.

Cwen gave Wat and Hermitage a rather worried look. 'But people might be gone because they died?'

The nun frowned now, as if she hadn't thought of that. She considered some more and then shook her head. 'If she'd died, we'd have had prayers.'

'And you didn't have prayers?' Hermitage was surprised at that. If a sister had died, the abbess would surely have had prayers said.

'Well,' Wat said. 'That's that then. No prayers, must be alive.'

Even Hermitage could see that this was somewhat fragile ground on which to base an assumption. The sister seemed to be clinging to a hope that if one nun had escaped then others might follow.

If something untoward had happened, Cartimandua might well try to keep it quiet; by cancelling the prayers, perhaps. Or even not telling anyone that the sister was dead at all. This didn't seem to be the sort of place where the leader of the community discussed things with their flock. Or even spoke to them very often.

He didn't want to raise the possibility of death directly with this sister, who seemed a bit fragile herself. He looked to the others and could see that they were thinking what he was thinking; he was quite pleased about that. Abbess Cartimandua, that's what they were thinking.

'This sister, the one who escaped, she was in charge of the tapestry?' Hermitage asked.

Another nod. Followed by a quiet whisper.

'You'll have to speak up a bit,' Wat was impatient and got a punch on the arm from Cwen. 'What?' he complained.

'She was,' the nun repeated, managing to get her voice as loud as barely audible.

'So the tapestry stopped?' Cwen asked, much more quietly herself.

More nodding. 'But the abbess sent for a replacement.'

'A replacement?' Hermitage couldn't help the question. Where did you go to get replacement nuns? Especially weaving ones.

'Sister Osgifu,' the very quiet one managed to say.

'Who wasn't born here and so is allowed a name,' Cwen almost spat.

'So the tapestry could start again,' Hermitage prompted.

The nun shook her head now.

'Why not?' Wat asked the nun.

'You're safe here. And with us.' Cwen was protective.

'An argument,' the sister said, as if horrified by the very idea. 'With the Abbess.' That was even worse. 'And she left.'

'Osgifu argued with Cartimandua,' Cwen said. 'And then she left as well?'

'Didn't Cartimandua try to stop her?' Hermitage couldn't imagine this abbess just letting someone leave.

The nun nodded once more, but this time with almost the barest hint of a smile at the abbess's problems with nun retention. 'There was a fight,' She even sniggered.

'Osgifu sounds like my kind of woman,' Cwen noted.

Hermitage reflected that there were two missing nuns now, even if one of them might well be dead. They still didn't know that she was murdered though. Although he had concluded that Abbess Cartimandua had something to do with this, he really couldn't see any abbess murdering one of her own nuns. His prior Athan, hated him deeply but hadn't tried to kill him. Well, apart from that once, obviously.

'How do you know about the argument and the fight and this sister Osgifu leaving?' Wat asked, gently. 'Did you hear anything?'

The nun cast her eyes firmly to the floor as that glint of the smile disturbed her lips even further.

'What happened?' Cwen lowered her voice.

Throwing her eyes from side to side, as if making sure that the walls weren't going to tell on her, the sister beckoned with a finger that they should all draw even closer.

'Outside,' she said. 'Sister Osgifu was outside the walls in the morning, as we were walking to chapel. She shouted.'

'What did she shout?' Cwen asked.

The anonymous nun dropped her voice even lower. 'You disgrace.' And she sniggered and clamped a hand to her mouth.

'She shouted "you disgrace"?'

The nun nodded. She pursed her lips and repeated the words that had obviously been ingrained on her memory. 'Cartimandua, you are a disgrace. I know what you've done. I'll be back for you. You see if I'm not. Then you'll get what you deserve.'

'I know what you've done,' Hermitage mouthed, almost as quietly as the nun.

'What did the abbess do next?' Cwen asked.

'Got very cross.' The sister quickly recovered her poise and the humour vanished.

Wat subtly beckoned that the three of them should step away from the quiet nun for a discrete discussion. The sister didn't seem concerned and went to the altar to kneel in prayer, as if luxurious times like this didn't come along very often.

'Well, well,' Wat said, when they were out of earshot. 'Dear Abbess Cartimandua tells us that one nun is dead and buried but we can't see the body.'

'She might have escaped for all we know,' Hermitage said hopefully.

Wat and Cwen both looked at him to say that they thought this was very unlikely.

'She wouldn't let us see the body,' Hermitage argued. 'Perhaps that's because it ran away?'

'I think even the most pious abbess, being asked if strangers could have a look at a dead nun, would treat them with suspicion,' Cwen observed.

'And she made no mention of a replacement. What do abbesses get for lying?' Wat asked Hermitage. 'Lying about anything must be pretty bad, but dead nuns must be worse.'

Hermitage was too confused to answer that, not that the question made any sense anyway. 'What is going on?' was all he could say.

'Very good question,' Cwen nodded. 'A lying abbess, a most likely dead nun who should have been leading the tapestry. A replacement who falls out with the abbess straight away? And Odo's tapestry in the middle of it all. I think we should, you know,' she nodded again at Hermitage.

'What?' he asked, looking around.

'Investigate.'

'Oh. Really?' And he'd just been developing the idea that they might not have to. 'The nun might still have escaped.' Even as he said this, he knew that he didn't really believe it. 'We could just go back and let people know? It makes such a nice change to be asked to investigate a murder and find no one's dead after all. In fact, in this case we were expecting lots of dead nuns, and there's barely one. That's even better. Surely?'

'We all know what we're thinking,' Wat said. 'Cartimandua killed the first nun, probably in a fit of temper because she wouldn't do what she was told or was too demanding because she was in charge of the tapestry. So, the abbess must find a new nun; Osgifu. What happens then? More temper but this one manages to storm out. We've only met the abbess once, and we don't like her, do we?'

They had to agree that no, they didn't.

'And why does anyone think there's a host of dead nuns anyway? Because that's what Cartimandua has told them. And why has she told them that? To hide the fact that she's just killed her chief tapestry maker and has had to rush out to find a new one.

Who she also lost. I can't imagine Odo being very happy with the abbess if he found out.'

'I can't believe any abbess would kill a sister, not really.'

'Could have been an accident,' Cwen suggested. 'Argument near a high window gets out of hand, that sort of thing? You have to admit, Cartimandua would be up for a good argument.'

Hermitage shrugged his acceptance of this.

'But,' he formulated his arguments. 'Running away isn't very serious. And if the abbess is simply trying to cover her own troubles, it's really nothing to do with the King's Investigator.'

'The king sent you to find out.'

'And I have found out,' Hermitage protested.

'There could be a dead nun out there and a killer abbess in here.' Cwen said.

Wat snapped his fingers. 'Where do they bury nuns?' he asked.

Hermitage wondered at the question. 'In the ground, generally. Like everyone else.'

'I know that. Which bit of ground?'

'Oh, I see. Well, if she was an important nun, she might be interred in the stones of the abbey itself.'

Cwen cast her eyes nervously around the stones.

'Other than that, there will be a private burial ground somewhere.'

'Not outside then?' Wat sounded disappointed.

'Certainly not.'

'I was just thinking we could go looking for a fresh grave, see if the nun is really dead.'

'The sister here thinks she ran away. I don't think even Cartimandua could bury a nun without anyone noticing. If she did kill her, she's just disposed of the body somewhere.' Cwen was quite matter of fact about this.

Hermitage sighed. His hopes had got so high as the number of dead nuns kept falling. And the one who was dead might even not be. Still, he knew his duty was to investigate. Sometimes he wished duty was a complete stranger.

'And it's all to do with a tapestry,' Wat said. 'Tapestry that should be made by weavers in the first place, not nuns. Odo's lesson here is weavers for weaving and nuns for, erm, nun things.'

Hermitage and Cwen shared looks of contempt for Wat's attitude.

'Cartimandua is obviously not going to tell us anything more about the nun presumed dead. We could look for the body but might not find anything. Particularly if Cartimandua's disposed of it properly. The only track we have is this Osgifu. We could look for her.'

'That's the spirit,' Cwen encouraged.

Wat stepped in. 'And we'd still have the opportunity to tell Odo that he needs some proper weavers looking after this. It's obvious that the nuns aren't up to it, what with dying and running off.'

Hermitage frowned that Wat's self-interest was starting to take over.

'Osgifu did say she was coming back.' Cwen said.

'Yes, but that was to get Cartimandua, not carry on weaving,' Wat noted.

Hermitage remembered the worst bit of the tale, a bit he had put to the back of his mind, probably hoping that it would stay there. 'Osgifu said she knew what the abbess had done. Did she discover the death?' He looked to the nun, who still had her back to them.

'Sister,' he called quietly.

The nun left her prayers and came back to them.

'Why would Osgifu say she knew what the abbess had done? Do you know what that meant?'

The nun simply shook her head.

'I expect the abbess has done a lot of things she should be ashamed of,' Cwen suggested.

Now the nun nodded.

'Did you talk to this Osgifu at all?'

Another nod. 'She led the tapestry and gave us our orders for the work. Just for the one day before she went to see the abbess and had the fight.'

'And was she,' Cwen searched hard for just the right word. 'Nice?'

The sister moved her head from side to side at this. 'Not nice, but not nasty either. She was too good for this place.'

'And she told you that, did she?' Wat asked.

'She only came to help out with the tapestry.' She beckoned them to come close for a great secret. 'Osgifu is really the queen.'

Well, that made no sense at all.

'Queen?' Cwen asked. 'Queen of what? Where?'

'England,' the nun replied. 'She's disguised as a nun so that she can see how her subjects are getting on.'

'I see.' Wat said this very slowly and looked to the others with rolling eyes. 'That's what she told you, is it?'

The nun nodded. 'But I wasn't supposed to tell anyone.'

'It's all right,' Wat said sympathetically. 'We won't tell anyone either.'

'And being the Queen of England, she probably didn't like being told what to do by an abbess.' Cwen could not hide her disappointment that Osgifu was turning out to be a bit odd, to say the least. Either that or the nun they were talking to was one bat short of a belfry.

'Did anyone bring her here? Osgifu, I mean,' Wat asked. 'A lot of people who perhaps had her tied up at the time. And was she jumping up and down telling them all she was the Queen of England and they had to let her go?'

'She told no one,' the nun reported, seriously.

'Except you.'

'She was a friend. Of sorts.' The way this was said brought them all to their senses. It sounded as if anyone who wasn't actually horrible, was considered a friend. And the nuns weren't allowed friends. Just a shame that this friend was as mad as a March Hare who woke up to find he'd missed March.

Wat spoke to Cwen and Hermitage. 'This Osgifu was obviously put here to keep her out of trouble.'

Cwen nodded towards the nun with the downcast eyes. 'Either Osgifu was or, everyone already here is a bit, erm…,' she let the thought linger.

'Some establishments do care for the confused,' Hermitage said.

'She sounds a bit more than just confused,' Cwen added.

'Is there really any point in going chasing for Osgifu the Queen of the May as she's probably out dancing with the pixies?' Wat was dismissive. 'If she's out there telling the Normans that she's the Queen of England, there really will be a murder.'

'We've still got the, er, missing sister to deal with,' Cwen pointed out. 'Even if Osgifu is gone with the clouds, she may be able to tell us something. I say we go and confront the abbess again.' She was all for confronting people most of the time.

The silent nun put an urgent hand on Cwen's arm.

'If we do that, she'll know where we got Osgifu's story.' Hermitage said. 'And then who knows what will happen to the poor sister here.'

'She can come with us.'

The grip on Cwen's arm tightened.

'Wouldn't you like to leave?'

The nun shook her head.

'But it's horrible in here. With a horrible abbess in charge.'

'And it's pretty horrible out there,' Wat said. 'If this is the only place you've ever known, why would you risk stepping outside?' He did give the nun a look of sympathy for her plight.

Cwen was looking thoughtful; thoughtful and scheming; thoughtful scheming and conniving. 'So, we go and look for Osgifu and get the dirt on Abbess Cartimandua.'

Hermitage didn't at all like the idea of getting dirt on an abbess, whatever it meant.

Cwen carried on slowly. 'It's obvious. Osgifu found out that Cartimandua had, erm, dealt with the missing sister.' She clearly didn't want to alarm the nervous nun. 'Problem is, we have no idea where Osgifu has gone. Did she say anything?' she asked the nun.

'Back to her throne, where she was going to rally her forces and return to deal with the abbess.' The slightest gleam lit up the nun's eyes at this prospect.

'I see,' Wat said, his voice falling with disappointment. 'Back to her throne, eh? Gather her forces. And I expect they'll all fly here on their unicorns.'

The nun looked at Wat as if he were mad.

'All right,' Wat invited the explanation. 'Where is her throne then? Did she tell you that?'

The nun nodded. 'Oxney.'

'Oxney,' Wat said blankly. 'The Isle of Oxney.'

'That's what she said.'

'I see. The Queen of England's throne is on the Isle of Oxney. Of course, it is.'

'You know this place, then?' Hermitage was slightly intrigued now, despite his best endeavours.

'Oh, I know of it. Never been though.'

'Really?' This was a surprise to Hermitage as Wat seemed to have been everywhere in the country in pursuit of his trade.

'Remember that marsh Ulf the ancient warned us about?'

'Erm, yes,' Hermitage's worry stirred deep inside.

'Well, if we want Osgifu, that's where we're going.'

The Marsh Mellows

'I still can't believe this.' Wat said. 'A nun who's been locked away since she was two tells us that the Queen of England turned up one day to help with the tapestry. And what do we do? Do we say, "that's nice dear" and all go home? No, we go and look for the queen?'

'We're looking for Osgifu,' Hermitage pointed out. 'We know she's not the queen.'

'Oh, good,' Wat didn't seem placated. 'As long as we're sure she's even real.'

Standing on the hill overlooking the marshes was a sobering experience for Hermitage. He had the idea of a marsh in his head, after all, he'd seen them in the east.* He hadn't even known there were any in this part of the world but imagined that they'd be the same. They weren't.

From this high vantage point, standing on a roadway before it took the plunge onto the flat lands below, Hermitage could see for miles. Miles and miles. Every one of them very flat and very wet-looking.

Some distance off to their left they could see the remains of a Roman construction of some sort, perhaps a fort. This sat on the hillside looking out over the marsh, as if waiting for its soldiers to return from what had been a very long mission indeed.

Still, Hermitage thought, if the Romans had thought nothing of establishing themselves in this area, it couldn't be that bad,

---

*   Variously in *The Case of the Clerical Cadaver* and *The Case of The Curious Corpse* - very marshy titles

could it? Unless, of course, the Romans had all drowned in the marsh.

He gazed out at the morning sun glinting off the bodies of water that lay below them; and there was an awful lot of glinting. Never mind the three of them getting lost in this place, a whole Norman army could vanish.

'Oxney's out there?' he asked, disbelief plain in his voice.

'So I believe,' Wat replied.

'Where?' Hermitage couldn't see anything that looked like an island. He couldn't even imagine an island in this blank landscape.

'Quite a way off, I think. On the other side of the marsh.'

'The other side, eh? Perhaps we should go round then? Instead of across. I mean, where marshes are concerned, around sounds like a much better idea than across, wouldn't you agree?' He could even hear himself babbling.

'Around would take days. And we won't be going through the worst of the marsh, just across the top.'

'Going across the top of a marsh does seem best.' Hermitage whimpered slightly.

'Come on.' Wat wasted no more time and led them down the hill, away from the nice safe trees and hills and roads that didn't have horrible sinking bogs on them.

'What do we do when we find Osgifu?' Hermitage asked from the back. 'She's hardly a reliable witness if she thinks she's Queen of England.'

'She might still know the truth about Cartimandua, the nun killer,' Cwen said. 'Even if she wears a crown of berries most of the time.'

'We still may not have a body,' Hermitage said. 'You know how awkward it is accusing someone of murder when the murdered isn't to hand.'

'That abbess needs dealing with,' Cwen replied.

Hermitage couldn't help but think that the king probably

already had an abbess-dealer-with. The Archbishop of Canterbury perhaps? 'We could just go and tell Stigand that we think she killed a nun, and he can deal with her.'

'She's been awful for years,' Cwen said. 'All of the years when Stigand was in charge. He didn't do anything about her before, why would he do it now?'

'And there's the tapestry to think about,' Wat said. 'We don't want Odo getting more nuns to weave tapestry for him, do we?'

'Don't we?'

'No, of course we don't. We find Osgifu, show that the abbess is finishing off any nuns that can weave and Odo suddenly needs to have a long chat about his tapestry. His great big tapestry.' Hermitage could almost hear Wat licking his lips. 'The biggest there's ever been. Just think.'

'I am thinking. I'm thinking you want to investigate so that you can get paid to make this Bayeux tapestry, and Cwen wants to do it so she can get revenge on an abbess. Neither of them very wholesome motivations, if I may say so.'

Neither of them had an answer to that.

The way through the marsh was actually a lot better than Hermitage had been fearing, and his hopes rose slightly. Only slightly though, as he started to worry about what would happen when they got to the other side.

There was still no sign of any island, not even a modest rise from the surrounding blandness. There was a lot of water, but it all seemed to be channelled and managed effectively. Rivulets, streams and even small rivers criss-crossed their path, but each had a bridge of some sort in just the right place. This was clearly a well-trodden route.

The bridge might be a simple tree trunk, dropped across a gap, or might be a properly constructed crossing, either way they all appeared to be strong and safe.

There was even more evidence of Roman presence. Stones and whole sections of wall emerged here and there, apparently to no purpose, but at least it was evidence that someone had been here before them. One thousand years before them, so it wasn't actually much comfort.

'Salt,' Wat said.

'Sorry,' Hermitage replied. 'I haven't got any.'

'I meant the Romans.' Wat pointed to a section of wall that had sunk into the land. 'You know how much the Romans loved a marsh. Build a wall, let the tide in and dry up, gather the salt.'

Hermitage nodded that this could well be the case. He also half expected a Roman to pop up from behind a wall at any moment because what they didn't see was any other people at all. He could tell that this was a place to be crossed, not loitered in, but even so he thought there might be some traffic. This did appear to be the only east-west route across the marsh, after all.

'It is very quiet,' Hermitage found himself whispering to the others.

Cwen seemed to agree. 'Anyone who lives out here all the time is bound to go mad sooner or later. Perhaps the rest of the population think they're Lords and Ladies.'

'They certainly wouldn't be bothered by the Normans,' Wat said. 'I know Hastings is not far away, but you can see why they'd leave this place be.'

'There could even be Roman soldiers who missed the message to go home.' Cwen made the familiar quip. It was often directed at folk who lived in the more remote areas of the country; folk who tended to live in a bit too much harmony with their animals. To find such a place here, so close to the site of the Norman invasion, seemed a complete anachronism.

Their journey continued in silence, each of them feeling shrunk by the land around them. They were insignificant blots on the landscape and could vanish forever without anyone even knowing. They also felt a growing dread, warning them not to draw attention to themselves, in case something jumped out of the marsh to get them. It was completely unreasonable, but then being unreasonable always made things worse, somehow.

'Water,' Cwen called after quite a while of silent walking. She pointed ahead.

'Oh, good,' Wat replied. 'Some more water, eh?'

'Shut up. I mean real water, proper water, lots of it.' She nodded her head in the right direction.

In the distance, the familiar shine of water was certainly larger than anything they'd seen to date. The horizon itself shimmered invitingly; or was that in warning?

Cwen squinted, her young eyes trying to catch some feature of comfort as they walked on. 'And buildings,' she called with enthusiasm. 'People.'

They all felt relieved at the thought of people. Not that they knew what people who lived out here would be like, but they would be better than an empty marsh, surely?

Recognition that their journey across the marsh was coming to an end hastened their steps, and soon the buildings ahead of them were clear.

Whatever this place was, it appeared to be quite a significant port. As they entered the edge of the village, some fine buildings watched them pass by. Fine buildings that were somewhat past their best, but still, it indicated trade and a normal sort of life.

If the buildings watched them pass with little interest, the same could not be said of the people. The first indication that the sight of strangers was uncommon was when one couple, standing talking in the street, simply dropped silent and opened their mouths as they studied the three people walking down their street.

After that, a child ran screaming for its mother, an old man made a very peculiar gesture in their direction, and even a dog ran off with its tail between its legs.

'Don't get many visitors, then,' Wat observed.

They carried on towards the water, Wat and Cwen ignoring the stares and the pointing, Hermitage bowing every now and then in acknowledgement of a particularly blatant examination.

Once at the waterfront they could see that this was indeed a busy place, or had been, quite a while ago. Wharves stood ready to receive great ships as they plied their trade across the oceans. Warehouses close at hand would store the goods before onward travel. Workshops would offer repair of the vessels before they made their return journeys.

Well, they would if there were any ships. From the state of the place it looked as if the last busy day had been when the Romans sailed away.

There were still small craft, bobbing in the high tide; local fishermen and traders who dealt with the nearest villages up and down the coast, most likely.

An old man sat with his back to them, his feet crossed in front of him as he repaired his nets. Wat approached him and coughed.

'What's the name of this place, old fellow?'

'Ah,' the old fellow screamed in surprise. 'Don't sneak up on people like that,' he said, as he screwed his head round to look at Wat.

When he did look at Wat his eyes immediately went quickly from side to side, as if seeking some help in dealing with the vision that had just appeared in front of him. The eyes then narrowed. 'Are you Segnar's boy?'

'Erm, no,' Wat said. 'We're not from round here.'

The old eyes considered this statement carefully. 'Yes, you are,' the man assured Wat.

'Eh?' Wat didn't understand that at all.

'You must be Burdon's cousin?'

'No. We are not from round here.'

''Course you are.' The man had it. 'That brother of Dolsar, the one who went off into the marshes.'

'No, no,' Wat explained. 'We're strangers. We've never been here before.'

Now the man looked puzzled, as if the idea made no sense at all. 'Yes, you have. You've just been keeping yourself to yourself.'

Cwen whispered in Wat's ear. 'Why don't we just ask the way to the queen's palace. I'm sure he'd know.' She gave him a worried look that said they'd now arrived in a whole village of mad people and might not be able to do anything about it. Apart from go mad themselves.

'We just wondered what the name of the place was.' Wat persisted.

'Ekley's long lost father?'

'No,' Wat was firm now. 'We are not from this place. Whatever it's called.'

'Whatever it's called,' the man repeated with a laugh, seeing that Wat must be kidding him.

'Yes. And what is it called?'

'This place?'

'This place.' Wat held his hands out towards the place in question.

'Fisherman's wharf, isn't it.' The man chuckled again.

'The village.' Wat's patience was running out with the tide. 'What is the name of this village?'

'Why, it's Appledore,' the man said, sounding very puzzled that he was being asked such a question.

'Appledore.'

'What else would it be called?'

'I don't know, do I? I am not from round here.' Wat's raised voice was attracting attention and several people were coming close.

'Is it the same Appledore that the Danes landed at many years ago?' Hermitage asked, the history of an old manuscript coming to his mind.

The heads in what was now a small crowd nodded. Heads that Hermitage noticed seemed to be predominantly blonde and rather Danish-looking.

'Danes?' Cwen asked, rather cautiously.

'That's right. They landed here but were then defeated in battle by King Alfred.'

There was an audible hiss from the audience at this.

Several of the local folk, the ones who had gazed upon the new arrivals with wonder, now came even further forward, probably satisfied that these people weren't going to eat anyone.

'Where you from then?' one woman asked, sounding very offended that anyone had the temerity to be from anywhere else at all. 'Brenzete?' The crowd gave a little gasp at people coming from such distance.

'That's three miles away,' someone almost fainted in awe.

'We're from Derby,' Wat said.

The woman thought about this for a moment. 'Is that in Denmark?'

'What?' Wat sounded appalled by the ignorance. 'No, of course it isn't in Denmark. It's in England.'

'Ain't no such place,' the woman concluded.

Wat simply shook his head in despair.

'Ain't no such place as Daarbee.'

'And you'd know, would you?'

'Fridiswid has travelled.' The old man explained that this woman's knowledge of the outside world was not to be challenged. 'She's been to Romney.'

The small crowd was now getting in a bit of a frenzy with all this talk of distant lands and exotic places.

'We've just come from Dover,' Wat hit back. And before that Canterbury. But that was after we'd come through London. On our way from Derby.'

The crowd sniffed at this nonsense.

'And now we need to go to Oxney.' Hermitage put in, helpfully.

The crowd fell silent. Then they took a step backwards.

'Do you know which way it is?'

No one in the crowd seemed prepared to answer, but the old man stared at them and held out a withered old arm and pointed away from the wharf.

Hermitage followed the directions and across a short stretch of the river in front of them saw another land mass, rising from the waters. 'Ah. That's the Isle of Oxney, is it?'

'It is,' the man confirmed. However, he confirmed it in such a grim and fearful tone that Hermitage quivered. 'But you don't want to be going to,' he paused, 'that place.'

'Why not?' Hermitage could tell that the people of Apple-dore considered Oxney to be a place of dread. That was obvious from the way they were behaving; obvious even to him. Still, they must have reason for their fear.

'You just don't.' The old man said. 'No one does.'

'Someone must do. Aren't there people who live there?' Even from here Hermitage could see signs of cultivation in the fields across the river.

'Not proper people. Not real people like you and me.'

'What's wrong with them?'

The old man looked about the crowd of his fellows, as if seeking their permission to continue.

'You mustn't,' one voice said.

'They've got to know,' the old man called back. 'If they're thinking of going there.'

'Know what?' Hermitage asked, thinking that he'd very much rather not know.

The old man beckoned them to draw near while he told his dread tale.

When they were all close, and the tension in the crowd was almost palpable, he imparted the knowledge they would need. 'They's funny folk over there.'

There was an awful silence.

'Is that it?' Cwen demanded. 'They's funny folk?'

'Well, they are,' the old man defended himself. 'Really funny.

And they have funny ways. And do funny things.'

'Such as?'

'Things as ain't natural.' The old man seemed to think that was enough explanation.

'So, I don't suppose anyone is willing to take us over there.'

The crowd joined the old man in his gasp at that suggestion.

'We should have brought More with us, after all,' Cwen said.

'Do you know a lady called Osgifu?' Hermitage asked, thinking that she must be known here, and may be well thought of. Or not, if she thought she was the Queen of England.

This brought no response at all. The faces all around them were completely blank.

'Osgifu,' Hermitage repeated. 'We were told that she lives on Oxney and may have travelled back there from her abbey.'

Although Hermitage had the old man's attention, he could see that the man's eyes had drifted their attention to somewhere in the crowd.

Hermitage turned and saw some movement there. Perhaps someone who knew Osgifu was coming to give information. He turned back and smiled at the old man.

Then he felt a searing pain on the back of his head and reasoned, very sensibly he thought, that someone had just hit him. Then he wondered why someone had hit him on the head. Then he stopped reasoning altogether.

Caput X

The Hit Parade

ermitage's mind told him to wake up. His head told him to go back to sleep; it didn't hurt so much when he was asleep. Then the pain told him that it wasn't going to let him go back to sleep anyway, so he might as well wake up.

He was flat on his back somewhere or other, and he was not at all comfortable. As the discomfort and the pain ganged up on him, he recalled the reason for going to sleep in the first place. He managed to keep his eyes closed, in case the person who had hit him on the head was there and wanted to do it again.

His hands seemed to be tied behind his back and were dragging pain through his shoulders and arms. As he tested his feet, he found them bound as well. Tied so effectively that he knew his legs had gone to sleep and that if he tried to stand up, he would fall over immediately.

He also knew that if he moved to make things easier, anyone watching would know he was waking and might do some more hitting. He forced himself to stay still and listen to what was going on around him.

Perhaps the people who had done this were still there and would now discuss their intentions in detail with each other, thinking he remained unconscious. That way, he could discover their dastardly plan and, when he escaped, thwart it. Or perhaps he'd just lie still and hope they went away.

The only thing he heard was a groan, and he wasn't even sure that it hadn't come from him. It could be the attacker was also in some pain. Perhaps he'd hurt his hand when he hit Hermitage.

'What bugger hit me on the head?' It was Cwen's voice, and it was nearby. Hermitage now opened one eye and saw that the three of them were alone. He opened the other eye.

They were in a rude hut of timber and thatch, lying on the earth floor. Wat was still asleep but Cwen was awake and struggling against her bonds.

Hermitage now moved and relieved the pressure on his arms.

'Where are we?' Cwen asked. Most unreasonably, Hermitage thought.

'No idea,' Hermitage croaked back. His mouth was completely dry, which told him he must have been asleep for some time.

He watched as Cwen squirmed around, her hands and feet obviously tied as well. She managed to roll over on to her front and shuffled to get her knees under her. After that she sat back against the wall of the hut, which bowed alarmingly. The moan and the expression on her face said that her head felt much the same as Hermitage's.

'And who hit us?' Again, Hermitage didn't know how he was supposed to have this information.

'And why?' At least Cwen didn't seem to expect any actual answers to her questions.

'We're still in Appledore, I assume,' Hermitage said. There was no clue to justify this assumption. The country was full of rude huts and they could be anywhere. There was still a tang of the sea in the air, so it was reasonable to conclude they had not been moved too far.

'As to why anyone would hit us, I have not a clue. We hadn't done anything.' Saying this made Hermitage think how unjustified and unfair the hitting had been. And hit from behind, how despicable was that?

'And why's he still asleep?' Cwen gave the back of the sleeping Wat a disparaging look. He was hunched against one side of the hut, his face to the wall. She clearly thought about kicking him but couldn't reach.

'Perhaps they hit him harder.'

'Hm.' Cwen didn't seem to think that was a reasonable excuse.

'Did you see who hit us?'

'Of course, I didn't. They got us from behind. Well, they hit me from behind.'

'Yes, me too. There must have been several of them to have done us all together. But it still doesn't explain why. We were only asking about Oxney.'

'And Osgifu.' Cwen said with some significance. 'It was only when you asked about her that we got hit.'

'Perhaps they'd been planning it for a while and that was their opportunity. It could be they hit all strangers.'

'Wouldn't be surprised,' Cwen complained. 'And they think the people on Oxney are funny.'

There was a groan from Wat at this moment.

'About time,' Cwen said.

'Cwen,' Hermitage cautioned. 'I am sure Wat is in as much pain as the rest of us.'

Wat rolled over to face them.

'Or even more,' Hermitage said, looking at the huge black eye that covered most of the right side of the weaver's face.

'They missed your back, then,' Cwen said.

Wat opened the one working eye and gave her a look of withering disdain. 'I put up a fight,' he croaked. 'Didn't fall over at the first little tap on the head.' He moaned some more and moved himself around until, like Cwen, he was resting with his back on the wall. The look on his face said that pretty much everything hurt to a greater or lesser degree. Mainly greater.

'But as there were three of them,' Wat went on, 'and you two had decided to have a little rest, I didn't last long.'

'Who were they?' Hermitage asked. He thought he'd better get in before Cwen said something unhelpful.

'Soldiers,' Wat said.

'Soldiers?' That was the last thing Hermitage had been expecting. He wasn't sure what the first thing was, but soldiers wasn't it. 'What were Normans doing here? And why would they hit us?'

Wat shook his head, even though it caused him obvious discomfort. 'Not Normans.'

'Not Normans?' That really didn't make sense. 'What other sorts of soldiers are there?'

'I didn't think there were any,' Wat said. 'Until they started hitting us. But they were definitely soldiers. Uniforms, weapons, very practised at hitting people.'

'Saxons?' Cwen asked. 'Could there still be a force of Saxons down here, hiding from the Normans?'

'Not Saxons, either.' Wat said. 'I've never seen anything like them.'

'Vikings?' Hermitage asked, quickly running through all the soldiers he'd ever heard of.

'They were big fellows, but they didn't look like Vikings. They were dressed all in black with round shields across their backs. And they were black as well. A black field with a stream running through it.'

'Erm,' Hermitage said.

'Not a real field,' Wat groaned. 'The shields were painted black with the blue line of a stream running across. Some sort of emblem.'

'Like William's lions?' Hermitage recalled the very poorly drawn lions that William displayed as his arms. They looked more like cats that had had something nasty done to them.

'Like that but very plain.'

'Some local lord, probably,' Cwen said. 'There must be one down here somewhere, despite the fact the whole place is virtually underwater. Could be one who didn't fight for Harold and, as we said, the Normans won't have bothered him down here, so he's carried on as normal.'

'Hitting strangers on the head and tying them up? Hardly a reasonable way to behave towards visitors.' Wat stretched his neck and tipped his head over, grimacing at the pain.

'Not when the visitors might be Norman, come to stop you being lord anymore,' Cwen suggested.

Wat managed a painful shrug. 'We'll find out soon enough, I expect. They didn't actually kill us, so they must want us for something.'

'And the tying up stops us leaving,' Cwen pointed out.

'Quite. Can you see out of the door?' Wat nodded his head towards the opening to the hut that was just to Cwen's right. He immediately regretted moving his head at all and released another moan.

Cwen looked over at the door, which was hung with a simple skin, rather than closed with anything more solid. Frowning at the pain in her own head, she got back onto her knees and shuffled over. Nosing the skin to one side with her head, she looked out.

She turned and sat once more. 'It's definitely outside,' she reported.

'What a surprise. Anything of note? Apart from sky and air?'

'No. We could be anywhere. Just a field with a house across the yard. Some sort of farm, I expect. But I think we'll know more soon.'

'How's that?'

'The man who saw me stick my head out will probably come and explain.' Cwen just gave Wat a glance that said it had been a stupid idea to look out of the door.

'They'd have come soon anyway. You don't tie people up and leave them in your hut for good.'

Forewarning did nothing for Hermitage's surprised squeak as a large man ducked into the hut, pushing the skin to one side. He was just as Wat had described, dressed all in black. He didn't have his shield with him though; probably didn't need it for three people tied up in a hut.

'Awake, eh?'

Hermitage could tell that Wat had some impertinent response on his lips, but he kept it to himself this time. After all, these people did have history when it came to hitting other people on the head. And Wat probably needed to keep his left eye to see out of.

'I'll fetch bald Osred,' the man said, and ducked out again.

The three looked at one another, a single question on their lips.

'Why does he have to be bald?' Wat asked.

'He probably shaves his hair off to be more fearsome,' Hermitage said, thinking that the state of this Osred's head wasn't the most important thing at the moment. 'Osred though, that's a northern name, mainly.'

'It's not Norman, that's for sure. Perhaps best not mention you're King William's investigator.' Wat said. 'Or that we've come from Odo.'

'What are we doing here then?' Hermitage hated this bit. There was always some part in his investigations when they had to make up some story in order to get at the truth. Either that or to avoid being murdered themselves. He'd never been good with stories, making up a load of nonsense that people were expected to follow when it was absolute rubbish. But it was all the lying that really put him off. He needed something as near to the truth as possible.

'I am a monk,' he started off.

'I think they're going to guess that bit,' Cwen said.

Hermitage tutted. 'I am a monk just travelling these parts and you are weavers I met on the road.'

'Excellent,' Cwen nodded. 'And we just happen to be trying to get to Oxney and are asking about Osgifu.'

'Oh, yes.' Hermitage hadn't really thought it through.

It was too late for any more fabrication as the door skin was thrown aside and bald Osred entered.

He could well be called Osred, there was no reason to doubt it. He too was dressed all in black, but why he was called bald was a complete mystery as he had a full head of hair; hair as dark as a jackdaw and as smooth as a frog. The full mane was slicked down with something pretty greasy - and pretty smelly.

'Right,' bald Osred said. 'Time for some explanations.'

'Good,' Wat replied. 'It would be nice to know why we've been attacked and tied up.'

'Not explanations from me,' Osred snapped. 'Explanations from you. What are you doing here?'

'We don't even know where here is.'

Osred just looked at Wat, very coldly 'And if I hit you in the other eye you won't be able to see where you are either. Why were you asking about Oxney?'

Hermitage knew what he would say if he was the first to answer; the complete and unadulterated truth. He also knew that the complete and unadulterated truth was seldom helpful, even though it should be. He tried to make sure that he was not the first to speak.

'All right,' Wat sighed. 'Although you only had to ask. All the hitting and the tying up was completely unnecessary.'

'We like hitting and tying up,' Osred replied with a horrible grin.

'This is Cwen,' Wat said, with a painful nod towards Cwen. Cwen looked back and it was not a look of encouragement. 'We were searching for her sister.'

Hermitage didn't know Cwen had a sister.

From the look on her face, it was a bit of a surprise to Cwen as well.

'Oh, yes?' Osred didn't sound convinced either.

'Cwen's a weaver and works with me, I'm Wat the Weaver,' Wat left the very faintest pause to see if Osred was impressed by this. He wasn't. 'And this is our monk, Brother Hermitage. For years we've been looking for Cwen's long lost sister, Eadrin.' He paused to let this fact sink in.

'So, we had some business in the south and heard about the abbey at Lyminge and the way that the abbess, Cartimandua, runs the place. Keeping girls captive, locking them up, that sort of thing. Well, that's quite common, obviously, but whenever we hear about places like that we go and have a look, for Eadrin, you see?'

Osred was giving nothing away.

Hermitage was quite fascinated by this tale, although he wasn't too sure about the idea of being Wat's personal monk.

'And would you believe we found her? In the abbey. She'd been there for years, held by Cartimandua.'

'Go on,' Osred said, which seemed to indicate that he saw something in this tale.

'We'd made up a lot of nonsense about being sent from the Archbishop of Canterbury and got in to the place to see the abbess. There was quite a bit of turmoil going on as Cartimandua said one of the nuns had just died. Before we left, we asked to go to the chapel; we always do that, so we can have a good look around without raising suspicion. That's when we found Eadrin. Ah, it was a happy reunion.' Wat smiled and nodded towards Cwen who also smiled, just with a bit more difficulty.

'Where's this Eadrin now, then?' Osred asked, having only tied up three people.

'That's why we're here. Eadrin said that the only nun who had ever been her friend was called Osgifu, and this Osgifu had recently had a fight with Cartimandua and had left.'

Although Osred looked thoroughly annoyed with Wat's telling of this tale, it seemed that he might believe it.

'Well, we couldn't escape with Eadrin there and then as the abbess was watching us all the time. So, we thought we'd find Osgifu and see if she'd help rescue Eadrin. This Osgifu had said she was going back for Cartimandua, it seems.

'The only thing we knew was that Osgifu was from Oxney. And there you have it. That's why we're here, it's why we're asking about Oxney and about Osgifu.'

Hermitage was very impressed, and not a little charmed by the heroic tale. He had to remind himself that it was a complete load of nonsense.

'And,' Wat went on, with a little anger this time. 'I assume that's the same reason we've been hit on the head and tied up. Are you in league with Abbess Cartimandua?'

Osred narrowed his eyes at them all in turn, presumably weighing up whether any of this could be true. But even if it was, what would he do about it?

Eventually, he seemed to reach a decision and stepped over to stick his head out of the door. 'Osred,' he called. 'Prepare the barge.'

Hermitage, Wat and Cwen exchanged puzzled looks. 'Probably brothers,' Hermitage mouthed.

'Both called Osred?' Cwen wasn't convinced.

There was no time for further discussion as bald Osred returned and considered them.

'We shall see how much of this is true,' he said. 'And if it's not, the hitting and the tying will be the least of your worries.'

'Fine,' Wat said, confidently. 'The barge will take us to Oxney then? And Osgifu?'

Osred gave Wat a really worrying look, full of foreboding. 'You're already on Oxney. Now we're going to take you to the Sacred Isle of Ebony.'

'Sacred Isle, eh?'

Osred smiled, which was really worrying. 'And those who go to the Sacred Isle and tell lies, never come back.'

Island Hopping

As they emerged from the hut, they could see they were on Oxney. Across the now swirling waters of the river sat the community of Appledore, probably waiting for the next stranger to hit on the head.

Osred did not seem interested in conversation and had removed the bonds on their feet with the clear indication that he preferred putting them on. He didn't even cut them away, he untied them carefully and rolled them up for the next time.

'Sacred Isle eh?' Wat asked as he was shoved along a narrow path. 'It'll be an isle, then?'

This only got him another shove.

'Nearby, I expect.'

For every snarl that Osred gave them, he got another back from Cwen, who looked very ready to put some bonds on their captor and see how he liked it.

Hermitage was too busy speculating about a sacred isle. It sounded quite charming really. An isle of peace and holiness. But then he recalled sacred groves and the like, the sort of thing favoured by Druids. There was no telling who held this isle sacred. He rapidly concluded that it wasn't likely to be a friendly group of Benedictine monks.

With no further information, Osred marched them on across the island, leaving the view of Appledore behind.

The river broadened here, the far bank receding away from them. The falling tide was also showing the first signs of what would be left behind once it had departed; mud, mainly. Hermitage hoped this sacred isle was close and that there would be enough water to get there.

'Hurry up,' Osred grunted with another shove for Wat.

'Why don't you shove one of the others for a change?' Wat asked.

'I like shoving you,' was Osred's conclusive reply.

They rounded a small rise in the land and saw that ahead of them, down at the water's edge, a jetty stretched out across the mud and into the water. It was a very long jetty and had obviously taken considerable effort to construct. Whole tree trunks had been driven into the bed of the river and planks were laid across these. It looked as if the water would go out a long way, if a jetty this length was needed.

Along the side of the jetty a rather magnificent boat was moored. When Osred had instructed that the barge be prepared, Hermitage had imagined a simple slab of wood with sides on it; the sort of thing used to move goods. This was clearly a passenger craft, and one made for passengers who expected to move in comfort.

It was very well made and maintained, being scrubbed clean with rows of carved benches down its middle. It must be at least thirty feet long and ten wide. On each side, single benches were occupied by oarsmen, all dressed in the ubiquitous black, and clearly keen to be off as they glanced nervously at the racing tide.

The prow of the vessel was decorated with a figure of some sort. It wasn't the dragon of a Viking, but more like a cat with its tongue hanging out. It seemed an odd thing to put on a boat, given cats' general hatred of water.

Like a Viking vessel, this one did have its shields along the sides of the boat. All these were in very good order and displayed the image Wat had described; a plain black background with a thin blue line, meandering across the middle.

Most surprising of all was that high in the stern, looking down on everything that went on below was what could only be described as a throne. It was a heavy carved chair, the size of a small hovel but clearly intended for just one person. It was unoccupied at the moment and looked like it was reserved for someone much more important than them.

'Get on,' Osred ordered.

Wat moved before he could be shoved again.

As soon as their feet were on the boat, it was untied and the oarsmen pulled and fended away from the jetty. They were clearly used to this as they soon heaved out into the fast-moving stream.

The three of them were directed to one of the benches in the middle, where Osred stood over them, daring them to move.

Hermitage looked out at the waters and huddled as close as he could to the middle of the craft.

Another black-dressed man came up from the prow of the boat and stood by Osred.

'A few more moments and we'd have been too late.'

'I know, I know,' Osred replied.

'We'll not get back before the next tide.'

'Then so be it.'

The man from the boat didn't seem too happy about that.

Hermitage chanced a whisper to the others while Osred was talking. 'They're very well equipped.'

Wat and Cwen looked hard at him, clearly thinking that this was hardly the most interesting topic of conversation at the moment.

'I mean, they've all got uniforms, those shields aren't cheap and then there's the boat.'

'So this local lord is rich,' Cwen said. 'Nothing unusual there.'

'I've never seen any local lord go to these lengths.'

'What are you suggesting?'

'Nothing really,' Hermitage shrugged. 'Just saying it's a bit odd.'

'Oh, good,' Cwen said. 'Thanks for that.'

'Yes,' Wat agreed. 'Being hit on the head, taken to an island

and tied up isn't odd enough?'

'I'm only saying.' Hermitage thought there was no call for them to be rude. It really was odd. And he had never heard of any lord having a sacred isle. He wasn't going to mention that though, if they were going to be all snappy about it.

'Quickly men,' Osred's companion called to the oarsmen, who doubled their efforts. 'We don't want to spend the night on the mud banks,' he said. 'Again.'

The oarsmen glanced over at the waters and heaved with renewed strength.

Ahead of them, the three tied-up passengers could see a far shore approaching. From this angle it wasn't clear that this was an isle at all. To its right, receding waters filled a gap some hundred feet or so wide, before rushes and low scrub indicated that the ground over there was more regularly land than water.

To the left, the main body of the river ran down towards them, but whether the land ahead was joined to the mainland behind or not was impossible to tell. Hermitage could only think that the title "Sacred Isle" would be a disappointing name for a spot that wasn't actually an isle at all. Sacred Promontory didn't have quite the same ring to it.

Another jetty, reaching out from the isle like a grasping finger was obviously their aim, and it was only some fifty feet away now. Two or three good strokes from the oarsmen would see them there.

The boat was moving at such pace that Hermitage feared they would hit their destination, rather than arrive at it. In fact, they did neither. Almost within walking distance of the jetty, the boat suddenly ground to a halt; or mudded to a halt, more accurately.

The oarsmen, who had been pulling backwards with all their strength, now found that the boat under them wasn't going anywhere. Rowing a boat that was fixed to the bottom of the river was not a tenable activity. Oars skipped out of the water and every one of them fell off their seat as they lost their grip.

'Oh, bloody hell,' Osred swore. 'Not again.' He considered his collapsed crew and the gap from the boat to the shore, which was not wide, just too wide to jump.

'Told you so,' his companion helpfully informed him.

Osred glared. 'Fetch the planks,' he ordered.

The oarsmen, who were now back on their feet but were rubbing bruises and strains, went to the prow of the boat and extracted four planks of varying lengths from brackets where they were stored.

Osred went over to the edge of the boat closest to the jetty and looked over the side. 'I think a number two will do,' he called to the men.

The oarsmen sorted through their planks until they found the one they were looking for. Two of them lifted this and took it over to Osred. Under his direction they hoisted it over the side of the boat and then moved it around, squinting at it to confirm that it would reach the jetty before they settled it in place.

Satisfied that their sight lines had been accurate, they hoisted the plank the last few inches and dropped it into place.

They then quickly leaned over the side of the boat as they watched the plank slip neatly between boat and dock and fall to the mud below.

No one said anything for several moments until one loan rower made the obvious observation. 'Should have been a number three then?'

Osred's growl was enough to make people keep their distance. 'Whoever said that is on plank recovery duty,' he announced to a groan from the back

'I had to get the last one,' the rower complained.

'Teach you to keep your mouth shut,' Osred concluded as another plank was brought up. 'Now, everyone shut up, and get the prisoners out.'

Three oarsmen moved to the back of the boat to get Hermitage and the others.

'This sort of thing happen a lot?' Wat asked, containing a smirk.

'The river's not what it was,' one oarsman explained. 'It's silting up badly. There's some as reckon the Sacred Isle won't be an isle at all much longer.'

'I told you to shut up,' Osred shouted. He pointed a finger at the oarsman who had spoken. 'I'm watching you, blind Osred,' he said.

Hermitage had to look to Wat and Cwen again. Another one called Osred and this one blind? When patently he wasn't blind? And a bald Osred who had hair? What was wrong with these people?

Wat just shook his head slightly and whispered to them both. 'I think we've been captured by the island where they put all the idiots.'

'Well done us,' Cwen said.

'Right,' Osred ordered. 'Get over the plank.'

'Bit difficult with our hands tied,' Wat complained.

'Dangerous, even,' Cwen added.

'What are you going to do?' Osred asked. 'Fall in the mud?'

At least he helped them climb up the side of the boat until they could get their feet on the plank. One by one they walked across the very solid wooden walkway, which was obviously used quite often. Once ashore, they were marched down the jetty while the men from the boat tried to haul it closer with a sturdy rope.

'Short Osred, unready Osred, you're with me.' Osred called.

'Are all your men called Osred?' Wat asked.

'Of course,' Osred said. 'Outsiders may have their different names, but we're better than that.'

'And what are all the women called?' Cwen asked. 'Oswilda?'

'Pah,' Osred scoffed as he walked ahead. 'Idiot.'

'Maybe they're taking us to the head Osred,' Wat speculated. 'Who's doubtless called head Osred.'

'You'll find out soon enough.'

The path from the jetty was wide and clear and well-trodden. The trees and bushes had been cut back and the road led straight and true into the heart of the island.

As they walked up the very slight incline, they caught glimpses of the surrounding river. The tide had dropped significantly now, and a sea of mud was revealing itself. If this place was hard to get to because of the water, it was now even more difficult. At least people could row on water. The mud looked as if it was ready to swallow whatever was thrown at it.

It was still impossible to see to the back of the island, but they had to assume that it really was an isle. Whatever their captors had planned for them, there was no point trying to run away; they'd only end up back where they started.

After only a few dozen paces, they emerged from the low trees and scrub to a clearing, presumably in the middle of the island, in which sat a house.

It really was a house. A proper, well-made house of timber and wattle and daub with a good strong thatch roof on top. And it was large, certainly big enough to house all the Osreds that had come with them in the boat. A fine oak door sat in the front, studded with iron, and windows either side gave the place quite a friendly character - even to people who were being brought here against their will.

There were even two stories to the house and it looked like it had several rooms on each floor. It was certainly the sort of place that a minor lord would consider fitting. And, like the rest of the place, it was very well maintained. The whitewash was fresh, the glass clean and the surroundings neat and tidy.

'Osred's house?' Wat asked. This only got him a fresh shove towards the main door.

Osred pointed his finger at them each in turn, in what was a clear warning to behave themselves. When they were suitably contrite, he knocked on the door.

After a few moments it was opened by a tall, thin man, very well dressed, who looked down his nose at the people who had the impertinence to knock on his nice clean door.

'Thin Osred?' Wat asked. 'Ow,' he added as their Osred clipped him round the ear.

'These people were found in Appledore,' Osred reported. 'They were asking about Oxney and Osgifu.'

The snooty man seemed to take some interest in this.

'Their story is that this one's sister knew Osgifu when she was out there.' He nodded to Cwen, who smiled, rather horribly.

He had said *out there* in a rather peculiar manner, giving it an emphasis that said it was somewhere special.

'And you brought them here?' The thin man didn't sound too happy about this.

'Best we deal with them here if their story is false,' Osred said. 'Lest they spread their lies.'

Hermitage didn't like the sound of that. Being dealt with was bad enough. Having it done on a sacred isle had horrible connotations.

'True, true,' the thin one agreed. 'We shall find out.' He stood back from the front door, which seemed to be the signal that they could enter.

With a glare from Osred that they really needed to be on their best behaviour now, he indicated that they should go in.

The inside of the place was as impressive as everywhere else. It was very neat, clean and well furnished. Whoever had built this place on this island had gone to a lot of trouble.

'Wait in here,' the thin Osred instructed as he directed them to the room on their right.

They went in and saw another comfortable room, this one with benches around the walls and under the window, while a large padded chair stood at the far end.

Boat Osred stood guard while the other Osred left them and closed the door behind him. After a few moments they could hear the sounds of muffled conversation in the room above. This was soon followed by footsteps coming down the stairs before thin Osred opened the door once more.

As he did so, he stepped back and bowed low as a woman walked in behind him.

Osred from the boat also bowed, but not before hitting each of them in turn to indicate that they should do the same. With very little enthusiasm, they did so.

The woman walked past them and went to the comfortable chair, where she sat.

They were now allowed to stand up straight again.

Hermitage looked at this woman, who was clearly the lo-cal lord all this fuss was about. Like her men, she was very well dressed. She wore a thick long gown of deepest red and doubt-less of great expense. She must be at least forty years old and had a look about her that said she was used to being in charge. Any discussion would only start when she was good and ready.

Her face was completely expressionless, but in a very expect-ant way; the main expectation being that she was about to be disappointed. Her men had work to do to impress her, and it was highly likely that they weren't going to succeed.

She gave the very slightest nod towards boat Osred.

Osred bowed once more. 'Your Majesty,' he said. 'These peo-ple came to Appledore with a tale of the Abbess Cartimandua and information from this girl's sister concerning Osgifu.'

The woman did raise an eyebrow at this.

'Your Majesty?' Wat mouthed at Hermitage and Cwen. It seemed that they had found the loon who thought she was a queen and simultaneously discovered that she had a whole is-land of loons to keep her company.

He got another clip round the ear.

'Be silent,' Osred instructed. 'And show respect. You are lucky to be here at all. Listen to the wise words of Queen Osgifu, you oaf.'

'Oh, Queen Osgifu?' Wat managed to sound really excited about this, as if it explained everything. And as if it was a great honour, one he'd been waiting for all his life.

'Of course,' Osred confirmed, while Queen Osgifu looked on.

'This is Queen Osgifu?' Wat's wonder went on. 'The Queen Osgifu of erm..,'

'Queen Osgifu, Queen of England, you fool.'

The Problems of 'Out There'

ueen of England,' Wat repeated slowly, as if memorising the fact as he would need it later.

'And you are?' Osgifu asked.

'I am Wat the Weaver, Majesty, and this is Cwen, she's also a weaver.'

'Wat and Cwen the weavers.' Osgifu repeated it as if it was the last time she would ever need it.

'Well, not quite,' Wat explained. 'I'm Wat the Weaver and this is Cwen, who's also..,'

'Wat and Cwen the weavers is right, Your Majesty,' Cwen spoke up. 'In fact, one might say Cwen and Wat the Weavers, if one was being polite.'

'And a monk?' Queen Osgifu asked, before Wat could go any further in outlining the correct nomenclature for weavers.

'Brother Hermitage, Majesty.' Hermitage gave a slight bow. He knew this woman wasn't the Queen of England. Knew for certain as it was only a little while ago he'd been in the presence of the king. And William had never mentioned that there was a queen living on an island in a marsh. Still, she believed it, and so did the uniformed men with weapons who were all over the islands. He'd let William and Osgifu sort out any disagreements over monarchy between themselves.

'Odd name for a monk,' the queen observed, with a slight smile. 'I imagine you would rather be in quiet contemplation over a volume of sacred text than running around chasing nuns to strange islands.'

Hermitage could only gape at her perspicacity. His overwhelming urge was to say, "yes please."

'And you claim to know me through your sister?' She asked Cwen.

'That's right, Your Majesty,' Cwen replied.

Hermitage could only hope that she meant it was right that she claimed it, not that it was actually right. He didn't want her lying as frequently and with as much nonchalance as Wat.

'And your sister's name?'

'Her name, ah yes.'

'I assume she has a name?' The queen's eyes narrowed as they honed-in on the real problem here; that it was all made up.

'Of course. She has a name, or rather she did. Erm,' Cwen paused for thought, which would appear to be unnecessary for someone trying to recall the name of the sister they've been searching for all their life. Wat mouthed the required information. 'Eadrin,' Cwen blurted. 'That's it, Eadrin. Her name's Eadrin. But she was taken into Lyminge Abbey as a baby and doesn't know that's what she's called anymore. Abbess Cartimandua has never told her what her name is, and now she has none.'

The effect on the queen of this only blatant and stumbling lie was immediate. She leaned forward on her throne and stared intently at Cwen.

'You left this sister with no name there? You didn't bring her out with you?' This was pretty much in the nature of an accusation.

'She was too scared to leave, Majesty. She's been there all her life and now it's the only life she knows. The world outside must be a terrifying place. But she told us that you had been her friend and that you had escaped the place after dealing with the abbess.'

Osgifu's eyes were doing their narrowing again. She gave Cwen a very careful examination. 'I would say that you are several years younger than the sister at Lyminge. How is it that you weren't given to a nunnery as well?'

'Ah, yes, that. Well, my mother, Eadgyth, had my sister out of wedlock you see. There was a great shame and the baby had to go. Then she married my father, Stigand, so I was all right.'*

'Hm.' The noise said that the queen was still not completely convinced. 'So, why come looking for me? You found your sister, she wants to stay where she is. Why not go home again?'

'Because Abbess Cartimandua must go.' At least Cwen was honest and sincere about this. 'If my sister doesn't want to leave, or rather, can't leave, it's because of what the abbess has done to her. And done to dozens of other girls, I imagine. If you're the same Osgifu, you were there. You know the truth but escaped. My sister told us that you called out to the abbess that you would be back, that you knew what she'd done. We thought that together we could deal with Cartimandua.'

Hermitage was relieved that she'd managed not to mention the possibility that Cartimandua might be killing her nuns. They'd need to see if Osgifu knew this, rather than give her the information. He was quite pleased with this thought, considering it to be just the sort of thing a real investigator would come up with.

Osgifu nodded gently at this. 'That may be possible,' she said. 'I was indeed in that place. I discovered that Cartimandua was the most awful woman. She was treating her sisters in the most shocking manner and was a traitor to her calling.'

The three of them just nodded at this.

'How do I know that this tale of yours is true?' Osgifu asked. 'You could be sent from the abbess to deal with me. After all, I know too much.'

Hermitage had to agree that was a possibility. He didn't know what they could say that would persuade Osgifu. Even though she wasn't the Queen of England, she did seem to be quite sensible. They hadn't found her in a ditch throwing dirt over herself so she couldn't be that mad. It must just be a misunderstanding.

---

*   For the partial, but still pretty shameful history of Cwen's family, read *A Murder for Mistress Cwen*

He couldn't immediately think what sort of misunderstanding would make an island full of people think she was Queen of England, but he was sure they'd get to that. In the meantime, they had to convince her that they were not Cartimandua's agents, somehow.

'Your Majesty,' he said. 'We suspect that Cartimandua has done something far worse than treat her sisters badly.'

Osgifu just looked at him but did it quite hard.

'But we cannot be sure, yet. We think you may know what this thing is, as you were there shortly after it may, or may not have happened.'

'You talk in riddles,' one of the Osreds complained.

Osgifu held a hand up for silence and addressed Hermitage. 'And you want to know if I know what this thing was. But you do not want to prompt me, in case you put the idea in my head.'

'Exactly.' Hermitage was impressed.

Everyone else in the room just looked confused.

'But if I say what it is, am I not putting myself in danger if you are Cartimandua's people?'

'You are the queen with all your men around you,' Hermitage pointed out. 'And we are at your mercy.'

Osgifu considered this very carefully and her eyes bored into Hermitage. 'You seem to be a trustworthy monk.'

'Thank you.'

'Very well,' Osgifu said. 'But if I find that you are not as you say, it will go badly for you.'

Hermitage nodded his agreement to this.

Osgifu took a breath. 'I will tell you what I know. But explanation is required. You are from out there, as we call anywhere that is not Ebony or Oxney. You are doubtless confused by discovering who I really am.'

'The Queen of England,' Wat said, as if it was perfectly reasonable.

'Just so.' Osgifu ran a hand over her eyes and a great weight seemed to fall on her. 'After many years, and a clear prohibition going back centuries, I decided to go out into the world, against the advice of my court.' She acknowledged the thin Osred at her side, who responded with a look of profound I-told-you-so.

'For generations, the kings and queens of England have resided on the sacred isle, protected by our personal guard and shielded from the ordinary world.'

'And the ordinary world was shielded from you,' Wat said.

'So it would seem. You can imagine my horror at what I discovered out there.'

'It is pretty horrible,' Wat agreed.

'I could not imagine how this had come to be.'

Hermitage put his hand up.

'Yes, Brother?'

'If you don't mind me asking, Your Majesty, how long ago was it that the, erm, kings and queens came here?'

'The isle was first made sacred by King Osred the second.'

'Oh,' Wat said, nodding towards the local men in the room. 'Hence all the Osreds.' He seemed very happy that this had some sort of explanation.

'Osred the second?' Hermitage scoured his brain to see if there was any King Osred in there at all, first or second.

'He was briefly exiled here before returning triumphant to his throne out there. That was in the year of our Lord seven hundred and ninety-two.'

Hermitage's brain dropped everything. 'That's over two hundred and fifty years ago.'

'Precisely,' the queen said, with some annoyance. 'And in that time, while we have been observing the sacred rituals and taking our responsibilities very seriously, it seems that out there we have been completely forgotten.'

'You've been on these islands for two hundred and fifty years?' Wat was as staggered as Hermitage. 'And you only thought to go and find out what was going on this week?'

'We are on the sacred isle.' Thin Osred spoke up. 'Great King Osred brought his court here and established it in perpetuity. He left instruction that we were never to leave. The kings and queens that followed him would remain here in glorious isola-tion. And not be corrupted by contact with the common folk.' He clearly thought that Hermitage, Wat and Cwen were very common folk.

'Didn't anyone notice the Danes sail through Appledore?' Hermitage had to ask. 'According to the chronicles, hundreds of them went right by here, off to battle in Wessex. And then they probably came back again.'

'Our records do make mention of something like that,' thin Osred admitted. 'But we do not concern ourselves with out there.'

'You mean you hid in the reeds while the Vikings went by,' Wat said. 'We've all done that, nothing to be ashamed of.'

Osred glared.

'And in all those years the common folk out there got on per-fectly well without you and forgot where they'd left their kings and queens.' Wat summed up the situation.

'It matters not,' thin Osred sniffed. 'The queen will remain here and out there can do what it pleases. We shall maintain the proper standards.'

Wat snorted. 'At the rate this river is silting up you'll be part of Kent soon, whether you like it or not. Then you'll find the Earl of Kent isn't half as shy and retiring as you lot. And the last thing he'll want is a queen popping out of the mud.'

'Watch your tongue,' thin Osred hissed.

Osgifu raised her hands for calm while thin Osred and Wat exchanged looks; different varieties of contempt.

'As I see in most disputes, you are both right.' She nodded her head towards thin Osred. 'We do maintain the standards of the monarchy and have thrived. But the books tell us that in years gone by the river was much broader. It is true, the tide gets shal-

lower each year and the islands will soon be joined to out there.'
Osgifu and Osred gave a little shudder at this. 'So, it is timely
that I should discover what I could.'

'Not good news, is it?' Wat said.

'Osred the second,' Hermitage's mind had been following a
much more important track. 'King of Northumbria?'

'Just so,' thin Osred confirmed. 'After his exile here, he returned to rule over his kingdom and to unite the whole country
into one land of the Angles. England.'

'I see.' Hermitage had recalled the relevant chronicle. He
didn't know how to break it to these people that Osred had indeed returned from exile, only to be promptly murdered by King
Aethelred. Who himself was done for four years later.

He turned to the queen. 'So, you know about William and
the Normans now?'

'I do,' Osgifu sighed. 'I went out there disguised as a nun. Osred did not want the queen to go at all, let alone to be recognised.'

'Very wise,' Hermitage said. Although there was no risk of
anyone recognising her as no one knew who she was. Mind you,
wandering the country claiming to be Queen of England would
have been not very wise.

'I slipped through Appledore, where people do know us, naturally. And headed east.'

'Towards Lyminge.'

Osgifu nodded again. 'Where I came upon the abbey and its
abbess.'

'Bad luck.' Cwen said.

'Being a nun, I thought it would be a suitable place of shelter and so made my lodging there. In conversation, Cartimandua
explained that she had secured a commission from the Earl of
Kent to make a great tapestry showing the history of his people.
Well, I had no idea who the Earl of Kent was supposed to be
but kept my counsel. A tapestry showing history could be very
informative and might give me all the information I needed.

'So, I said that I was quite an adept seamstress and would be fascinated to see this tapestry.

'Cartimandua was overjoyed and offered to show me what they had done so far. Of course, I agreed. Then she tried to lock me in a cell with seven or eight other sisters, all of them sewing through day and night.'

'Sewing?' Wat asked with a frown.

Osgifu ignored the interruption. 'The sisters had been given the tale they had to tell and were working their way through it. You probably know it well, but to me, it was utterly appalling. The whole thing begins with someone called Edward.'

'That'd be King Edward,' Wat said.

'No mention of Osred at all,' Osgifu complained. 'Then there's someone called Harold.'

'King after Edward,' Wat explained. 'But not for long.'

'And then William.'

'And here we are.' Wat held his arms out to show that they were now up to date.

'And the things these people do is quite revolting.'

'We know,' Hermitage muttered.

'At least I found out who this Earl of Kent is,' Osgifu was contemptuous. 'He wants to appear in his own work. A picture of him holding a club in the middle of battle has to be included. And him a bishop as well.'

'Odo,' Cwen said.

'So it seems. Hic Odo episcopus baculum tenens confortat pueros. The man has even sent the words he wants included.'

Wat and Cwen looked to Hermitage.

'Here Odo the bishop with a club strengthens the boys,' he translated.

'Lucky boys,' Cwen said.

'It must have all been a terrible shock,' Hermitage sympathised.

'Of course. It was clear that I had to get away from Cartimandua. Unfortunately, I had to leave your sister behind.'

Hermitage was pleased to see Cwen cast her eyes to the floor.

'And here we come to your question, Brother.' She gazed intently at Hermitage, probably to judge his reaction. 'When I arrived at the abbey, a nun had gone missing; the one who managed the tapestry, which is why the abbess was so keen to keep me there.

'Some of the sisters said that this nun had escaped but in my arguments with Cartimandua she gave too much away. I have no evidence for it, but from the things she said, I suspected that the nun was dead. I also think Cartimandua had something to do with it. She is a woman with a vicious temper and it may have been an accident, but I cannot say for sure.'

Hermitage breathed and nodded. 'Just so, Your Majesty. We suspect the same thing, and may be in a position to bring Cartimandua to justice, with your help.'

Osgifu seemed satisfied with this.

'You mentioned sewing,' Wat said.

Everyone gave him very odd looks.

'So, what now, Your Majesty?' Cwen asked, ignoring Wat. 'About the Normans and the rest of out there?'

Thin Osred spoke. 'Her Majesty has returned to the sacred isle and will reside here. We shall send emissaries out there who will apprise these strange new folk of the situation. Queen Osgifu will be restored to her rightful place.'

Hermitage, Wat and Cwen exchanged painful looks.

'A problem?' Osgifu asked.

'Well,' Hermitage stretched the word out, the way people do when they want to alert the listener that they are about to get bad news. 'I'm not sure the Normans will be very welcoming. William went to an awful lot of trouble to become king and isn't the sort to give things up lightly. Anything at all. Let alone the kingdom.'

Osgifu nodded and beckoned Osred to close conversation.

They whispered to one another and it seemed that they were resolving some issue that had already been discussed. Neither of them seemed very happy with the result.

They turned back to Hermitage. 'How many are these Normans?' Osred asked.

'Oh,' Hermitage had never counted. 'Lots,' he said, helpfully.

'More than two dozen?' Osred asked.

Hermitage looked but saw that the man was being serious.

'Oh, yes.' He nodded as sombrely as he could. 'More like, oh, perhaps, erm, thousands, at a guess. Wouldn't you say?' He asked Wat and Cwen, who nodded.

'Thousands?' Osred was seriously disheartened. He returned to his whispered conversation with the queen.

After a few moments they came to another conclusion, even more distasteful than the first.

Osred announced the result. 'You are honoured to be the first to know that there will be a royal wedding.'

'A wedding?' Cwen had clearly not expected that at all. 'Between who?'

'Queen Osgifu of England and William of Normandy.'

Three faces simply looked very blank, and not a little sickened.

'Marry William?' Cwen tried to get the bad taste out of her mouth.

'He will be honoured to join the ancient line of Osred and secure his place on the throne at her side.'

'I think you'll find he's already secured his place on the throne,' Cwen said. 'And he has a proven method for doing it; he kills whoever was sitting there before him. If you send word that the rightful Queen of England is on Ebony, he'll send some of his thousand men to trample it into the mud of the river.'

Osred and Osgifu seemed to be running out of ideas.

Hermitage had a piece of information that might cast further doubt on their scheme. He had to say it, they'd find out sooner or later. 'And anyway,' he said quietly. 'William's already married.'

Wat and Cwen turned to him. 'Is he?'

'Of course.' Hermitage couldn't believe that they didn't know this. 'Matilda. Queen Matilda?'

'I've never heard of her,' Wat protested.

'He doesn't talk about her much,' Cwen said.

'Nonetheless she's there. They've been married for years. She spends most of her time in Normandy.'

'If I was married to William, I'd stay further away than Normandy,' Cwen huffed.

Wat looked at him. 'How do you know this stuff?'

Hermitage shrugged. 'I listen to people.' He quietly thought that Wat might like to give this a try once in a while.

While they were considering William's marital status, Osred and Osgifu had returned to their quiet discussions.

The queen turned back to them with a heavy expression on her face. 'Then there is nothing left.' She shook her head. 'I despair that it should be I, Queen Osgifu the Seventh, who sees this sorry day.'

Hermitage, Wat and Cwen were all mouthing "seventh" at one another in some considerable surprise.

'Osred,' the queen said. 'It is decided. Take word to my son, Osred.'

Hermitage had already worked out that this meant her son was called Osred as well. This must be a very confusing place to live.

Osred bowed and left the room.

Hermitage just gave Osgifu a curious look. Even though she wasn't really the queen, it seemed rude to ask direct questions.

'We are left with only one course of action,' Osgifu said.

He was glad that they had come to their senses. He just hoped that William would be merciful when he saw what a harmless bunch they were, really.

The queen gave a resigned nod. 'If we cannot negotiate with

these Normans and there is no route to an alliance through marriage, there is only one thing for it. They have got to go. We shall attack the Normans and drive them from our land.'

'Ah.' Hermitage remained as calm as he could manage in the circumstances. 'Attack the thousands of Normans and drive them from your land?' His wide eyes begged Wat and Cwen for some help here.

'Well,' Wat said. 'It's a plan, I'll give you that.'

Caput XIII

The Best Form of Attack is Attack

ermitage wondered if this was the moment to let Osgifu and all the Osreds know that their original king had been murdered within weeks of leaving Ebony. On balance, he thought not. They'd had enough bad news recently. He really didn't want to make things any worse for them.

But attacking the Normans and driving them from the land? If King Harold and all his army couldn't do it, what hope would a tiny island full of Osreds and Osgifus have. (He had already concluded that all the women here would be called Osgifu).

'Majesty,' he said thoughtfully. 'May I counsel against this idea?'

Osgifu smiled at him. 'You seem a learned and thoughtful fellow. I will take your counsel.'

Hermitage smiled back, and out of the corner of his eye saw Wat giving him a rather lewd wink for some reason.

He had never ever seen himself as being invited to counsel a monarch. The one he had to deal with most of the time simply gave him impossible orders and then complained when they weren't completed immediately. He'd come to conclude that sort of thing was normal for kings and queens.

'The Normans are many,' he began. 'We have already reported that there are thousands of them. There were thousands and thousands at the battle of Hastings and more have come since then. How many men do you have?'

The queen spoke brightly. 'It is not only the men who are capable of fighting,' she said. 'The women of Ebony and Oxney take arms as soon as they can walk.' She suddenly looked quite doleful. 'We have had some losses recently, though.'

'Losses?' Hermitage couldn't imagine this place being bothered by anything.

'Our young men and women,' Osgifu explained. 'They see the bright lights and gay life of Appledore and are drawn to it.'

Wat chose this moment to have some sort of coughing fit.

'How many remain?' Hermitage asked.

'At the moment we have some sixty of travelling age.'

'Sixty. Against thousands.'

'Just so.' Osgifu didn't seem too concerned about this. 'But many of them have never left the islands at all. I am not sure how well they will perform.'

'I don't think that really matters, Your Majesty.' Hermitage did give serious thought to how sixty could overcome the entire Norman army. His serious thought didn't last long.

'If you were in the north perhaps, sixty may be enough to rally support. But you are in Kent. Well, I mean you're on the sacred Isle obviously, but, erm out there, over the water is Kent. It's full of Normans. It's just down the road from where they arrived and it's the first county they took. It's already got an earl and he's well established. I just caution that sixty people, landing in Kent to attack the Normans might not even make it as far as Lyminge before they were erm, you, know, defeated? Defeated to death, most likely.'

It was a shame his first counsel to a monarch had to be quite so depressing.

Osgifu was nodding as if she knew this perfectly well but was going to go ahead with it anyway. Was that really her plan? To lead her men to their final defeat? To see her realm dissolved in one last glorious battle? That was all very well, but Hermitage knew that sixty Osreds and Osgifus fighting just the Kent contingent of the Norman army would not be very glorious at all. At least it would be quick.

'You counsel wisely, friend Hermitage.' The queen leaned towards him slightly.

Wat snorted for some reason.

Osgifu gave Wat a scowl. 'Of course, our force cannot defeat all of the Normans, that would be a ridiculous hope.'

Hermitage was relieved to hear this. Osgifu seemed to be a thoughtful and intelligent woman who cared for her people. But what other options did she have?

The queen beckoned that Hermitage could come and stand at her side, the space previously occupied by thin Osred.

As he stepped up, he saw that Wat was now nudging Cwen and nodding his head towards Hermitage and the queen. He really was behaving in a most peculiar manner today. Well, slightly more peculiar than normal.

'You are quite right. Sixty against thousands of Normans would be a completely hopeless task.' Osgifu explained.

Hermitage nodded sadly.

'But we don't have to kill thousands, do we?'

Hermitage considered this for a moment and concluded that actually yes, you probably did need to kill thousands. Particularly when it came to Normans. Knocking a few down wouldn't do at all, it would only make the rest of them cross.

Hermitage knew about William's trouble in the north and had heard what his plan was to deal with that. Even the slightest provocation got the most outrageous response. He supposed that was one way of stopping provocations, but sixty armed men and women arriving in Kent uninvited would get one of William's really special responses; one that left sixty armed people dead, followed by their families, their livestock and their crops.

'Erm?' he did his best to sound as if he were trying to come up with something.

'We only have to kill two,' Osgifu said.

'Two?' Killing two Normans really wouldn't achieve anything at all. Apart from inviting trouble to rain on you from a very great height.

'William and this Earl of Kent.'

'Odo,' Hermitage said, while he tried to comprehend what the queen was suggesting.

'Ah yes. The bishop who strengthens boys with his club.'

'You plan to go over there and assassinate William and Odo?' Wat was joining in the serious business of the day again.

'Assassinate?' Osgifu asked.

'A word we came across from the east,' Wat said. 'It means sneak up and kill one person and then get away.'

'Ah,' Osgifu clearly liked the word. 'Just so. We shall assassinate William and then do it again to Odo.'

Hermitage started to think she wasn't quite so intelligent and thoughtful anymore.

'It's not just them, Majesty,' he said. 'There are other important Normans who would avenge their deaths.'

'Such as?'

'Well, there's Le Pedvin. He's a really horrible man, always at William's right hand. And then there's Robert Beaumont, rumoured to be made Earl of Leicester, Roger de Montgomery, he's another one.'

'Hm.' Osgifu gave this some consideration. 'This does make it more complex.'

Hermitage breathed a sigh that some sense was coming through.

'Perhaps you could draw up a list?'

Hermitage wondered what sort of list the queen could possibly want just now.

'If we knew the ones we need to assassinate, we could do them all in one trip.'

'Majesty, that's awful.' Hermitage couldn't stop himself. In all conscience he couldn't go round handing out lists of people to be murdered. He couldn't do it as a monk or as a human being. He was absolutely positive he couldn't do it as King's Investigator.

Osgifu was clearly working it through in her head. 'You are right.' She laid a grateful hand on Hermitage's arm.

And now Cwen snorted. What was the matter with the two of them?

'There's no need to go too far,' Osgifu said. 'I am sure that with William and Odo dead, one of the others would be interested in a marriage to the throne.'

'Is there no consort Osred then, your Majesty?' Wat asked, with a most impudent smirk on his face.

'My husband took on the mission of exploring out there before me.' The queen bowed her head. 'He did not return.'

'If you land in Kent, intent on killing William and Odo, Your Majesty, you will not return either,' Hermitage pleaded.

'We are grateful for your concern Brother,' Osgifu said, patting his arm now. 'But we will not go as we are. We shall cast off our arms and go as ordinary folk. My time out there has taught me what ordinary folk look like.' She had an idea. 'Monks and Nuns. We shall go dressed as monks and nuns, that way we will not be stopped until it is too late.'

Hermitage's horror at this idea could not find words.

'No,' the queen said suddenly. 'I have had another thought.'

Hermitage breathed again.

'We shall attend to Odo first, as he's closest. And then find William before he knows what's hit him.'

'A monk or a nun, presumably,' Wat said with a shake of the head.

Osgifu gave him a dark look. 'Where will we find this Odo?' she asked Hermitage.

'Find him? I think sixty monks and nuns arriving in Kent will get his attention.'

'He surely has a base somewhere? A sacred isle?'

'Normans tend not to go in for sacred isles,' Hermitage said. 'They prefer to be closer to the people they need to kill. They build castles on hills wherever they go.'

'And where is Odo's?'

'Dover, your Majesty.' Hermitage didn't like to think that he now knew where Osgifu was going to meet her death.

'Dover,' the queen mused. 'And that is?'

'Oh, erm, east. Along the coast as far as you can get.'

'Excellent. So we must cross the marsh and pass Lyminge?'

'Just so.'

'Well, as we are going that way we shall depose the Abbess Cartimandua, avenge the murder of the nun and release your sister.' She gave her smile to Cwen.

'Who? Oh, right, yes, thank you. I'm sure she'll be pleased.' Cwen's smile was weak. 'She's been there so long she's probably even forgotten she ever had a sister.'

'But you only saw her recently.'

'Ah, yes, that's right. We did, didn't we.'

'We can take care of her,' Wat offered. 'Once she's released.'

'Don't worry, master weaver,' Osgifu said. 'We shall return triumphant. You shall be our guests until then.'

'It's all right, really,' Wat said. 'We found you, that's all that matters. And now you have big plans of your own, we can all cross the river together and then we'll, erm, leave you to it.'

'No, no, I insist.' The queen was quite clear on this. Clear in the way that only a queen can be. She nodded to the door behind them.

The Osred who had been standing there all this time stepped across the door to bar their exit.

'Your Majesty?' Hermitage asked.

'I am sorry, Brother,' Osgifu said. 'It is only an inconvenience, I assure you. Our plan is not known beyond this room and it must stay that way. The only precaution I can take is to make sure that there is nothing that will warn the enemy of our intentions. I am sure you are honest and true, but I still have nothing to show that you are not in league with Cartimandua.'

'We aren't, we wouldn't..,' Hermitage began. Although he thought that actually he might warn the enemy, if only to save all the Osreds and Osgifus from being very quickly slaughtered by some Normans.

'Of course, you wouldn't. But you are from out there and your ways are strange. It is best that you stay here while we complete our mission. I will leave my son and Osred in command.'

With no obvious action on anyone's part, three more Osreds entered through the door. These ones looked very fit and well, and carried rope to go with the weapons that hung at their side.

'Not again?' Cwen complained, looking at the rope.

'A necessary safeguard,' Osgifu said. 'We will not be defeated, but if we are, it is best that the Normans find you here as prisoners. That way your lives will be safe.'

'Thank you very much,' Hermitage said as one of the Osreds with the rope came towards him.

◆ ◆ ◆

'Can't you talk to her?' Cwen asked. 'She likes you.'

Once more they were tied up in a hut. This time the hut was on Ebony, not that there was any way of telling from the inside. It seemed there was no way back to Oxney until the tide came in again, so a hut on Ebony it was.

'She likes you a lot,' Wat grinned.

'I have tried talking to her,' Hermitage said, ignoring the nonsense that the two of them were spouting. 'You saw me talking to her. She even took my counsel. And then she ignored it.'

'At least we now know that Cartimandua is the one we came for,' Wat said. 'The one who's been killing all the nuns.'

'All the nuns being just the one. And what good is that doing us, tied up in a hut?' Hermitage complained. 'While these people go off with their mad plan to assassinate William and Odo.

'It's not really mad,' Wat said. 'Well, not totally mad. If someone could get rid of William it would cause chaos. The rest of the Normans do rely on him.'

'But this lot aren't going to manage it,' Cwen said, disparagingly. 'Not dressed up as monks and nuns.'

'Not when they've been living on an island for two hundred and fifty years.' Wat added. 'A half decent contingent of Normans will do for them in five minutes.'

'And we'll be left here, tied up with only a couple of Osreds to look after us.'

'We can hardly stop them,' Hermitage said, wriggling against his bonds to test their limitations. 'And she obviously doesn't like me enough not to tie me up.'

'When do we think they're going?' Cwen asked.

'I'd reckon as soon as they can. You saw Osgifu; she's all fired up to become an assassin. They'll be off with the next tide, I'd say.'

'We've still got a few hours then.'

'A few hours to do what? Get out of these ropes and fight off sixty Osreds and Osgifus hell bent on slaughtering Normans? Just the three of us?'

'What do you suggest then?' Cwen demanded. 'Master Wat of Wat and Cwen the weavers?'

Wat scowled at the name. 'We obviously can't do anything until the next tide either. If we got out of here now, we'd only have to sit and wait.'

'And come high water?'

'We do get out of here, find a boat and head for Hastings.'

'Why Hastings?' Hermitage asked, thinking that going to the source of all their troubles didn't sound like a very good idea.

'It's west,' Wat explained. 'The opposite direction from Lyminge and Dover. We head back to William and tell him that Cartimandua killed the nun. Leave him to sort it out with Odo.'

'I thought you wanted to get this tapestry work?' Cwen was clearly critical of his change of heart.

'It seems to be more trouble than it's worth, quite frankly. And what's all this about sewing? Who sews a tapestry?'

'And we leave Cartimandua to the Normans?' Cwen asked, with feeling. She'd clearly prefer dealing with the abbess in a much more personal manner.

'I think she's about to be surprised by sixty nuns and monks knocking on the door. They'll get to her before they hit Odo. Or rather miss Odo.'

'God knows what she'll do to the sisters if that happens.' Cwen was angry.

'We run away?' Hermitage checked.

'Got it. Run away and stay alive. And the quicker we run away, the more likely it is we stay alive. If the Normans found us mixed up with the mad queen of Ebony, they'd kill us without blinking.'

Hermitage shook his head. It wasn't like him to want to step into danger. Or even have a look at it from a distance and behind a tree. But there seemed to be more at stake here. 'We cannot let these people walk to their deaths.'

'I think they'll take a boat, actually.'

'They are innocent. They have been here for all these years living under a delusion. That delusion is going to lead them to their ends. They have no idea what the Normans are really like, or what the rest of the world is like, come to that.'

'So?' Wat said, making it sound as ridiculous as possible. 'What you're suggesting is that we escape these ropes and the hut, find a boat and take off after the Ebony army. Once we catch up we somehow stop them killing two horrible Normans and persuade them to live a life of peace and harmony? And we deal with the murderous abbess and save all the sisters of Lyminge Abbey while we're at it.'

'Erm, yes.'

Wat coughed.

'Good,' Cwen said. 'We're agreed then.'

'Thank you,' Wat said.

'We do Hermitage's plan.'

'What?'

A Dressing of Nuns and Monks

band of wandering nuns and monks?' Wat asked, incredulously. 'Where on earth are these people going to find sixty nun and monk habits in the middle of an island? It's all very well saying we'll go in disguise, but you have to think about the practicalities.'

Cwen looked at him askance. 'Is that really our main worry at the moment? Where the murderous band of mad people is going to get its clothes?'

'The monk's habit is simple garb,' Hermitage put in. 'It's hardly a tailored garment. Just a simple piece of rough cloth cut to shape.'

'There you are.' Wat was triumphant. 'Cut sixty habits before high tide? I don't think so.'

'Maybe it won't be a very good disguise,' Cwen said fiercely. 'Can we perhaps discuss getting ourselves untied and escaping from the island, instead of what the modern assassin is wearing these days?'

'Please yourself. I'm only saying that I don't think they're going to get far. If they don't actually look like monks and nuns, Odo is hardly likely to welcome them with open arms, is he?'

Hermitage had to admit that was a good point.

'Even if they take their uniforms off, they still don't look much like monks or nuns. And if they're all carrying weapons, I think even a Norman will get suspicious.'

'Hm.' Cwen grunted her disappointment that Wat might be sensible after all.

'You know what the Normans are like with large gatherings.

They like to make them smaller by any means possible. The first encounter with a Norman or two will see the whole plan collapse, mark my words. They'll be running back here as fast as the mud will let them.'

With his argument made, Wat leaned back with a rather satisfied air.

He was disturbed by thin Osred, who entered the hut and considered them all. 'Ah,' he said, peering down his nose at Hermitage. 'Would you come with me please, Brother?'

'He's a bit tied up at the moment,' Cwen said with an angry snort.

Osred considered her as if she were a talking cat; remarkable and unexpected, but with nothing to contribute to any conversation. He went over to Hermitage and helped him to his feet, loosening the rope at his ankles so he could walk.

'Erm,' Hermitage didn't like to ask why he was being singled out. He was pretty sure he wouldn't like the answer. 'Where are we going?'

'We just need to get you some new clothes,' Osred said, which was not at all what Hermitage had been expecting. Perhaps it got cold on the island at night and they wanted to make sure he was all right. 'We need to borrow your habit, for our monk, you see?'

'Borrow my what?'

'Habit,' Osred repeated disdainfully, as they walked through the door. 'Osgifu has her nun's habit and we have yours. We tend not to keep a stock of monks' habits on the islands. The rest of our band will wear their work clothes and be postulants on their way to their monasteries and abbeys.'

Cwen stuck her tongue out at Wat once Osred had gone.

Wat shrugged as much as he could in his bonds. 'That could work,' he said.

Only a few moments later, Hermitage returned. Wat and Cwen could do nothing but gape as he stood before them. He

stood very awkwardly and with great embarrassment, as if that
dream he sometimes had, had come to life. He really was standing naked in the middle of a village while people went about
their daily business; hundreds and hundreds of people.

He might as well have been naked; the clothes he now wore
felt as peculiar as nothing at all. He was dressed in the normal at-
tire for a man of Ebony, black leggings and jerkin with a dark un-
der-shirt. Dark boots rose up his leg to just below the knee and
a black leather belt completed the ensemble. Unfortunately, they
had not given him the sword or knife that usually went with it.

A new Osred appeared behind him and roughly gestured
that he needed to tie Hermitage's legs again.

Reluctantly, Hermitage stood while he was bound, and then
accepted Osred's assistance to lower him to the floor once more.

The Osred checked that they were all still tied, then grunted
and left.

'Hermitage,' Cwen was aghast. 'You look like a completely
different person.'

'I feel like one,' Hermitage complained.

'I mean, you look, sort of, normal.'

Hermitage didn't know whether that was good or bad.

'The hair gives it away a bit.' Wat nodded his head towards
Hermitage's tonsure.

'I don't think I've ever seen you out of your habit,' Cwen said.
'If you know what I mean,' she added hurriedly.

'It's a nice outfit though.' Wat nodded appreciatively. 'I don't
know where these people get their money, but they spend it
wisely.'

'I feel awful,' Hermitage complained. He had worn the habit
for as long as he could remember. To be denied it now, in this
fashion, was very disturbing. Obviously, he took it off sometimes, just to wash it, and himself, but that was a very private
affair. He felt as exposed as a newborn babe. He really did not
feel himself.

'Mind you,' Wat said, with a sly look in his eye. 'They've now got a monk, right?'

Hermitage and Cwen nodded.

'And we've got a soldier.'

Hermitage tried very hard to think where they'd got a soldier from, and where he was now.

'You,' Wat said brightly. 'Apart from the hair, you look just like one of them.'

Hermitage had to accept that this was true. What use it was, was more of a mystery.

Wat explained impatiently. 'If they've got one monk and one nun leading a whole population of postulants, we've got one soldier leading two prisoners.'

Now Hermitage got it. 'I couldn't,' he said. 'I couldn't go outside dressed like this. People would see me.' He clamped his knees tight together.

'What people? They'll all be off to murder Odo. We'll only have thin Osred and this son of Osgifu. Plus a few old folk and children, I expect. We get you to lead us down to a boat under the pretence that Osgifu has ordered us back to Oxney.'

'Why?' Hermitage asked.

'So we can escape?' Wat seemed puzzled by the question.

'No, I mean why has she ordered us back to Oxney?'

'Does it matter?'

'Of course, it matters. What if someone asks?'

'Make something up,' Wat was impatient.

'Hermitage?' Cwen checked. 'Make something up?'

Wat saw the problem. 'All right. She's ordered us back to Oxney because, erm, we are desecrating the spirits of the sacred isle, not being sacred ourselves. There you are.'

Hermitage nodded that this seemed to be a good reason.

'And what do we do when we get back to Oxney?' he asked.

Wat hung his head and blew out slowly. 'We don't go to Oxney,' he said, very slowly. 'We go to Appledore.'

'Ah.' Hermitage now saw that this was quite clever. There was one problem though. 'Won't they be expecting us in Oxney?'

'No,' Wat said, as if instructing a puppy not to bite. 'Because we made that up, remember?'

'Oh, yes.' Hermitage nodded that he was content now. 'Ah.'

'Oh, God. What now?' Wat complained.

'How do we do all this when we're still tied up?'

There was a rather awkward silence.

'That is a good question,' Cwen noted.

'Obviously, we get untied first,' Wat said.

'Good.' Hermitage waited to hear how this was going to be achieved.

Wat wriggled and struggled against his ties, but they were strong and secure. He leaned towards Cwen. 'If we get back to back, I might be able to reach your hands.'

'With your fat fingers?' Cwen was surprised at the idea.

'I haven't got fat fingers.' Wat was offended.

'Yes, you have. Everyone knows that. My fingers are much better for fine work. Like untying knots.'

'My fingers are not fat.'

'Cwen, Wat,' Hermitage called. 'Could we deal with this later?'

They stopped arguing and started to wriggle around.

Hermitage sighed. 'I really think we're going to have to talk about how we prioritise things.'

The sound of scuffling footsteps came from outside and Wat and Cwen quickly resumed their normal positions.

They were only just in time as the animal skin door was thrown aside and thin Osred stooped in.

He looked at the three of them, as if disappointed that they were still cluttering up his hut. 'The tide has returned, and the party will depart shortly.'

'Thanks for letting us know,' Wat said.

'Personally, I think the less you know, the better. However, the young prince wanted to see our captives and the queen agreed.'

'Prince Osred?' Wat asked.

'Naturally.' Osred clearly thought that was a rather odd question.

'Do bring him in,' Cwen said, as if inviting visitors to her parlour. 'Excuse us if we don't get up.'

Osred gave her a dismissive sniff and turned away. He put his head out of the hut and spoke to what must be the prince.

He turned back into the hut and stood, stiff and upright by the door.

They all waited for the prince to enter. It was typical of royals to keep people hanging around like this. Not that they could go anywhere else at the moment.

After an interminable wait the animal skin twitched once more and they looked over.

'Boo,' said Prince Osred as he jumped into the room. He then ran round and round it a few times with his arms out, making screeching noises like a seagull. After that he stopped in the middle of the floor, looked at each of them and jumped up and down on the spot, pointing.

'What have we said about pointing, Your Highness?' Osred asked very wearily.

Prince Osred stuck his tongue out at Osred.

'And sticking your tongue out.'

Prince Osred now squatted down on his haunches opposite Cwen and studied her intently. He screwed up his nose and spoke. 'Yeuch,' he said. 'Girls.'

'Ah, bless,' Wat said. 'He's talking already.'

Osred glared.

'I can see the sacred isle is in safe hands.'

Hermitage was so taken aback, he couldn't think of anything to say. In his mind he had Prince Osred as a powerful young man, supporting his mother and ready to take over the very small kingdom once his time came.

He had never imagined a child who, they now knew following the royal proclamation, wanted a wee wee.

Osred snatched the young prince up and whisked him out through the door, before his young charge could drop his tiny leggings and perform the royal duty right on the prisoners' feet.

Hermitage, Wat and Cwen just looked at one another as they heard Osred announce that it was bed time and that there was to be no nonsense just because the queen was away. It sounded as if thin Osred was suddenly finding his duties more burdensome than normal.

When the sound of a screaming child had receded into the distance, Wat shook his head. 'I think our chances of escape just went up.'

'Stupid baby.' Cwen seemed to have taken the insult personally. 'Still, looks like Osred will be tied up for the rest of the evening. Now we just need to make sure that we aren't.'

Comfortable in the knowledge that thin Osred would be occupied for some time, they attacked the ropes once more.

Wat's disappointment was palpable when it was Cwen who managed to untie his bonds, rather than the other way round. Her triumphalism didn't help.

Wat quickly released his own feet and then stepped over and undid Hermitage.

He turned to Cwen and seemed to be considering her carefully.

'Don't even think about it,' she snarled. 'In fact, don't even look like you're thinking about it.'

He shrugged with a smile and bent to release her.

Rubbing wrists and hopping from foot to foot to get the feeling back, Wat indicated that Hermitage should have a look out of the door.

'Why me?' he whispered.

'Because you look like a local?' Wat said. 'Be a bit odd if Wat the Weaver sticks his head out when he's supposed to be tied up.'

'Except of course,' Cwen pointed out, 'no one here knows who on earth Wat the Weaver is. All they know is Wat and Cwen the weavers.'

'Yet another topic for another time?' Hermitage hissed at them. He very cautiously moved the very edge of the animal skin very slightly and peeped out through the tiny gap. 'I can't see anyone.'

'And it looks like it's getting dark,' Cwen said, peering over his shoulder. 'Even better.'

'Ah, yes.' Hermitage was thinking that escaping on a boat across dark waters was not really better than anything.

'Get back,' Cwen ordered urgently. She sat herself on the ground and put her hands behind her, pretending to be tied up. Without knowing why, the others followed suit.

After a few moments the noise of tramping feet could be heard.

'Sounds like the queen and her entourage off to defeat the Normans,' Cwen said.

They all kept quiet, fearful that someone would come to check on the hut and its contents. Nobody did, and once the noise of the passage had faded, they got back to their feet and returned to the door.

'So,' Wat said. 'We follow them.'

'Follow them?' Hermitage thought that sounded a bit risky.

'Of course. They're going to where the boats are. We want a boat, yes?'

'Yes, but, erm, won't they see us.'

'Not if we make sure they don't see us,' Cwen said with a blow of her cheeks.

'How do we know there'll be a boat? We came on that big one and they're probably going to take that away with them. And we wouldn't be able to row it on our own anyway.'

'There's bound to be some more somewhere. They live on an

island, they have to have boats all over the place.'

Their walk behind the queen's party was slow and cautious and they had silently agreed that they would find a hiding spot until they were sure that the group ahead had sailed away.

They were comforted that they would not be spotted from behind as the sounds of Prince Osred's wailing complaints drifted through the night. Thin Osred was clearly a man with a very short tether, and there was nothing like a small child to quickly find the end of a tether and keep you there all night.

The sound of embarkation and the placing of oars came to them, and it included the voice of one man who was insisting that he had recovered the plank and that if they couldn't find it that was hardly his problem.

Before long, the sounds became that of a large boat rowing steadily away from shore.

'Right,' Wat said. 'Here we go.' He stood from their cover and quickly walked down the short slope to the shore line. A glance about in the gloom of the evening revealed an upturned boat on the strand. It was only a coracle really, but it was a large one and would easily take the three of them.

Wat nodded towards it with a wide grin.

Cwen put a hand on his shoulder. 'Before we get carried away, can we turn it over?'

Wat looked at her. 'We'll have to anyway,' he said. 'They tend not to work too well the wrong way up. But why?'

'Silly, really,' she admitted. 'I just want to check that More's not underneath.'

'How could he be?' Hermitage asked.

'I don't know.' Cwen sounded quite angry with herself for worrying about this. 'He just keeps turning up. There's something unnatural about him.'

Wat walked over to the boat and easily lifted it over. There was no More. There was also no oar. 'Look for an oar,' he instructed.

'Don't we need two?' Hermitage asked.

'Not for one of these things. You move them along with one oar at the back. I've seen it done.'

Hermitage wondered where the back of a round boat was. He waited a moment for his next question. 'But you've never actually done it?'

'Well, no. I'm a weaver, not a boatman, but it looked pretty easy.'

'I see.' Hermitage chanced a glance out at the dark swirling waters into which they were about to venture in a flimsy boat under the command of a man who'd once seen a coracle rowed and who thought it looked pretty easy. The racing tide was quite fearsome in its own right, and as it was rising, it could take them in completely the wrong direction if they weren't careful.

'Are you sure More's not in there somewhere?' he asked, hopefully.

Caput XV

At Sea with The Weavers

hy are we going round and round backwards?' Cwen asked, with admirable restraint, considering their situation.

For a moment, Hermitage thought to point out that they couldn't be going both round and round and backwards at the same time; the boat having neither front nor back. The growing feeling of unease in his stomach told him that he had more practical matters to worry about.

'Ask the boat,' Wat snapped back.

'I thought it would be easier to ask the man with the oar who said that rowing these things looked pretty easy.'

'Very helpful.' Wat dug the oar into the water again, but the rotation of the boat simply dragged it sideways. 'Rowlocks,' he said.

Hermitage managed a tut through his tight shut lips.

'I mean there's no rowlock, nowhere to hold the oar against the boat.'

'What about these two sticks?' Cwen said, pointing out the two protuberances she was resting against.

'Oh, yes,' Wat said quite fiercely. 'That's what we're looking for. If you wouldn't mind moving away from the rower's position?'

With unhelpful noises, Cwen shifted herself around the side of the boat and sat on the single plank that bisected the vessel and on which Hermitage was groaning.

Once out of the way, Wat manoeuvred himself into position and slotted his oar between the two upright pegs. Now he had some leverage and when he dropped the oar into the water the wild rotation of the craft slowed immediately.

'There we are,' he said triumphantly. 'If you hadn't been sitting in the wrong place, we'd have been all right.'

'We're still going backwards,' Cwen pointed out. 'Appledore being in that direction.' She pointed forwards. 'While we seem to be going in that direction.' She pointed backwards. 'Along with most of the river.'

'One thing at a time.' Wat tried an experimental pull on the oar, which succeeded in sending them round in a circle again.

'Can you not do that, please,' Hermitage moaned, now feeling very unwell.

Wat looked at him. 'Don't you be sick on those clothes. They're good quality, they are.'

'I shall do my best,' Hermitage replied, not meaning it at all. The rolling in his stomach had given him a new-found contempt for anything that didn't involve getting off this boat as soon as possible.

Wat considered the oar with intense concentration, clearly trying to work out how one oar on its own was supposed make a boat go anywhere.

'I think you're supposed to wave it about a bit,' Cwen said.

'Wave it about a bit?' Wat looked at the oar and was obviously wondering how waving it about would move them at all.

'In the water. You sort of move it round in circles.'

'Really?'

'Yes. I saw some old fellow do it like that once, on the River Trent. I didn't mention it because you said you knew all about it.'

Wat pursed his lips but looked as if any idea was a good one just at the moment. He took the oar and moved the end round in a cautious circle. At first, the boat spun slightly to its left but as he continued it came back to the right. Taking the speed of the river into account he had achieved quite substantial progress; they weren't going anywhere anymore.

He repeated the action and the boat did the same thing. It swung a bit to either side but didn't actually move forward.

Hermitage swallowed, hoping that the contents of his stomach would stay where they were. 'Perhaps we could just wait here until the tide turns?'

Wat heaved around on his oar once more but achieved no forward progress. 'That might be the best we can manage.'

They were all resigned to a long wait in the middle of the river with Wat working hard just to keep them where they were. At least the endless circling had stopped, and Hermitage's stomach started to settle a bit.

Their predicament did mean that Queen Osgifu's party would be well ahead of them. By the time the coracle made it to Appledore, if it ever did, the Osreds could be knocking on Abbess Cartimandua's door.

'Found a good spot then?' A friendly voice called out in the darkness and nearly caused Hermitage to fall out of the boat. The voice was alarmingly close, and he looked to their left to see who was out walking on the river at this time of night.

As they all watched, a coracle, just like their own, sped out of the night and stopped neatly alongside. A young man stood in it, just as Wat did, the oar in his hand.

In this case the young lad, he could be no more than fourteen or fifteen, seemed to swing his hands around without thinking, and the coracle under his feet responded as if it was part of him. He peered over the side of their boat.

'You've got your feet all wrong,' he said.

'Oh, really?' Wat sounded as if he did not welcome the guidance.

'Absolutely. You want your left foot over there and the right up here.' He pointed at the right places.

Reluctantly, Wat moved to the correct position. He then continued to rotate the oar in the water, but this time it didn't move from side to side with each pull.

'Oh, yes,' he said, much happier now.

'And you don't pull the oar like that. Still, not bad for a beginner.'

Wat gave half a smile.

'You're not boat people, are you?' the boy said, it probably being blindingly obvious to the passing fish that they weren't boat people. 'Although you look like an Ebonite.'

'Ebonite?' Hermitage asked.

'The weird ones from Ebony. They all wear black. What one of them would be doing out here fishing is a mystery though.'

Hermitage had actually forgotten that he was still dressed as an islander. The discomfort in his stomach had taken his mind off everything else.

'What you doing out here then?' the boy asked bluntly. He considered Wat's black eye as he did so and seemed to notice Cwen for the first time. He gave her a broad smile and a wink. With a flick of his wrist, he spun his coracle around so that it moved to put him next to Cwen.

'These men bothering you, sweetheart?' he asked.

Hermitage cowered slightly in the boat, worried that there was nowhere to get out of the way when Cwen responded to this.

Cwen smiled back at him, which was a surprise. 'No more than you'll be bothered when I put that oar somewhere you won't be able to reach to pull it out again.'

Another twist of the hands took the lad's boat a few feet away. He gave Hermitage and Wat a look of shock. 'Better keep my distance, eh?'

'That would be wise,' Wat agreed.

'So,' the boy carried on, as if being threatened by every girl he spoke to was quite normal. 'You obviously aren't fishing. You can't row a coracle and you're stuck in the tide. Where you trying to get to?'

'Appledore,' Hermitage said.

'Really?' The boy sounded very surprised at this. 'You've got no chance. Sink before you get half way in that thing, rowing it like that.'

'What would you advise?' Hermitage asked.

The boy gave this careful thought. 'I could take you, I suppose.'

'Really? That would be most kind.'

'For tuppence.'

Cwen sighed. 'What is it about people in boats taking money off us. You're not called More by any chance, are you? Or related to him?'

'Never heard of him,' the boy replied.

Cwen looked as if she didn't really believe this.

'We have to get over into your boat?' Hermitage asked, with pretty naked terror at the prospect. He thought that staying here all night waiting for the tide was preferable.

'Nah, I've got a rope here, I'll tow you.'

Cwen and Hermitage looked pleadingly at Wat, who was the one with the money.

'Go on then,' Wat sighed. 'Be better than staying here all night.'

The boy controlled his boat with one hand while he reached down for a length of rope. 'You wouldn't have stayed here all night,' he assured them.

'Really?' Hermitage asked. Perhaps it wasn't so bad after all.

'No, when the tide turns it swings round the back of Oxney and takes everything with it. By morning you'd be three miles out at sea.' He grinned at them.

Hermitage happily took hold of the rope as it was passed over, now seeing it as a literal life line.

'You can tie it to the rowlock,' the boy advised as he started to move his boat away.

'I'd rather hold on, if you don't mind,' Hermitage replied.

Despite the fact that the young lad now had to pull his own

Coracle as well as another one with three people in it, all of them against the tide, they made good progress.

Hermitage felt hugely relieved that they were actually going in the right direction. Well, more that they were going in any direction with a measure of control. He even relaxed so much that the rope slipped in his hands slightly, and he let Wat take it from him and tie it to the rowlock.

They could now sit and let the boy and his coracle take the strain, not that it seemed to be much of strain as the lad kept up a constant stream of conversation as they moved steadily along.

He covered the boat, the landscape nearby, that they couldn't see anyway because it was too dark, the village he came from, his best friend who wasn't as good in a boat as he was, and how the coracle he was in had been made. He was an enthusiast for this aspect and went on at enormous length about a number of details in which they had not the slightest interest whatsoever.

'Of course, normally the stringers would be braced against the gunwale, but I wondered if we couldn't get pieces the right shape to begin with, which would reduce the strain on the skin once it's in place.'

'You were out fishing, then?' Hermitage asked, even his deep patience struggling against the tide of pointless detail.

'That's it.'

'Won't your family be put out when you return with nothing?'

'Ah, but I won't. With your tuppence I'll buy fish at the Appledore market and still have change for my purse. In fact,' he turned to face them. 'If you want towing back after you've done your business, I can wait.'

'No, no,' Wat spoke up very quickly. 'It's fine really. We're going on from Appledore.'

'Oh, yes? Where you wanting to go?' There was a clear intention that wherever it was, he could take them.

'We can't say.'

'Doesn't sound like much of a plan, if you don't mind me saying so.'

'No,' Wat went on. 'I mean we'd love to tell you, but we can't.' He tapped the side of his nose.

'Oh, yes? Secret is it? I wouldn't tell anyone. I can keep quiet.'

'I've seen no evidence of that,' Cwen said. 'Just get us to Appledore and we can say goodbye.'

'Please yourself,' the boy sounded offended now. He peered ahead into the dark. 'Do you want me to tie up against Queen Osgifu's boat? It's at the jetty.'

They too looked ahead into the night and couldn't see a thing.

'Can you see if there's anyone on board?' Wat asked.

'They're getting off. Don't know what they're all doing over there, they never leave the islands all together like that.' The boy sounded quite concerned about this.

'We'll wait till they've gone, and then go ashore,' Wat instructed.

'Oh ar? Like that, is it?'

'Like what?'

'Sneaking around the queen, are you?'

'No, we are not. And it's really none of your business.'

'You're wasting your time.' The boy was dismissive.

'Is that right?'

'Of course, it is. They're all mad as coots on mushrooms, that lot. Leave 'em alone, that's the best.'

'Osgifu thinks she's the Queen of England,' Hermitage pointed out.

"Course she does. And who's to tell her she ain't?'

'King William, perhaps?' Hermitage thought it would be interesting to see if this boy knew about the Normans. Very few people round here seemed to, which was a bit of a surprise. He momentarily thought about moving to the area himself.

'King William's not likely to come down here, is he? Nothing for him.'

'But you obviously know all about her, and about the Normans.'

'That's right. But then I'm from Smallhythe, up river of here. We're quite normal, we are.'

Cwen just coughed.

'Has no one thought to mention to Osgifu that there are new kings in England? After all these years?' Hermitage asked.

'Why would we do that then? They've got a pile of royal treasure somewhere on the islands. As long as they keep spending it with us, why worry them with details?'

Hermitage gaped. 'That's awful.'

'Very clever,' Wat said.

'Everyone's happy,' the boy explained. 'She thinks she's Queen of England, they all pay us for food and clothes and the like, why muck that up? Do you know how much they paid for that big boat of theirs?'

'They must know the truth, surely.'

'Oh, we don't like that round here.' The boy sounded very cautious. 'Always gets nasty when the truth comes out.'

'Treasure, eh?' Wat asked.

'You're welcome to have a go,' the boy said. 'There's been generations of people gone looking for it, not one ever found it; if they came back at all. Easier to take it one coin at a time than try and get the lot.'

'But we know all about the place now,' Hermitage pointed out.

'Lots of people do, but no one believes them. Queen of England living on a lost island in the marshes? You try saying that and you'll have to duck the rotten turnips as they drive the loon out of town.'

Hermitage just shook his head at this appalling deception. A deception carried out by so many people over such a long period of time. How was it even possible? He knew this spot was isolated, but really. He now knew why it stayed isolated and why strangers who asked questions tended to get hit on the head and tied up.

'They've all got off now,' the boy reported, and he rowed the two boats forward.

Wat handed over the tuppence as they climbed from their wobbly craft.

'At least you got a free boat out of it,' Wat said.

'Oh, no,' the boy replied. 'This goes back where you found it. Otherwise they'll be wondering what's going on. You going to see what they're up to, are you?'

'Can't say,' Wat repeated.

'Probably some meeting with the head man. Don't you lot go mucking things up. We need them back on the island pretty soon. We can't have her wandering off trying to be the real Queen of England; she wouldn't last a day. She's got us to look after.'

'And to pay,' Hermitage added.

'That's right.' The boy had no shame about this.

'We'll be careful.'

They left the boy standing on the jetty while they walked into the darkness of the town. The sound of the passage of sixty shuffling postulants was muffled as they moved ahead.

If the boy discovered the queen's plan, and that she now knew about the outside world, he would raise the alarm with the whole town. Hermitage wondered if that might not be for the best. Osgifu and her people would be saved from certain death, the truth of this place would come out and this grand deception would be brought to a halt.

It all sounded like the perfect recipe, but a recipe for complete chaos and an awful lot of trouble. Everyone would be angry with everyone else, there might even be fighting and death as arguments got out of hand.

No, he thought, as he followed Wat and Cwen along the shore on the trail of Osgifu. Better to say nothing, keep his head down and hope it all turned out all right in the end.

Caput XVI

After Them!

s they wandered on, Hermitage realised that his plan had already failed. He wasn't doing nothing. He was following a band of sixty people into the darkness in an attempt to stop them trying to assassinate the two most senior Normans in the country. What on earth had he thought they were going to do when they caught up?

They didn't have enough rope to tie up sixty people. They didn't have enough rope to tie up one person, so the question was irrelevant. And what would they do, the three of them? Ask people to form an orderly queue while they were restrained? One monk and two weavers?

And Queen Osgifu had already heard his counsel and rejected it. What new arguments did he have?

'They must stop somewhere soon,' Cwen said as they walked cautiously along. 'Probably want to get away from Appledore but they can't walk all night.'

'They probably can,' Wat said. 'They're all a bit odd, after all.'

'Even odd people sleep.'

'I suppose. And what do we do then? Hermitage?'

'Hm?'

'This is your plan. What do we do when they go to sleep?'

Hermitage considered it for a moment. 'Take a rest ourselves?'

'I thought we'd come to stop them walking into the hands of the Normans and dying a horrible death? Not going to achieve that if we're having a nice doze in the marshes.'

'Erm.'

'Surely, we bound up behind them, call out that they must stop and then you, erm, stop them?'

'Ah, well, that would be good.'

'How do we do it, then?' Wat's face was full of interest and looked as if he was ready to be fascinated by the answer.

'First we catch them up, as you say..,'

'Then?'

'Then we, erm, do, the, ah, stopping.'

'Good plan. How?'

'How?'

'That's it. How exactly do we stop these sixty fighting Osreds led by their queen? What is it that we do? Each of us? I think we need to know.'

Obviously, Hermitage had not the first idea what they were going to do. Actually saying that he had no idea did not seem terribly helpful, somehow. 'Something will occur to us.'

'Something will occur to us?' Wat was starting to sound quite worried.

'That's it. When we see the situation and are actually in it, something will occur to us.'

'Any one of us in particular or is this more of a widespread occurrence?'

'I'm sure it will become clear. When the moment arrives.'

'Good.' Wat sounded surprisingly happy with this proposal. 'That's settled then,' he said decisively.

'What is?'

'There is no plan. We have no idea what we're going to do and you're just hoping something will pop into your head before they tie us all up again. Am I right?'

'Well, I wouldn't say we have no idea what we're going to do. We know that we're going to save Osgifu and her people; we just haven't quite worked out how yet.'

'Not quite worked out how, eh?'

Hermitage tried to look as if he was thinking hard and the

details of the plan would be with them at any moment now.

'Here's a thought,' Wat said.

Hermitage looked at him, hopefully.

'Now we've actually escaped and got here and discovered that it's a lot trickier than we thought, why don't we leave them to it? Turn around, head west and hear about how it all went in a few months' time?'

'Your plan,' Cwen said with disgust.

'Erm, you know, I think it might be.'

'We are not leaving killer Cartimandua in charge of that abbey.' Cwen was definite on that. 'Do you want to be the one who tells Odo and William that we didn't bother doing what they asked because running away worked better for us?'

'I won't be in a position to tell Odo and William anything will I? I'll have been sent back to the island to be tied up again, while the only people who know I'm there have gone off and got themselves slaughtered. I suppose we could stay there and watch little Osred grow up.'

'We have escaped the island,' Hermitage pointed out. 'And we are on our way to Lyminge to deal with the abbess and the murder of the nun. Along the way we must save Osgifu's people.' It sounded quite simple when he said it like that. 'It's perfectly reasonable to have an aim in mind, even if you haven't worked out the details.'

'Tell that to King Harold,' Wat said. 'I'm sure he had a marvellous plan to win the battle at Hastings, just hadn't worked out the details of not being shot.'

'Take the lexicography of the post-Exodus prophets, for example,' Hermitage said, never for a moment thinking that he'd have the opportunity to bring up his favourite subject. 'I don't even know that there is one at the moment.'

'We don't even know what one is,' Cwen muttered.

'Or care,' Wat added.

Hermitage ignored them. 'But I will work my way through

all the prophecies and see if I can identify common features. I have an aim in mind but don't know if it's actually achievable until I start doing it.'

'That's all very well,' Wat said. 'But discovering that stopping sixty armed people is not achievable when you're in the middle of sixty armed people, is a bit more problematic than suddenly finding you've read the wrong book.'

'But it is still a laudable aim.'

'Laudable, yes. Doable? No. I'm all for laudable aims. I love a good laud. Getting knocked about again by Osred and his friends Osred and Osred, is not on my list of aims at all. Laudable or not.'

'We have to sort out Cartimandua,' Cwen was decisive about this. 'And Osgifu is connected.'

'Ah, now, perhaps we're getting things mixed up here?' Wat was a bit more enthusiastic. 'One abbess in an abbey is a different kettle of herring from a force of sixty intent on murdering Norman nobles. Do we have to do both?'

'It's probably going to be unavoidable.'

'Only because Osgifu's said she's going to get Cartimandua. We could go to the abbey and do the bit where Hermitage goes "aha" and accuses the killer, then we pop off to William and Odo, job done.

'Saving Osgifu is a different task completely. And one we can't do...,' Wat was getting impatient now and a little bit shouty. 'Because we have no idea how.' He took a breath. 'Osgifu has sixty people at her command and this is the course she has chosen. Why do we have to sort her problems out for her?'

'Because she has been tricked and deceived and doesn't know what she's getting in to.' Hermitage felt quite strongly that an innocent like the queen should not suffer for it. 'A meeting and argument with Cartimandua is not at all the same as understanding the Normans. If she only knew the truth, she would see that this course of action is madness.'

'Unfortunately,' Cwen said, 'when she does understand the Normans it will already be too late because they'll already have killed her. And all her people.'

'Exactly,' Hermitage concluded. That was that then.

Wat shook his head. 'Still don't see why she's our problem,' he muttered.

'At some point William and Odo are going to discover there's someone who thinks she's the Queen of England,' Cwen said. 'And who did this woman have tied up in a tent? Why, the king's own investigator and his two weaving friends. But they didn't mention it to the king or try to do anything about it? Gosh, I think William will be cross about that.' She folded her arms at Wat.

'I'm not sure he'll care.' Wat grumbled. 'We came looking for a collection of dead nuns and we might have found one. Now we end up chasing the Queen of England through the marshes in the middle of the night. How did that happen?'

Cwen snapped her fingers. 'We get ahead of them.'

'Excellent idea,' Wat said. 'Then we can watch them coming to their deaths instead of going.'

'No, no. They're going to stop somewhere for the night and we get round them. We get to the abbey and Cartimandua first.'

'That'll be nice. Then what do we do?'

'Erm,' Cwen said.

'No one is thinking this through, are they?' Wat complained. 'You're just making it up as you go along.'

'It's better than running away,' Cwen bit back.

'Not really.'

'We get to Cartimandua, say we know all about the murder of the nun, and that Osgifu is coming with a great force.'

'Which is true,' Hermitage said. He always preferred it when things were true.

'So she has to let us in.'

'Sounds like a few reasons to keep us out,' Wat said.

'Obviously we don't tell her that until we're in.' Cwen sniffed at his stupidity.

'Then, when Osgifu arrives, Cartimandua can confirm how awful the Normans are and how she's better off going home. And we get to free the sisters at the same time.'

'Is this before or after we accuse Cartimandua of murder?' Wat asked. 'I just worry that she might become a bit less cooperative?'

Cwen just tutted.

'And Osgifu is going to believe the abbess anyway, is she?' Wat picked up the problems. 'The one she hates, who locked her up and made her do tapestry against her will. Although I still don't understand what the sewing was about.'

'Can we forget the tapestry?'

'Certainly not. It's the only thing keeping my interest in any of this.'

'Well.' Cwen sounded very determined about this. 'That's what we're going to do, so there you are. You go west if you want, Hermitage and I will sort everything out.'

Hermitage wasn't sure he was going to sort anything out, even with all three of them.

'I've got a better idea,' Wat said. 'We let Osgifu get to the abbey and she deals with Cartimandua. We then pop off and tell Odo and William all about it.'

'Before they slaughter Osgifu's people, or afterwards?' Cwen asked.

Wat shrugged. 'Doesn't matter, really.'

Cwen's look was enough to indicate to Wat that his new idea was not really what she was looking for.

'All right, all right.' Wat surrendered. 'But don't blame me if it all ends in tears. Our tears, mainly.'

'You never know,' Cwen said, with a fierce gleam in her eyes, 'If we don't sort this out you might get an abbey full of dead nuns after all.'

The force of Osgifu did indeed stop for the night once they had passed well beyond Appledore. They didn't even pitch tents or make fires, they simply settled themselves down in the darkness to get whatever rest they could.

This made it more difficult for Hermitage, Wat and Cwen to slip by unnoticed. There was always the risk that they would trip over someone in the dark, and then have to explain why they were here and not tied up in a hut on Ebony.

With cautious steps, many of them a lot wetter than was comfortable as they stepped in the soggy ground of the marshes, they managed to find their way to the road on the far side of the make-shift camp.

'I don't suppose we get any rest?' Hermitage asked.

'Not if we want to get to the abbey before Osgifu,' Cwen replied.

'I don't understand why investigations require so much staying up all night. It's very tiring.'

'We have to keep one step ahead of the bad people.'

'Yes, that's another problem. Why can't we be ten steps ahead, or a few behind, even?'

'Honestly, Hermitage,' Cwen said with a wry smile. 'Anyone would think you didn't want to be King's Investigator at all.'

Hermitage had his answer ready for that one.

'And that we'd rather be at home making tapestry and not traipsing round the country chasing killers every time the king sneezes,' she added.

'In the dark,' Wat pointed out. 'And with wet feet.'

With grim acceptance of their fate, they tramped on towards the east, where the dark of the sky told them they had a lot of dark to get through before the sun was prepared to light their way.

The bright of the moon gave some help in avoiding the worst of the holes in the road, but it slipped behind the clouds every now and then, as if playing with them.

As on their outward journey, they had to cross numerous streams and small rivers. Spotting these in the grey of the moon was not straightforward and Hermitage wondered why they were suddenly walking down hill at one point; the landscape having been pretty flat until then. He quickly discovered the stream at the bottom of this particular hill and had to turn and clamber back up.

'I wondered where you'd gone,' Cwen said. 'Being dressed in black isn't good in this light; we could lose you altogether.'

Naturally, the thought of being lost in a marsh at night, dressed all in black so that no one could find him, was now foremost in Hermitage's mind. He stuck close to Cwen and Wat as they moved along.

The night was full as they tramped across the path, Hermitage constantly thinking that walking through an unknown marsh at night was a ridiculous thing to do in any circumstances. At least the path was well trodden and marked, and the small bridges they came to gave him the confidence that they were on the right track. Well, they were on a track. The morning would tell them whether it was the right one or not.

After what felt like hours, the moon did deign to make an uninterrupted appearance and showed them the side of the hill that led out of the marshes and on to Lyminge. It was still a little way off but gave hope that they were nearly out of this awful flat expanse.

'Can we rest now?' Hermitage asked. 'We must be way ahead of them and it's still night. I must close my eyes, even if it's only for a moment.'

Cwen agreed. 'Me too. We'll be no good in Lyminge if we're half asleep.'

'Please yourself,' Wat said agreeably. 'It's your plan. Personally, I'd find a hole and sleep until it's all over.'

'Excellent,' Cwen said. 'You can take first watch then.'

Despite their best intentions there really wasn't anywhere to rest just here, apart from lie in the middle of the road, which seemed a bit rash, and very uncomfortable. They tramped on until they came to the first trees at the bottom of the hill and found shelter among the trunks.

'If they do approach along the road, we should see them coming and be able to move without being spotted,' Cwen said. She pointed a finger at Wat.'And you do have to wake us if they appear. No hiding in the trees until they go by and then claiming that you never saw anything.'

'Would I do a thing like that?' Wat protested.

'Yes.'

'I want some sleep as much as you do. I'll give you half an hour and then wake you. Hermitage can do the last watch.'

'Why me?' Hermitage asked, thinking that there must be some good reason for this.

'Because if they are on the move they'll see you, and you look like one of them. They'll just think a scout has gone ahead. If they see us they could come running.'

'Ah, yes, good idea,' Hermitage said. Not at all liking the idea of being spotted by anyone, let alone people who went running after other people.

When the time came for his watch he felt as if he'd have been better off not sleeping at all. He was still groggy and disoriented as he leaned against a tree, looking out over the brightening marsh as the first slices of approaching day slid across its surface.

Wat had just laid down and was already snoring loudly. Cwen was clearly dreaming and was kicking things as she did so.

Hermitage blinked vigorously and stretched his arms out, yawning all the while. He wiped his hands over his face, rubbing his eyes hard and then settled to his watch over the path through the marsh.

His stomach rumbled, and he wondered if there would be anything to eat at the abbey when they got there. He thought he'd probably better ask before he accused the abbess of murder.

He also wondered what they were going to do afterwards. It would be just the three of them in an abbey with a killer abbess. When he had identified killers in the past, there was usually someone there to take care of the details; either that or the killer just ran off. He thought that the abbess would not be happy and might try to do something about it. Even though the evidence was circumstantial, this was a killer abbess, what if she had a go at them?

He then found himself wondering whether he would be able to escape by walking through the walls or flying over them on that giant crow that was carrying a basket of breads but wouldn't hand anything over until he was paid. But Hermitage didn't have any money, mainly because he was standing naked again, this time in the middle of an abbey full of nuns.

He almost fell off the tree he was leaning against as he woke with a start. He shook himself all over and moved away from the tree. Any point of rest would only make him fall asleep again.

He breathed deeply and cast his gaze back to the marsh.

'Run!' he called to Wat and Cwen as he saw that the sixty Osreds had got quite close while he was having his little doze.

It's Tapestry Time

here's my tapestry?' Odo, Bishop of Bayeux, Earl of Kent demanded of his Saxon retainer as he sat over his noon meal.

'What?' the retainer asked, surprised by the question that had come out of nowhere, and that Odo knew perfectly well where his tapestry was. He sighed. His short months in Odo's service should have prepared him for this sort of thing.

'It's not made yet, is it?' The retainer had learned that Odo seemed to appreciate direct talking; until it got too direct of course. The previous incumbent of the post of retainer would testify to that; if he was still capable of testifying to anything anymore. Not that anyone knew where he was; or even where the bits of him might be.

'Those nuns were doing it,' Odo snapped.

'The dead ones?'

'Oh, yes.' At least Odo recalled facts when they were thrown in front of his face. 'Why aren't there more nuns?'

'Abbess Cartimandua said she was working on it.'

Odo contemplated this excuse briefly, and found it wanting. 'That was days ago. And it's a stupid name for a nun. The woman will have to go. I shall deal with her.'

'The Archbishop of Canterbury tends to get irritated when you try to deal with his people. And then the king gets annoyed when you irritate the archbishop.'

'Archbishop! That man's the worst of the lot. I should do for him first.'

The retainer ignored this. Odo said a lot of things, most of them mad and horrible, but only actually did about half of them. If you ignored something, there was a very good chance it would just go away; until he asked you months later why that horrible thing he'd asked for hadn't been done yet. "Dealing" with the Archbishop of Canterbury really was best left alone.

Odo gnawed into the bone of some large animal or other until there was nothing more to be gained. He threw the bone on the floor.

A very small attendant scurried over with a basket and scooped the discarded bone up. He placed it carefully in the middle of his basket and then presented himself, very humbly, to the bishop.

Without pausing before the next bone, the bishop reached out into the air and blessed the basket and its contents.

The small attendant nodded happily and shuffled out of the room like a cross between a spider and a crab. A blessed bone from the table of the bishop would fetch a good price and help swell the coffers; and add weight to the small attendant's purse as well.

The retainer shook his head in sorrow.

'It's no good you complaining...,' Odo paused for a moment as if trying to recall the retainer's name. Instead he just waved his hand in the right direction. 'It all helps pay for people like you.'

The retainer made a note to give thanks for the money he was owed by Odo, never having actually been paid anything.

He had been quite happy as a very minor Saxon land owner, minding his own business in Dover before the Normans turned up. He'd managed to mind his own business in Hastings as well and slipped back to Dover as soon as it was clear that Harold wasn't going to be doing any more ruling of the country.

Then he had been enticed into the service of the Bishop of Bayeux. Not enticed by any material wealth, rather by the promise that service to the bishop was one of the more reliable ways of staying alive.

And if the retainer was busy retaining inside the walls of the Norman's castle, there was a good chance his wife and family would not be bothered by Norman soldiers. The local Saxons might be more trouble when they found out what he was doing with the enemy though. Still, better the Normans not kill you now and the Saxons threaten to do it later.

'This abbess has said nothing?' Odo asked, carrying on his previous conversation.

'We've had no word.'

Odo gave this some thought as he tried to extract a lump of animal from between two of his back teeth. 'We shall have to send someone.'

'We have sent someone. The king sent his investigator the monk, remember?'

'The monk?' Odo was clearly running through all the monks he knew. 'Oh, that one. What's he supposed to do?'

'Find out who killed the nuns,' the retainer sounded very bored with repeating this tale. His master might be very effective in the moment, but as soon as that had gone by, he forgot about it and got on with the next one.

'The king said that you were not to go, how did he put it? "stomping and slaughtering into the middle of a nunnery," I think that was it.'

Odo just grumbled to himself about this. If he wasn't allowed to do something as simple as go stomping and slaughtering into the middle of a nunnery, what was he allowed to do? He was Earl of Kent, after all.

'But the monk hasn't come back either?' Odo asked.

'He only left two days ago.'

'Hm.' Odo rubbed his chin. 'It's very suspicious.'

'What is?' The retainer knew what was coming now. Something horrible. Something horrible and unwarranted and doubtless against the direct instructions of the king.

'The monk disappearing like that.'

'He hasn't disappeared. He's gone to Lyminge. Where you sent him.'

Odo was on a track of his own now, and there was very little chance of getting him off it. 'And him the king's own man.'

'What are you going to do?' The retainer used the voice that said, "whatever it is you're going to do, you really shouldn't". He used it quite a lot.

'Serve the king, of course. How dare you suggest otherwise?'

'Let me guess. As the king's investigator has disappeared, which he hasn't, by the way, the very least you can do is go and look for him.'

'My thought exactly.'

'Just take fifty men or so, fully armed, and ride to the abbey.'

'Good idea, erm,' Odo tried hard to recall the name now.

'Just "you" will do.' The retainer had quickly concluded that Odo not remembering his name could be quite useful in the future.

'Good idea, you. Yes, we shall take men and demand that the king's investigator be returned unharmed. The king would want us to do that.'

'If you say so.'

'We can't have the king's men being taken captive and held hostage like this.'

'Like what?' The retainer squeaked a bit. 'Where did being taken and held hostage come from? The man walked out of here of his own volition, him and the other two. We've had no word that they've been captured by anyone.'

'Dangerous times,' Odo said, significantly.

'They certainly are,' the retainer muttered.

'It's our duty to erm, what's the word?'

'Investigate?' the retainer suggested.

'What the devil does that mean?'

'To track, apparently. The monk told me.'

'What monk?'

The retainer ran a hand over his face. 'The king's monk, the investigator. The one who's doing the tracking for the king. The one we're about to ride off to rescue?'

'Ah, right, good. Yes, we need to go and investigate.'

'And while we're there?' the retainer prompted.

'Oh, yes, while we're there we can ask this wretched nun where my tapestry is.'

'But we don't want any accidents, do we?' the retainer prompted.

'Accidents?'

'You know what I mean. Accidents with soldiers and swords and nuns. Accidents that come to the attention of the archbishop, and then the king, and then things fall on us.' The retainer didn't care the second hoot of an owl if the king got angry with Odo. It was the collateral damage that was of more concern.

'Punished by the king.' Odo said this in a very unfriendly and contemptuous manner.

Odo's way of dealing with being punished by the king was to punish some people of his own. And he didn't bother finding out whether they'd done anything wrong or not.

And he did tend to get punishments from the king quite regularly; nearly all of them well deserved. In his very darkest days he even muttered about him being a better king than William. That sort of talk really would lead to trouble. William's method of getting rid of people who thought that way was a simple execution. Followed by the simple execution of anyone who had even heard the thought expressed.

'We'll get the men, then,' the retainer said, hoping to divert Odo from treason by the thought of some happy wandering with a bit of casual violence.

'Excellent.' Odo clapped his hands and stood. 'To horse,' he called and strode towards the door. He stopped halfway, recalling something important. He turned back to the table, blessed the wreckage of his meal and left.

✦　　✦　　✦

'Nuns?' One of the soldiers in the courtyard questioned the degree of challenge in their mission. 'We're going after nuns?' He looked at the very large number of horsemen gathered around him, clearly thinking that you didn't need this many for a few nuns.

'No, we are not going after nuns.' The retainer, now sitting on his horse at Odo's side, recalled that getting ideas into the heads of Norman soldiers was slightly more difficult than doing it to their horses.

'We are going to Lyminge Abbey, to see what has happened to the king's man. An investigator monk.'

'Yeuch,' one of the soldiers expressed his profound disgust for such behaviour.

'It means tracker. The king's tracker. King William.' He knew that dropping the name into conversations always got their attention.

The soldiers nodded that they understood now. They understood that whatever it was they were going to do, it was for William. They still didn't understand what it was, but that wasn't important anymore.

The retainer had tried his best to convince Odo that fifty men was really a bit much for a visit to one abbey full of nuns. An abbey that was only a couple of hours away. If the nuns really did put up a fight it would be easy to send for reinforcements.

'And have these nuns taken the man?' one soldier asked.

His companions snorted crude and comprehensively disgusting suggestions as to what the nuns would have done if they had.

'We don't know what's happened to him,' the retainer said, ignoring the spittle that was coming more from the soldiers than their animals. He frequently marvelled at how these people had managed to walk up the beach at Hastings without falling over, let alone defeat Harold's army.

'There were two others as well,' he went on. 'Weavers.'

'Weavers?' Now the soldiers were in danger of getting really lost.

'King William sent the monk and the weavers to find out what has happened to Lord Odo's tapestry.'

The soldiers nodded at this. They knew all about the tapestry and were looking forward to seeing it. Several of them had been promised that they were going to be in it and couldn't wait to see how they'd come out.

Whenever the troop leader wanted something horrible done, he offered a part in the tapestry as reward. That worked for a while but there were rumours in the barracks that he'd promised everyone that they were going to be in it. In which case the thing would have to be two hundred feet long, which was plainly ridiculous.

'The weavers and the monk went to the abbey and we are now going to make sure they're all right.'

'And take decisive action if they're not,' Odo added.

The soldiers all knew what Odo's idea of decisive action was and looked forward to it.

They even noticed that he had his famous club with him. The one he used to kill people in battle. Being a bishop, it wouldn't be at all appropriate for him to carry a sword. A deadly weapon like that was only good for slicing people, which no Christian bishop should have anything to do with. Clubbing them to death was fine.

'But we need to keep calm,' the retainer urged. He could already see that the soldiers were girding themselves for a fearsome and bloody attack on a nunnery, one that put up no defence at all. 'King William will not want his monk or his weavers harmed. The man who does so can think what will happen to him.'

The soldiers looked very disappointed at that, as did Odo.

'And killing a nun is a sin,' the retainer reminded them. He knew that left them with no one to kill at all, which was always a risk with this lot, but better that than start the rampage nine miles out and have to explain a completely desecrated abbey to the archbishop and the king.

'We know why the tapestry is not done though,' Odo roused his men. 'And why the king has sent his own man to look into it.' He paused for effect. 'Someone is out there killing my nuns, boys. And if we find them, you know what to do.'

The boys did know what to do and cheered at the prospect. They also knew to hang back enough to let Odo and his club do it first.

With a throaty "to Lyminge", which wasn't the most fearsome battle cry ever, Odo led his men out of the castle gate and down the slope towards the town.

Once at the foot of the hill, he allowed the retainer to catch up so that he could point out which way Lyminge actually was.

Once they were on the right road, a road suddenly free of local people and their business, they upped their pace and thundered along.

As they started to climb the hill on the far side of Dover, the sea on their left being the only thing to blissfully ignore them, they came upon a lone monk, sitting at the side of the road.

This was an old fellow, clearly tired from his travel, with no energy to do anything in the face of the oncoming Normans. He simply raised his hand in blessing, hoping that they would ride on by.

Of course, they didn't. One of the soldiers in the vanguard, seeing the monk, swung his animal to a halt. As the others drew up, he pointed at the wizened old man who wasn't a threat to a dead rabbit.

'Is this the one?' the soldier asked.

'Is this the one, what?' the retainer replied, anxious to get in before one of the others said something along the lines of "yes, that's the one; let's kill him."'

'The king's monk?'

'No, it isn't. The king's monk is in Lyminge and we're not there yet. In any case, this man's old enough to drop dead at any minute. Hardly the sort of monk the king would send.'

'Are you the king's monk?' the soldier shouted loudly, as you had to with old people.

The old monk just looked bemused.

The retainer repeated the question in old Saxon English. The monk didn't look any the wiser.

'Acweþan na,' the retainer prompted.

'Na,' the monk said.

'He says no,' the retainer reported to the Normans, who were very disappointed.

Reluctantly leaving a very confused old monk by the side of the road, the Norman contingent rode on.

'That gives me an idea,' Odo said to his retainer.

'Ah,' the retainer said, expecting the worst.

'If we see any monks or nuns along the way, we should stop them.'

'Erm, why?'

'Because they may have something to do with all this.'

'Really?'

'Of course. They could be the ones who killed my nuns.'

'Other monks and nuns? Monks and nuns don't usually kill one another, being of a religious frame of mind. It's more usually soldiers.'

'Or they could be escaped weavers.'

The retainer was running out of sensible responses.

'Broken out of the abbey when they were attacked by the nun killers.'

Before he could interject, Odo had stood in his saddle and called out to his men. 'If we come across any wandering bands of nuns and monks, we stop them.'

'Yay,' called the men, obviously concluding that "stopping" meant stopping permanently.

Odo urged the men on toward the killing grounds of Lyminge Abbey that obviously awaited them. He did not catch a plaintive and hopeless 'Oh, God,' slip from his retainer's lips. Nor the words that followed. 'Here we go again.'

Caput XVIII

Pursuit of the Osreds

at and Cwen were very quickly on their feet but stumbled about as if they were still half asleep; or rather, they stumbled about because they were still half asleep.

'Eh, what?' Wat asked as he tripped over tree roots and brambles in his random struggle to make his legs work.

'I'll get you next time,' Cwen said, obviously to someone she had left behind in her dream.

'Wake up,' Hermitage called to the two of them, an odd thing to say as they were both standing and moving about.

'Hermitage?' Cwen asked, sounding surprised to see him. 'Where are we?'

'About to be chased by Osgifu and her Osreds.' Hermitage sounded insistent and in a bit of a panic; mainly because he was.

Wat shook his head to clear it of sleep. 'How did they get here?' He looked back over the path across the marshes and could clearly see the large group walking towards them. They could only be about half a mile away at most.

At least they were just walking and there seemed to be no urgency to their steps. They obviously hadn't spotted their erstwhile prisoners hiding in the woods. Yet.

'They walked, I imagine,' Hermitage said weakly.

Wat quickly gathered his pack and led the way out of the shelter of the trees and further up the hill away from the oncoming Ebonites. 'Obviously they walked. What I mean is, how did they get here so quickly.'

'Walked quickly?' Hermitage offered.

'Hermitage? Did you fall asleep?'

'Fall? No,' Hermitage was completely honest, as usual.

'Really?'

'No. I sort of leant asleep,' he confessed.

'Leant asleep?' Cwen's contempt was clear.

'I didn't mean to. I didn't do it on purpose. I was leaning against the tree watching the road. Then I woke up and there they were.'

'For goodness sake.'

'Sorry.'

'We will be if they catch us.'

'What shall we do?' Hermitage was anxious to make amends for his mistake, or at least find out that it hadn't really mattered because they had a ready means of escape.

'I think your idea of running is a good one,' Wat called back.

It was actually very difficult to run anywhere. The trees and bushes growing all over the hill covered every inch of spare space. The only way to move was to wind in and out of these and progress was slow.

Even the bushes and the trees seemed grateful to be out of the marsh and grew with abundance on the slopes. They looked down on the bleak landscape below them, mocking the poor grasses that only had a bog to grow in.

'Shouldn't we get on the path?' Hermitage asked. 'We'd move quicker.'

'And be visible to those on the path below us,' Cwen said.

If all this vegetation blocked their view of their pursuers, it also blocked the pursuers' view of them.

'We might make it to the abbey,' Wat said.

'That's a long way still,' Hermitage observed.

'The alternative being?' Cwen asked. 'Osgifu and the Osreds are heading there and we're in their way.'

'We could do as Wat said on the island.' Hermitage recalled the comment and saw its value.

'Me? What did I say?'

'You said the Ebonites hid in the reeds while the Vikings went by. There is a profusion of cover here. We could hide off the path and let them go by.'

'Let them go by?' Wat didn't sound too pleased with the suggestion.

'Well, yes?'

'So, why did we just wade through a bog in the middle of the night? While Osgifu and her band were sleeping?'

'Oh,' Hermitage said. 'So that we could, erm, get in front of them and head them off at the abbey.'

'There you are.' Wat congratulated Hermitage on recalling a key plank of his own plan. 'Hiding in the bushes and letting them go past would seem to defeat that object. Yes?'

'Yes,' Hermitage admitted. 'We keep going then.'

'We do. And we just hope that the Osgifu hunting party are having a nice gentle morning stroll. If they're on the path, they'll move faster than us.'

'Maybe they have scouts going ahead?' Cwen suggested.

'Ah, thanks for that,' Wat said. 'Yes, they may have scouts ahead of them who will find us before we've even got to the top of the hill.'

'We need to know where they are,' Cwen said.

'Really?' Hermitage preferred not to know where they were. Capture would be a bit of a surprise, but it was somehow less worrying than knowing someone was right on your heels.

'Of course. Know your enemy.'

Hermitage knew his enemies quite well, he couldn't immediately see how this helped.

'If we know where they are and how fast they're coming, we can take the appropriate action.'

'Like hide and let them pass because it's too late to keep ahead,' Wat said. 'Or run like hell.' He stopped beside a tree that was more solid than those that had been perching on the slope down to the marshes. 'Who wants to climb a tree?' he asked.

Hermitage only briefly thought that this was an odd time for climbing trees. 'I'll do it,' he said, hoping to make some recompense for the brief doze that had caused all this trouble.

'You?' Cwen asked in some surprise.

'I can do it,' Hermitage assured her.

'I never saw you as the tree climbing sort.'

'I'm not, really.' Hermitage examined his black Ebonite outfit to see if there was anything to get in the way of tree climbing. A habit was a most inconvenient garment for this sort of thing, but then it had been a long time since he'd been chased up a tree while wearing that.

'When the other children wanted to climb trees, I usually went home to read a book. Well, to read the only book we had. But when the other children got a bit more boisterous, I found that climbing trees could be quite useful.'

'Well, I'm not going up it,' Wat said, looking at his fine clothes and making it clear he wasn't going to risk dirtying them on some tree. 'And you mind those clothes,' he warned Hermitage. 'I don't want you tearing a hole in your leggings climbing trees.'

Hermitage had already got his foot on the trunk of the tree and had grasped a limb above him. It wasn't a tall, or even very substantial tree, but that made it easier to climb, and he was confident it would hold his weight.

'Go on then.' Wat stepped over and put his shoulder under Hermitage's backside and added lift.

'Ooh, thank you,' Hermitage said as he was almost thrown into the lower-most branches.

He threw one arm over a solid looking limb and hoisted his left leg over after him. From the position of laying on the tree, he slowly brought his feet and knees up and levered himself more upright with his arms.

He looked out from his vantage point and realised that all he could see was the rest of the tree. He would have to go higher.

As he prised himself up to his knees and cautiously looked for his next climbing point, Cwen gazed up at him. 'Are you sure you've climbed a tree before?'

'Of course.'

'You're positive it was a tree? It wasn't a bookshelf or just something made of wood.'

'Was it a ladder?' Wat asked.

He ignored them and was now on his feet on the branch. He found another one further up and grasped this to haul his view higher.

'Well?' Cwen asked. 'Can you see anything yet?'

Hermitage could. Through the top branches of the tree he could see the path across the marshes, although the route it took up the hill was mostly hidden by other trees.

'I can see the main party of Ebonites. They seem to be moving more quickly now.'

'More quickly?' Wat asked suspiciously.

'Yes,' Hermitage was cautious. 'I think they do have a scout.'

'Blast,' Wat grunted. 'Can you see him?'

'Er, yes. And it's a her, I think.'

'What's she doing?'

'Nothing, really.'

'Nothing?'

'No, she's just sort of standing there, on the path.'

'Why's she doing that?' Cwen asked.

Hermitage could only make an assumption, but it seemed a reasonable one in the circumstances. 'I think she's wondering why someone from Ebony got up this tree and is looking at her.'

'Get down,' Wat barked, and Hermitage did so quite quickly. 'Come on.' Wat barged off into the woods. 'There's no point keeping off the path now. The only thing we can hope is that we can make it to the abbey before they catch us.'

'But the scout?' Hermitage gasped as he ran to follow.

'It's only one scout,' Wat called. 'I'm sure Cwen can deal with her.'

'Oh, yes,' Cwen said in a positively enthusiastic tone.

Hermitage was going to suggest that they should take a measured approach to their current problem. He then recalled that their current problem was that they were being chased by sixty people who thought they were tied up on an island miles away. And that they were the people who had done the tying up.

He imagined that being caught by these people would result in something a bit more than just an awkward conversation. He sped to keep up with Wat.

They were back on the path now and rounded a corner where a large oak had grown out and had to be circled.

'I'll wait here,' Cwen said, and stopped behind the tree.

Hermitage knew perfectly well what she was planning to do, and he didn't approve at all. Lying in wait for some poor woman to come along the path so that she could be attacked and stopped from following them was outrageous. It was not the sort of thing he could lend any support to at all.

Wat had simply nodded, and Hermitage followed him along the path, finding himself hoping that Cwen got a good hard blow in first, so that they could get away.

He and Wat trotted on, putting as much distance behind them as they could. He imagined that the large party of Ebonites would not be running hard. The scout could only have indicated to them that they needed to hurry. Unless, of course, there were two scouts and one had been sent back with word that one of their own was ahead of them, up in the trees.

'At least they won't know it's us.' Cwen said, as she caught up with them.

She had a rosy glow about her and a look of quiet satisfaction.

'She didn't recognise you?' Wat asked.

'She didn't see me,' Cwen boasted. 'The expression "never

knew what hit her" was made for occasions like this.'

Hermitage just shook his head with a mixture of sorrow and gratitude.

'Only the one scout, as far as I could see,' Cwen went on. 'So all they'll know is that there's someone up here.'

'Good,' Wat said. 'We're still in with a chance then.' He carried on at a slow running pace, the sort that could be kept up for quite long periods of time. Unless you were a monk who wasn't used to running anywhere.

'Can we rest for a moment?' Hermitage panted.

'No,' Wat said.

'But.' Hermitage simply didn't have the breath to argue for his preferred course of action.

'We have most of the population of Ebony on our heels. And they're probably going to find their scout laid out in the woods at any moment.'

'No, they won't,' Cwen said with a horrible smile.

'Cwen, you didn't?' Hermitage's horror gave him breath.

'No, of course not. I just put her down a badger hole.'

'Down a badger hole?' Hermitage thought she'd gone mad.

'That's it. There was a huge badger sett on the slope just there. And she was quite a small woman, fitted just right.'

Wat coughed a laugh. 'I don't think the badgers are going to be very pleased.'

'Give her something else to worry about,' Cwen smirked.

Hermitage was starting to worry about Cwen. Well, slightly more than usual.

'All right,' Wat relented. He stopped at the next tree and slung his pack off so that he could stretch and take breath. 'Only a moment or two though. We don't know how close Osgifu is. The abbey can't be much further now.' He looked around as if expecting to see a sign saying "abbey this way."

They all took the time to recover as much as they could. Hermitage found his new clothing was hot and stifling. He was never very good running in a habit, but this outfit seemed to be worse. Why would anyone wear so much leather, he wondered? And all of it black? That seemed to make it even worse, somehow.

As their panting subsided and they started to ready themselves for the next leg of the journey, Wat held up a hand for silence. They held what breath they had and listened hard. There was no mistaking it. The noise of several dozen people moving along a path through some woods was clear. And it was a lot closer than comfort demanded.

'Oh, bloody hell.' Wat snatched up his pack and set off along the path once more. Hermitage and Cwen were quickly in pursuit.

'I could wait behind another tree,' Cwen offered with some enthusiasm.

'Not for all of them, you couldn't,' Wat warned. 'We have got to get to the abbey. They obviously know they're chasing someone now. They've probably set their fittest and fiercest after us.'

Hermitage thought that either the fittest or the fiercest would do the job perfectly well. Putting them both together seemed a bit harsh.

They entered an open clearing now, where the trees had been removed, probably for their timber. The old stumps littered the place while the new saplings poked their heads up in between. It was a large space, some three hundred feet or so from end to end, and Hermitage just hoped that they could reach the shelter of the trees on the far side before anything horrible emerged behind them.

They were only some dozen or so paces from the trees, and Hermitage had just started to get his hopes up, when a call came from behind.

'Stop,' a voice commanded.

'Why do people say that?' Wat asked as he didn't stop, and ran on into the woods. 'I mean, what do they think we're going to do? Actually stop?'

'What else are they going to say?' Cwen asked. 'We're behind you?'

Hermitage didn't have the breath to enquire how many times Wat had been chased for him to have an opinion on the proprieties of the process.

They were back in the woods now, but the pursuit had broken into a powerful run as it saw its quarry.

Hermitage had looked back as they were shouted at; he always looked at people who were shouting at him. He didn't recognise any of the Osreds or Osgifus so hopefully they wouldn't know who it was they were following; only that it was some people who were running away, one of them looking very much like an Ebonite; all of which was suspicious enough in its own right.

Wat and Cwen had got ahead slightly, and so he ran on to catch up. Which is why he ran straight into the back of Cwen and they both ended up on the floor.

'What?' Was all he managed to say as he started to sort himself out. 'Are we there yet?' He just assumed that they must have arrived at the abbey, although he didn't recall it being in the middle of the woods.

Cwen untangled herself and got back onto the path where Wat was standing. Hermitage joined them and saw exactly why they'd stopped.

They all walked very slowly backwards, towards the clearing and the oncoming Ebonites, emerging from the woods just as the first pursuer, another Ebonite woman, caught up.

'Aha,' she said.

Wat rolled his eyes in disappointment at the word.

'Aha, indeed,' the Earl of Kent said as he rode out from the trees and looked down from his magnificent stallion at the strange sight. He had his massive club in his hand for good measure, and four more horsemen drew up at his side.

The Ebonites stopped in their tracks.

'Our watchers on the hill sent word that people were coming

out of the marshes,' Odo explained.

Hermitage rather wished that the watchers on the hill had made themselves known a bit earlier.

'They were right.' Odo raised his club and pointed it at all of them.

His retainer now rode up to his side, his weary look of resignation temporarily replaced by genuine surprise.

Odo was confident and patronising. 'It looks like we have found our wandering band of nun murderers,' he announced.

The retainer considered the Ebonites suspiciously.

'And look how many there are.' Odo was very pleased. 'We shall have a marvellous execution and get everything back to normal.'

The growing band of Normans riding out from the trees considered the now nervous group of Ebonites who clearly knew that it was no good trying to run away from mounted soldiers.

There was a moment of slightly awkward silence as each group regarded the other, just waiting for the first move to be made.

As the two forces weighed one another up, each growing anxious for action, the atmosphere grew tense and even the woods joined the silence, as if the creatures of nature were holding their breath in anticipation of the first clash of steel. A sudden distraction dragged their attention away from the matter soon to be in hand.

The people from the marshes and the Normans both watched with interest and not a little puzzlement as a small woman ran screaming across the clearing, closely followed by three for four very angry looking badgers.

Caput XIX

Normans Meet The Ebonites

The Earl of Kent shook his head as the woman and her pursuers vanished into the woods. 'Bloody Saxons,' he said, as if being baited by badgers was some sort of national past time and he really wasn't interested in what Saxons did with badgers; or vice versa.

'Ah, look, sire,' Odo's retainer observed from his horse. 'That one's the King's Investigator.' He pointed straight at Hermitage. 'And he appears to be unharmed and uncaptured.'

Odo passed his glare over Hermitage, obviously disappointed that the monk was alive and well and didn't require some horrible act of retribution.

Hermitage gave a little wave of acknowledgement.

'Although why he's dressed like that, I do not know.' The retainer looked as if he was going to be very interested in the reply.

'What's going on?' Odo demanded. 'Why don't you look like a monk anymore?'

'A long tale, sire.' Hermitage hoped that there wasn't the time for long tales just at the moment.

'And who are these people?' Odo waved towards the Ebonites.

'Ahum,' Hermitage said, wondering how much he should even try and explain, and how much Odo would actually believe anyway. At least this was a new question and he could ignore his Ebonite clothing for now.

'We're on our way to the abbey,' Wat spoke up.

Odo looked to Hermitage for confirmation. At least he could nod honestly at this, not that it was an answer to the question he'd been asked.

'All of you?'

'That's right.' Wat sounded very nonchalant about the whole situation. 'We're going back there to deal with the matter of the dead nun and the tapestry. These folk are on their way to begin their devotions. They're postulants, you see?'

'Postulants?' Odo sounded very doubtful. 'What sort of postulant carries a sword?'

'A cautious one, I suppose. Dangerous country.'

'It is now.' Odo looked at them all, making it quite clear that the danger was sitting on his horse right in front of them.

'Why were you running?'

'Dangerous country, as you say. And we've got to get to the abbey quickly, haven't we, Hermitage?'

'Oh, er, yes, that's right.' Again, it was true that they needed to get to the abbey quickly, but that wasn't why they were running. He was in danger of getting very confused over which truth went with which fact.

'Why?'

'Stop more deaths,' Wat said confidently. 'Don't want any more dead nuns holding up the tapestry.'

Odo was at least happy with that as a reason.

'So there have been deaths?' the retainer asked. 'This Abbess Cartimandua isn't just incompetent when it comes to tapestry?'

Wat looked like he really wanted to offer some comment on the competence of nuns when it came to tapestry, but he was biting his tongue.

They all looked at Hermitage, who realised he was supposed to answer.

'Erm, yes. Well, that is, we, erm, there could be.'

'There could be? There's either a death or there isn't. It's probably a significant point to the one who's dead.'

'There is a nun who is missing,' he explained not wanting to leap to any unwarranted conclusions. 'And she was leading the work on the tapestry. We've not been able to confirm that she's dead.'

'Why not?'

'We haven't seen the body.'

Odo nodded that this was a very good reason.

'Do you normally go round looking for dead bodies?' the retainer asked.

'I'm afraid so,' Hermitage said. 'There tends to be one whenever there's a murder.'

'Not if the murderer's any good,' Odo explained. 'Hide the body. Obvious, isn't it. First thing you do.' He clearly held enormous contempt for murderers who couldn't even do the basics like hide the body.

'Our murderer is a good one, then?' the retainer said.

'As there is no body, we really aren't sure. Someone has told us that the nun simply left the abbey, another report is that she was murdered. That's why we need to get back there.' He didn't like to add that they were being chased by the Ebonites, one of whom thought she was the Queen of England and who was coming to assassinate Odo. He didn't think it would help. 'And we could stop any more happening.'

Odo nodded that this was a reasonable plan.

'We were told there were swarms of dead nuns.' The retainer didn't sound happy that there was only one.

'Not that we've been able to find,' Hermitage said. 'I mean, obviously there could be more, but no one has said there are any others missing.'

The retainer frowned at this news while Odo looked a little sheepish and was examining the state of the trees in this part of his demesne; the ones that weren't there any more.

The retainer turned to his master in a very deliberate manner. 'Did we report a host of dead nuns to King William for any good reason?'

Odo coughed. 'There could be more. You heard the monk.'

'The king would be much more forgiving of slow progress on the tapestry if he thought half the nuns in Kent had been slaughtered.' The retainer raised questioning eyebrows. 'Rather than one had just gone missing.'

'We've got more nuns now.' Odo waved his hand towards the group of armed postulants who looked as if they were hoping that they'd be forgotten at any moment now. 'They can do the tapestry.' He nodded to himself in a very self-satisfied manner. 'All is well,' he concluded.

'All is well?' the retainer muttered his disbelief quite quietly. 'They don't look like nuns,' he observed.

'That one does,' Odo pointed over their heads towards the back of the clearing.

The remainder of the Ebonites, the ones who hadn't set off in hot pursuit of Hermitage, Wat and Cwen, now appeared through the trees at the far end of the clearing. Osgifu led the way, looking very nun-like, accompanied by Osred dressed in Hermitage's habit.

It was a very strange experience, watching his own habit walk towards him with another man's body inside. His habit had identified him for so long that he suddenly felt giddy. Was he in the habit walking towards himself dressed as an Ebonite, or was he outside looking back? The confusion was so profound that he felt expelled from his own body, whichever one that was, and was now floating above the field looking down on everyone.

He could see himself as an Ebonite standing with the earl, and as a monk walking towards them. His eyes and his head could not flick between the two fast enough to make any sense of this. All he knew was that he had to sit down.

'Hermitage!' Cwen called. 'Are you all right?'

Odo considered Hermitage as he sank to the floor. 'Faint at the sight of a nun? What do you monks get up to?'

'I'm fine. Really.' Hermitage recovered his poise.

'Do you know these people?' Odo asked, sounding very suspicious.

'Oh, er.'

'You were all running as fast as you could to the same abbey, it seems. Be a bit odd if you didn't.'

Hermitage took the hint. 'Of course. The, erm, postulants and then there's the nun and the monk of course.'

'Who are?'

'Well, I think that's erm, Sister Osgifu and there's Brother Osred with her.'

'I see.'

Osgifu, Osred and the other Ebonites had stopped now, and were looking over to the other side of the clearing with interest.

Hermitage couldn't imagine what they were thinking. Their own band was now simply standing there looking at a lot of men on horseback. A lot of men with weapons on horseback. Men with weapons on horseback who suddenly seemed to be in charge. Would they recognise Normans, never having met any? Hermitage thought it was quite likely. Osgifu had heard all about them, after all. Who else was likely to be riding about on horses waving swords in the air.

Clearly concluding that they couldn't simply walk slowly back into the woods and pretend that none of this had happened, Osgifu beckoned her party to follow her across the clearing.

Now Hermitage was really worried. Would Osgifu announce herself as Queen of England come to assassinate Odo? That wouldn't go down at all well. It would also be a pretty stupid thing to do and Osgifu did not strike him as stupid.

'Ah, Sister Osgifu,' he almost shouted across the clearing as they drew near. He thought that this would at least give her enough warning to play the right part. 'And is that Brother Osred with you? And the postulants, I see.'

'I don't think we need a commentary,' Odo observed.

They waited in awkward silence until the rest of the Ebonites joined them. Osgifu and Osred came to the front.

Osgifu nodded to Hermitage. 'Brother Hermitage. Why are you dressed like that?' She asked this question so innocently, yet with such intense venom that Hermitage was almost tempted to reply honestly; just for Odo's benefit.

That was a bit unfair, he thought. She knew exactly why he was dressed like this, and it was her fault. 'Oh, you know. My habit got, erm, damaged and this was all there was. Do you know the Earl of Kent?' He thought the introduction was needed, in case Osgifu decided to do something stupid after all. He also thought that it would put her off her guard just as she had done to him. And he felt bad about doing it, of course.

Osgifu ignored Hermitage and bowed her head to Odo. Well, the head moved downwards a bit, but it didn't look much like a bow.

'A nun, eh?' Odo said. 'Are you a weaving nun?'

'I can weave,' Osgifu replied, making it quite clear that she wasn't going to.

'Excellent,' Odo called for all to hear. 'This nun here can re-place the missing one. Take her.'

Before the Ebonites could do anything, three horsemen rode forward, two of them springing down from their beasts to take Osgifu by the arms.

'And take these peoples' weapons,' Odo instructed. 'Can't have postulants wandering around the country armed like they rule the place. We rule the place.'

The Ebonites obviously realised that they had no chance of fighting off fifty Normans on horseback. Osgifu also gave them a warning look not to resist.

Hermitage hoped that she was getting the idea that defeat-ing the Normans was simply beyond her people. Unfortunately, he suspected that she was still planning something; probably in-volving the death of Odo at any moment.

'There we are, that's better,' Odo said as the Ebonites handed over their swords and knives. 'Now, we can all go to the abbey together, can't we?' He made it sound like quite a nice day out.

He gave a wave of the hand and the troop turned to head back the way they had come. A good contingent of the fifty men loitered until they could come along behind the Ebonites. This may be a group of unarmed nuns, monks and postulants, but that didn't mean the Normans weren't ready to attack at a moment's notice.

Hermitage, Wat and Cwen walked along behind the front horsemen, not really with the Normans but not with the Ebonites either.

'Here we are,' Wat said brightly. 'All our problems solved. Osgifu's not killing Odo, Odo's not killing Osgifu. The tapestry gets done, even though it'll still be nuns doing it instead of proper weavers, and we can get the Normans to deal with Cartimandua.' He beamed at them both.

'I think Osgifu still has plans for Odo,' Hermitage said.

'Plans that he won't be too keen on when he finds out,' Cwen added. 'And now she knows what he looks like, she'll know where to aim.'

'And I don't think she's going to quietly settle down to a bit of weaving and not mention at some point that she's the rightful Queen of England.'

Wat continued smiling. 'But the marvellous bit about all of that is that it's not our problem anymore.' He held his hands out as if to show that a problem he had been holding, had vanished.

'I need to talk to Osgifu again,' Hermitage said. 'Now that she has seen just a small portion of the Norman force, she will realise that her mission is hopeless. Even if she did manage to kill Odo, which I doubt, the remaining Normans will deal with her.'

'And all her people,' Cwen added.

Wat had a look on his face that said Hermitage could do

whatever he liked. It didn't really matter anymore.

Hermitage allowed himself to slip slowly backwards in the entourage until he was alongside Osgifu and Osred.

'How did you escape?' Osred hissed at him.

'Well, as we'd all been tied up but not tied to anything, we shuffled around..,' Hermitage began to explain.

'That hardly matters now,' Osgifu's voice was authoritative and Osred's lips closed tight. 'What's important is what you have told the Norman.'

'Told him? I haven't told him anything. Well, I've told him we're going to the abbey, but that's all.'

'You haven't told him who I am?' Osgifu sounded a bit confused now.

'Of course not. I think he would deal with you most harshly if I did. The whole reason we escaped and got here ahead of you was to warn you away. You've seen the Normans now, what they're like and how many they are. And this is only one small band. There are thousands of them out there. If you try to do anything against them you will fail, and you will fall. You and all your people.'

Osgifu was thoughtful.

'And you can see that if you killed Odo, one of the other fifty odd men would stick a sword in you without even thinking about it.'

'So, you are simply trying to save us?' Osred said this in a very sarcastic tone.

'Exactly.' Hermitage was glad that he'd got it at last.

'He thinks we really are postulants going to the abbey?' Osgifu asked.

'Possibly. He's still a bit suspicious, particularly as the postulants were better armed than postulants generally. But then he's Norman. They seem to think carrying weapons, and using them regularly, is normal.'

Osgifu said nothing.

'His Saxon retainer might be more of a worry. He could pick up on any clues that there's something going on.'

'But would he report us to his master?'

'Who's to know.' Hermitage certainly didn't. 'Some Saxons are with the Normans completely, others only out of necessity. From their conversation so far, I'd say this Saxon was of the reluctant variety.'

'So he may keep confidences.'

'It's possible.'

Osgifu looked very pensive as she walked along. There was clearly some internal debate going on and a decision was about to be reached.

'You have served us well, Brother Hermitage,' she said in a very regal sort of way. 'You proved your worth by not revealing our plan to the Normans.'

'Erm, thank you?' Hermitage said, starting to worry that this was going to go in a rather worrying direction at any minute.

'Your advice is sound. Now that I have seen the force of Normans, I can see that we will need to take care.'

'Well, that's good.'

'Just so. Killing Odo and making a public example of him to his people would only lead to dire consequences for us all.'

'Exactly.' Hermitage felt huge relief, and quite a bit of surprise, that this plan of his had come to fruition. He had not been so optimistic to think that Osgifu would give up her ideas at the first sight of a Norman, but it was working out that way. He couldn't wait to tell Wat and Cwen.

'So, this is what we will do,' Osgifu went on.

Hermitage's worries came straight back to bite him. But they hadn't gone far anyway.

'We take this Saxon retainer into our confidence. Then, when we arrive at the abbey we watch for a moment when Odo can be separated from his men and got on his own. The Saxon can help us with that.'

'And then?' Hermitage asked, already knowing full well what "and then" was going to be.

'Then we kill him. When no one is watching. We let the Normans find the body and they won't for a moment believe that nuns or monks could have done it.'

Hermitage could only sigh. 'What they will probably believe is that a Saxon did it. Then they'll kill all the Saxons they can find. Namely us.'

'They can try,' Osred growled defiantly.

Hermitage had something else he needed to tell Wat and Cwen now. He only had one thought he could leave with Osgifu and Osred. 'The problem is that when the Normans try to kill Saxons, they generally succeed.'

Caput XX

A Better Form of Attack
is a Slightly Different Attack

till don't see why it's our problem,' Wat said, when Hermitage had given the details to them both. 'Osgifu tries to kill Odo, she either succeeds or she doesn't. 'If she does, the Normans will deal with all her people. If she doesn't, they'll just deal with her.'

'And us?' Hermitage asked.

'We're the King's Investigator. Well, you are.'

'I'm not sure that's going to help.' Hermitage had never found being King's Investigator a help in any other situation, he didn't know why it would start being useful now. 'And I'm not sure King William will accept it as an excuse for standing around while his brother gets murdered.'

'If she does manage to finish him off,' Cwen said, 'the rest of the Normans are going to be pretty cross. And we don't know that the Saxon retainer will go along with it anyway.'

'You go and tell the Ebonites then,' Wat suggested. 'They seem pretty keen on this course of action.'

'Oh, what do we do?' Hermitage gave a quiet wail. 'If we go and warn the Normans, they'd probably want to kill her anyway. The whole business of being Queen of England will come out and then there'll be all sorts of new trouble.'

Neither Wat or Cwen had anything to offer.

'I obviously can't persuade Osgifu not to do this. I've had at least two goes now.'

'She may not be able to get him alone,' Cwen said. 'You know what the Normans are like. They seem to think that everyone they know is trying to kill them most of the time anyway. Enemies, friends, relatives, doesn't seem to matter. They spend most of their lives on their guard. He's hardly likely to allow himself to be caught alone.'

'By an innocent nun on her way to the abbey?' Wat questioned the thinking. 'And a nun who's going to do his weaving for him? He probably wants a chat with her, so he can tell her what he wants done.'

'Oh, Lord,' Hermitage fretted.

'Would she even do it herself though?' Cwen asked. 'She is queen, after all. Surely queens have people to do things like that for them. They don't get their own hands dirty.'

'William doesn't mind.' Wat said.

'But he's not a queen,' Hermitage pointed out, helpfully. 'Cwen could be right. She wouldn't do this herself, she'd have an Osred or two do it for her. And Odo is unlikely to let them gang up on him.'

'And they don't actually have weapons anymore,' Cwen said. 'What are they going to do, strangle him with their bare hands?'

They walked on for a few more minutes, the wood enveloping them and taking the prospect of arrival at the abbey out of Hermitage's head. He knew they'd get there soon enough though, and then what?

'This is completely ridiculous,' was all he could say. 'First of all, we're looking at a host of dead nuns and then there's only one. Then we find the so-called Queen of England and have to try and save her from being put to death by the Normans. Now we're trying to save a Norman from being put to death by her. Who thought we'd ever have to do that?'

More paces were taken without anything helpful coming forward.

Wat seemed to be enjoying the stroll through the woods, as if none of this was anything to do with him and he wouldn't be affected. Hermitage, on the other hand, was worried that everything was to do with him and he would be affected in ways he hadn't even begun to imagine.

Cwen was looking very thoughtful and was starting to nod to herself. 'We need to make sure that Odo is never alone,' she said. 'Well, never alone with Osgifu or an Osred.'

'Never alone?' Hermitage didn't like the idea of staying close to Odo at all. You could never tell with Normans. They did all sorts of peculiar and unpleasant things when you were least expecting it.

'Just watch him,' Cwen explained. 'Most of the time he'll be with his men, or with that retainer of his. If it looks like Osgifu or a couple of Osreds are sneaking up, we step in.'

'Step in, how?'

'Just appear. Like the nuisance at a carnival who keeps bothering you to buy his apples.'

'I heard about you and the apple seller at the carnival,' Wat cautioned.

'He soon recovered,' Cwen dismissed the problem. 'We just have to make sure the Ebonites don't get a chance to murder Odo.'

'They've already tied us up once,' Hermitage pointed out. 'If they think we're interfering with their plans, goodness knows what they'll do.'

'Excellent,' Cwen said, as if it was all settled. 'Any other ideas?'

There weren't any.

'There we are then.' She sped up a bit until she was at the back of Odo's retinue, from which point she smiled back at them. If Odo had seen that smile, he would have sped up as well.

◆　　◆　　◆

It wasn't as long as Hermitage had hoped before they saw the abbey rise up over a hill in front of them. He considered the building as they approached, perhaps as a distraction to what was likely to happen when they got there.

He imagined that Cartimandua would throw the doors wide to welcome Lord Odo. Well, she would if she had any sense. Keeping Normans at bay was never advisable. When they got in, and they would, the person doing the keeping-at-bay would count themselves lucky if they died quickly.

Presumably, all Odo intended to do was deliver Osgifu and get the tapestry going again. He might have some harsh words for Cartimandua for holding the whole thing up in the first place, but that would be about it.

Any concerns that the King's Investigator was here to resolve the murder of nuns would be a minor concern. Mind you, that Saxon retainer seemed more aware of what was going on. He would probably remember that King William was involved in all of this somewhere.

And then there was the problem of protecting Odo from the murderous intentions of Osgifu.

'Make camp,' the retainer called out as they drew up below the walls of the abbey.

Hermitage didn't think that they'd be staying here for any length of time, but inviting fifty armed Normans into a modest abbey full of modest nuns was a recipe for something slightly worse than a disaster. Very wise to camp the men outside while Odo got on with his business.

The Normans started to sort themselves out and dismount from the horses. Packs were taken down and the soldiers prepared themselves for a bit of leisure time while Odo got on with this tapestry/nuns/monks/weavers business.

Odo himself had some quiet words with his retainer and then looked around the field.

The Ebonites had all gathered together and were milling around the figure of Osgifu, who had a couple of the larger Osreds at her side.

'Ah,' Odo called over. 'You, nun.' He beckoned that she should draw near.

Osgifu gave him a charming smile and, with a rather secretive nod to an Osred, walked over.

'My Lord,' she said with a bow.

'Exactly. Now then. This is the abbey where my tapestry is being made. The last nun who was in charge of it all has vanished.'

'Vanished?' Osgifu sounded interested.

'Vanished, murdered, something like that.' Odo didn't sound very interested at all. 'So, before we go and see the abbess and find out what a mess she's made of the work so far, you and I need to have a discussion.'

He wandered away from a small group of his men and Osgifu tagged along.

'The whole thing goes back to King Edward,' Odo said as he led the two of them away.

'Hello,' Hermitage said as he popped up in front of them.

'What do you want?' Odo was as much startled as disappointed.

'Oh,' Hermitage said. 'You know, this and that.'

'No, I do not know. Get out of my way. I'm talking to this nun.'

'Precisely,' Hermitage said. He cast his hardest glance back at Wat and Cwen, once again questioning why he had to be the first one to interrupt Osgifu's murder attempts.

Odo just looked at him. It was the sort of look that said he didn't want to see him anymore.

'The nun,' Hermitage said.

'What about her?'

Osgifu looked a picture of innocence in front of Odo.

'The dead one,' Hermitage specified.

Odo considered Osgifu. 'No, she isn't.'

'Not this one,' Hermitage said. 'The other one, the one who's gone.'

'Vanished.'

'That's it.'

'What about her? I've got another one now.' He nodded his head towards Osgifu.

Hermitage thought that was a very good point. There had to be something else he could say, other than "Wat and Cwen would like a word." 'The king,' he said. Which worked very well indeed.

'Where?' Odo almost spun on the spot.

'No, no. I mean the king sent me to find out what happened to the nuns, er nun.'

'Well, you have. She vanished.'

'There's usually more to it than that,' Hermitage said, drawing on his horrible experience as King's Investigator. 'And the king will want to know what I found out.'

'And what have you found out?'

'That she may have been murdered.' He said this with as much solemnity and seriousness as he could muster. This was a very significant suggestion and Odo should take it to heart.

'Well done,' the earl congratulated Hermitage.

'Well done?'

'Yes. You can go and tell the king that the nun might have been murdered. Now. If I could get on with the tapestry?' Odo had his priorities and murdered nuns were not included.

'Exactly,' Hermitage said, for no immediately obvious reason.

'Exactly, what?'

'The tapestry.' Hermitage knew the word worked on Odo, he just had no idea why he'd said it.

The Norman's eyes narrowed. 'What about the tapestry?'

Osgifu was now looking impatiently at Hermitage, giving him the clear impression that she wanted him to go away. Which made him determined to stay.

'The tapestry and the murder,' Hermitage said, rather grandly, he thought.

'Are they connected?' Odo was interested now.

'Are they connected?' Hermitage repeated, asking himself the same question.

Odo considered Hermitage quite carefully now. 'Are you an idiot?' he asked, looking ready to move away if necessary.

'Not at all, sire.'

'Not even a little bit?'

'The tapestry and the murder could be connected,' Hermitage announced. What the foundation for his announcement was, he had not the first idea. He was frantically hoping something would occur to him.

'How?'

How? That was a very good question indeed. Hermitage would have to listen carefully to himself, just to find out what the answer was.

'It is a bit suspicious, isn't it?' he said.

'What is?'

'The very same nun who is in charge of your tapestry is the one who gets murdered.' Actually, that was quite a good point. Hermitage would have to follow it and see where it pointed.

'I thought she might have just vanished,' Osgifu said, sounding as if butter wouldn't melt in her mouth if she was on fire.

Hermitage gave her a puzzled look. After all, she had reported Cartimandua's guilt. She was clearly quite desperate to get Odo on his own. He chanced a look around and saw two Osreds not far off. They were trying to look as if they were fascinated by the Normans and their camp, but it was obvious that they were loitering.

'Why would the nun who was doing your great tapestry disappear at all?' Hermitage asked. 'Murdered or vanished, it's still suspicious.'

The look on Odo's face said that he agreed it was suspicious. He just had slightly less of a clue why it was suspicious than Hermitage did.

Hermitage hated to even think about asking the next question, but it was key. He had a very strong feeling that Odo would not take it well.

'The tapestry, my lord?'

'What about it?'

'Yes. Or rather, what's it about?'

Odo just stared at him. 'What's it about?' He said these words very slowly and very deliberately, as if unable to understand how anyone could ask such a question. He took a very deep breath.

'I've told you once,' Odo huffed. He explained again, as if Saxons couldn't be expected to understand anything as complicated as a picture. 'It is about the triumph of the Norman people.'

Hermitage just nodded, hoping this came across as a resounding endorsement of such a noble subject.

'And the brazen treachery of the Saxons,' Odo went on. 'Particularly Harold.'

'Ah.' Hermitage surprised himself by reaching a conclusion on this quite quickly. And all on his own.

'I even want a bit showing him shot in the eye,' Odo enthused. He turned to Osgifu. 'Can you do people shot in the eye?'

'Of course, sire,' Osgifu said, as if the shot in the eye was a speciality of hers.

'The Norman folk must be looking forward to the work,' Hermitage said.

'Of course.'

'Perhaps not so much the Saxons?'

Odo looked puzzled. 'The defeated Saxons,' he corrected.

'Well, obviously. Defeated. Quite. But there are still a few left.'

'Too many. And the tapestry isn't for them anyway.'

'But there may be some who aren't quite so keen on having a tapestry made showing their, erm, treachery. Never mind all the eye business.'

Odo shrugged that he really didn't care about that.

'Some who might take steps?' Hermitage proposed. 'Steps to

stop the tapestry being made at all?'

Now Odo got it and didn't look at all happy.

'Someone murdered my nun?' His voice rose as he seemed to be unhappy about the event he hadn't cared half a quack for two minutes ago. 'Rebels. Just as I said.'

'I only suggest it might be possible,' Hermitage said, thinking that it might be very possible indeed. He would have to see what Wat and Cwen thought about his new idea.

'Are they going to kill this one as well?' Odo nodded towards Osgifu as if she were a pheasant on a fence.

Osgifu was now giving Hermitage a most unfriendly look.

'I don't know, sire.'

Odo turned away from them. 'Oy, you,' he yelled to his retainer.

The man wandered over, showing little interest or devotion.

'Gather some men,' Odo ordered. 'We need to find out what's going on in this abbey. Someone's killing my nuns.'

The retainer sighed as he gave Hermitage and Osgifu a look of despair. 'Right back where we started then,' he mumbled. 'Bloody typical.'

'Bring the monk and the weavers as well as this one,' he tipped his head towards Osgifu. 'No point loitering if we can get the tapestry going again.'

As Odo strode off, Hermitage thought that he'd better go and update Wat and Cwen. He found his path impeded by two of the larger Osreds.

'Our Majesty has plans,' one of the big Osreds hissed at Hermitage. 'Plans for the Normans. And if you interrupt them again, it will not go well for you.'

Hermitage swallowed as he got the message. He looked to Osgifu for some support, but she too had walked off.

Naturally, he worried about this as he was left alone. But now there were bigger problems. He'd made the suggestion that Cartimandua may have killed the missing nun, and now he considered her fine, traditional name. If she was descended from a family who thought Cartimandua was a nice name, they were probably Celtic and considered the Saxons to be late-coming ne'er do wells. What she'd want to do to Norman invaders who were using the tapestry to glory in their victory, did not bear thinking about.

Caput XXI
Into the Abbey

Odo's approach to the abbey was straightforward and matter of fact. Even though the place looked quite capable of defending itself, he behaved as if it was his own stables. With a dozen carefully selected men, carefully selected because they were the ones who looked keenest to storm an abbey full of nuns, he rode up to and through the main gate.

He was followed by his dozen men, all on their horses. By the time the last of them arrived, it was blindingly obvious that the courtyard of this abbey was simply not big enough for a dozen anything, let alone fully armed Normans on horses, every one of whom was keen to get stuck in to something or other.

The last of the horsemen had ridden in full of bravado and martial intent, only to find that they were riding into the back of their companions.

The horses, the ones at the front now being pressed against the buildings, made it quite clear that they weren't happy with this arrangement and were anxious to leave. One or two of them even started to jump and kick in discomfort at their confined surroundings.

The Normans were struggling to control their beasts as Hermitage, Wat and Cwen walked up, followed by Osgifu and her favourite Osreds.

There was no way they were going to try and press themselves into a courtyard full of rolling horse flesh. Even the riders found that their feet were jammed against the animal next to them and they couldn't get off if they wanted to.

'Get out, get out.' Odo ordered in a loud voice. As he had

been the first to arrive, he was now right at the back of the yard and was being comprehensively pressed into the walls of the abbey. If he could stand on his saddle, he'd have been able to step in through one of the windows.

'What's going on down there?' a female voice called from above. Presumably it was a nun, but it didn't sound like a happy one.

'Lord Odo, Earl of Kent attends and demands your presence,' the retainer replied, his voice heavy with sarcasm as he tried to control his own beast.

'Mother Abbess, Mother Abbess!' The voice from above called back into the building. 'There are horses all over the courtyard.'

There was obviously a reply to this but those down below couldn't hear it.

'I don't know,' the first nun said. 'One moment it was all quiet, now it's full of horses. Hundreds of them.'

Another silent question from within.

'Yes, they've all got men on them. Oh, wait a minute, one of them has fallen off. Now they've nearly all got men on them. One of them said it's the Earl of Kent.'

A pause.

'No, the man, not the horse.'

Further instructions.

'I don't know. Shall I ask?'

The nun called down to the courtyard. 'The mother abbess wants to know if it's the Earl of Kent who's fallen off his horse?'

'No, it is not, damn you,' Odo called out.

'Well, really. There's no call for profanity,' the nun replied. 'This is an abbey and we don't tolerate language like that here.' This was a nun to be cowed by neither horse nor earl. 'The mother abbess wants you to get the horses out of the courtyard.'

'What do you think we're trying to do?'

'I'm sure I don't know. You're the ones who tried to get too

many horses in in the first place. In any case, we don't allow horses in the courtyard. Let alone ones with people on top who use
foul language.'

Odo's reply to this would have made the horses cover their
ears.

'Well, really,' the nun expostulated. 'I think you'd better go
away and come back when you've a civil tongue in your head. I
never heard the like.'

The Norman who had fallen from his saddle in the melee
now managed to worm his way around and underneath the
horses until he could lead the one closest to the gate away by the
bridle.

Far from encouraging those that remained to leave as well,
it seemed to startle them into pressing further in. Perhaps they
thought their companion had been taken by a lion, or something.

'Stupid bloody animals,' the walking Norman muttered as he
led first one, then another horse out of the courtyard.

'And don't you start with the language,' the nun called from
above.

At one point, the equine brains obviously worked out that
the exit was now available and so they went for it. All of them.

Hermitage, Wat, Cwen and the Ebonites watched with interest as all the Normans left, including Odo and the retainer
who appeared to be squirming and tugging on their horses to
make them turn back.

The horses were having none of it. Getting out of the courtyard was now top priority, and no man on their back was going
to stop them.

'Mother Abbess, they've gone now,' the nun from above called
out. 'There's just some people.' She looked down on Hermitage
and the others, who now wandered into the courtyard unim-
peded.

They looked up and could see the face of a nun peering at

them through a stone opening high in the wall. Even from that height they could see the nun's eyes widen as she noticed Osgifu.

'Sister Osgifu?' The nun sounded very surprised. 'Oh, bloody hell and damn my backside,' she said as her head quickly withdrew.

'I don't think they're expecting you,' Wat observed.

'We know you left in awkward circumstances,' Cwen sounded as if she was pressing Osgifu. 'You don't seem very popular at all.'

Osgifu looked at Wat and Cwen as if they'd been trodden in on the bottom of the horses' hooves. She turned away and beckoned her Osreds to follow.

'Well, really,' Hermitage said. He was disappointed at this behaviour from Osgifu. He thought that they had built up some sort of rapport. Obviously, she had had them tied up and left on an island and had stolen his clothes, but still, he thought they'd been getting on quite well.

'Whatever it was, we'll find out when Osgifu and the abbess meet,' Wat said. 'Should be an interesting event.'

There was a commotion of noise behind them and they turned to see Odo and two other men returning to the abbey gate on their horses.

As the animals approached and recognised the scene of their recent unpleasant experiences, they shied away and stamped their objection to going any further.

'For God's sake!' Odo swore once more. He heaved on his beast's reins, which did absolutely nothing to calm the situation, and eventually gave up and let the horse turn away. He dismounted, and his two fellows did likewise.

'Here,' he handed the reins of all the horses to one of the men. 'Stay here and keep the wretched things ready. We won't be long. You, with me.' He turned and headed for the abbey on foot, his retainer following with no enthusiasm whatsoever.

'Now then,' he said, as he saw Hermitage, Wat and Cwen

loitering in the courtyard. 'Where's this abbess and the weaving nun? Let's get them together and we can leave this wretched place.'

He strode forward, looking all around the place as if weighing it up for demolition.

'Here I am, my Lord,' Osgifu called from somewhere towards the back of the courtyard.'

'Aha.' Odo beckoned that his man should follow, and they left Hermitage and the others without a backwards glance.

'You know,' Hermitage said. 'I don't think he's in the least interested that a nun may have been murdered to stop his tapestry. And that this abbess might have done it. As long as the work starts again, he'll be happy.'

'Really?' Wat said, looking thoughtful. 'What's that expression for when you want to let someone know that you told them so? Oh, I know, it's "I told you so". There you are, Hermitage, I told you so.'

Hermitage frowned at Wat's rambling.

Cwen went on, 'And I further suspect that you telling him that the abbess must be taken away from her tapestry duties simply because she's killed a nun won't be well received.'

'But..,' Hermitage began to say that such a response would be completely unreasonable. He quickly gave up all hope that reason was going to bother anyone, let alone the Earl of Kent.

'I suppose we had better follow,' Hermitage said, thinking that he'd rather follow the horses. 'If Cartimandua is to be confronted, I suspect that we'll be the ones who have to do it. Odo is not going to bother.'

'We?' Cwen asked. 'What's this we?'

Hermitage looked at her with some alarm but saw that she was winking and smiling.

Before they could move more than two or three steps away, a door opened to their right and the figure of Abbess Cartimandua blocked the space.

'So.' The abbess produced a single word with a booming authority that only the body of an abbess could generate. 'Osgifu has dared to show her face again, has she?'

There was no answer to this, so Hermitage didn't give one.

'Where is she?' Cartimandua demanded, giving him a glare so fierce he shied away. If the horses had run at the sight of the abbey, they'd have provided instant manure in the face of its abbess.

'Erm, over there,' Hermitage bleated, pointing away and hoping the abbess would go that way.

'Where?' Cartimandua asked, clearly thinking she was being deceived.

'Over there.' Hermitage turned to look where he was pointing now. 'Oh, she was there. With a couple of her, erm, companions. Lord Odo and his retainer went over to join them.' He was now puzzled by this. 'Where can they have gone?'

It only took a light cough from Wat to make Hermitage realise perfectly well where they might have gone. This was the Osgifu who was planning to murder Odo after all, and only needed to get him on his own to do so.

'Oh, dear,' he said.

'Oh, dear?' Cartimandua was not happy. 'What do you mean, oh dear?' She considered the three of them with her penetrating gaze. 'What are you three doing back here anyway?'

'Oh, it's a complex and confusing tale,' Hermitage said, desperately hoping that Cartimandua didn't want to be confused just at the moment.

Cartimandua's folded arms said different.

'We were just erm, travelling and, that is, we ah..,'

'Bumped into Osgifu on the road,' Cwen spoke up. 'She was coming back here with her postulants.'

'Postulants?' Cartimandua was dismissive. 'I have my doubts that woman is a nun at all.'

'But where have they gone?' Hermitage asked, needing to get

the conversation away from areas where he knew it was likely to go horribly wrong.

'Probably into the abbey,' Cartimandua snorted. 'Osgifu knows she is not welcome, yet she meets the Earl of Kent here and enters my abbey.'

'Perhaps we should go and look for them?' Cwen suggested. 'In case they got lost, or something worse.' She nodded vigorously at Hermitage, making it quite clear what "something worse" was likely to involve.

'Ahm, yes, quite. It won't do for the earl to be wandering the corridors with Osgifu, when he should be dealt with by the abbess.' He only hoped that playing to Cartimandua's authority would do something useful.

The abbess snorted like a bull with a very heavy cold and turned off to the corner where Odo had last been seen.

'Oh, dear, oh, Lord,' Hermitage fretted to the others. 'What are we going to do? What's happened? What's Osgifu going to do?'

'That's quite a few different questions,' Cwen said. 'Perhaps follow the abbess, is the only answer we have at the moment?'

The first question was the easiest. It was the other two he really wanted answering.

'The Osreds might be going to kill Odo.'

'They certainly might. That is what Osgifu said she wanted to do.' Cwen did not sound as worried about this as Hermitage felt. Or as much as he felt everyone else should be.

'In which case we'll be having to explain the death of his brother to the king.'

Cwen did raise her eyebrows at this and gave a polite gesture that Hermitage might like to go first.

With a deep sigh, he did so.

He led on in Cartimandua's wake until they reached the far corner of the courtyard and a small door set into the wall. This was an older part of the abbey, where the original walls of wattle and daub had been gradually replaced with more solid stone as it became available. The resulting construction was an absolute mess, the door clearly having been made for an opening that was a completely different shape. The thing had then been chopped and altered to fit so that there wasn't a straight line or neat corner anywhere.

Nonetheless, the abbess took the handle and pushed hard against it so that the door ground open against the floor behind.

'They can only have come through here,' she reported, making it quite clear that they were going to be coming out of here again as soon as she laid her hands on them.

'Where does this lead?' Wat asked.

'Into the abbey,' Cartimandua replied with weary disappointment at the idiocy around her.

'I suspected it might,' Wat said.'Any bit in particular?'

'The stores, mainly.'

The passage they entered was narrow and little used. The floor was a covering of loose dust and stone with doors off to each side clearly opening into stores. The smells of fruit and meat intertwined with logs and a musty underlay of things that had been stored for far too long.

'Does this lead anywhere else?' Cwen asked.

'The corridor comes out near the refectory,' Cartimandua replied as she hurried on. 'That must be where they're going. Though goodness knows why.'

Hermitage, Wat and Cwen exchanged looks that said they had best check these store rooms to see if any of them had a dead earl inside.

Wat pushed the first door, peered in and then came out with a shrug of the shoulders.

Cwen did the second and emerged holding her nose.'Cheese,' she explained.

Hermitage very cautiously did the next one, naturally convinced that a dead body was going to drop on him as soon as he stepped over the threshold.

In fact, this was the log store and it was so full of logs there wouldn't be room for anything else. They moved on.

Cartimandua had gone on ahead and the corridor was their own. There only seemed to be seven store rooms in total, and none of them had anything interesting to reveal. Apart from the wine store, which Wat reported was very well stocked for an abbey.

'Where would she take him?' Hermitage asked Wat and Cwen. 'If they overpowered the earl and his retainer, why not finish him off straight away?'

'And be caught standing over the body?' Cwen said. 'She said herself that she needs the earl to be found dead, so that no one comes after her.'

'But we know she's got him. And I am the King's Investigator.'

'But she doesn't know that, does she?'

'Ah, no.'

'She probably thinks we'll thank her for getting rid of Odo,' Wat said.

'And if she is standing over the body with a couple of Osreds holding bloody knives, she'll probably ask us not to mention it to anyone.'

Hermitage was feeling quite sick by the time they got to the end of the corridor. There was another door here that they quickly pushed open to find themselves at the back of a large refectory, empty tables ranked across the room, just waiting for nuns to come and enjoy the cheese and wine.

Hermitage could only gape at the scene before him.

At the far end of the chamber several of the benches had been overturned and there was a nun, sitting on the floor amongst the wreckage. Cartimandua was kneeling there, tending to the nun who was making moaning noises and holding her head. She saw them approach.

'This is your fault,' she barked.

'Our fault?' Hermitage was about to say that he'd never seen the injured nun before, but quickly realised that wasn't what the abbess was talking about.

'Bringing Odo and that terrible Osgifu here.'

'Well,' Hermitage wanted to explain that he hadn't had much choice. 'We didn't exactly bring them.'

'More like they brought us,' Cwen said.

'It doesn't matter to the poor sister here, does it?'

'What happened?' Hermitage thought it was only reasonable to expect an explanation of whatever it was he was being accused of.

The nun moaned some more.

'They all barged through here,' Cartimandua said. 'The monk and another man who were with Osgifu were fighting Odo and his man.'

'Oh, Lord.'

'Quite. Tables were thrown over, the poor sister here knocked to the floor, and then they went out that way.' She nodded to the door at the far end of the refectory, presumably the one the nuns used to enter the room.

There was a new moan now, a deeper more resonant one, coming from underneath one of the benches.

Wat went over and pulled the wooden seat away to reveal Odo's retainer.

'God above,' the man complained as he rolled over. He got to his knees and then dragged himself up to sit on a bench that was the right way up.

'Oh, dear,' Hermitage said. 'This means Osgifu and the Osreds have got Odo.'

'Who, what?' the retainer asked, rubbing his neck at the same time.

'It's a rather long and complicated tale,' Hermitage said. 'Suffice to say that the nun called Osgifu and two of her men have captured Lord Odo.'

'Oh, yes?' the retainer sounded vaguely interested. 'And what do they plan to do with him?'

'Kill him,' Hermitage said, hoping that the man would respond accordingly.

The retainer gave this some thought. 'Good,' he said.

The Only Good Norman

ood?' Hermitage was appalled. 'What do you mean, good?'

'I mean good, Odo will be dead. You do know that he's horrible? He's probably killed more people than you've ever met. All of them while he's a bishop who mustn't use a sword because it's not fitting. If anyone deserves to die, it's him. I'm just surprised it's taken so long.'

'But, but,' Hermitage began. 'We can't allow it to happen. We can't allow a man to be murdered. Any man, good or bad.'

The retainer stretched his legs out in front of him and rubbed the back of his neck. He gave Hermitage's comment some consideration. 'I think we can you know. Well, I can, no problem.'

'It is the most awful sin.' Hermitage thought that was enough to convince anyone.

'What's this about murder?' Cartimandua barked at everyone. 'Why had no one mentioned murder of any sort in this abbey until you three turned up?'

Hermitage knew that wherever he went there was murder. It wasn't his fault, most of them happened before he even got there. Just as this one might have done. As he considered this, he remembered that Cartimandua was the most likely suspect and he didn't like to discuss murder with the murderers. They might be tempted to do it again; to him.

He thought that together with Wat and Cwen he would be reasonably safe but, despite himself, he would be more comfortable if he had Odo and a few Normans at his back when it came to that moment.

'We were only sent to consider the issues around the tapestry as you know. We met Osgifu when we were travelling.'

'And now she wants to kill the Earl of Kent?' Cartimandua was showing signs of excitement, which Hermitage always found awkward. He felt that it might be justified in these circumstances. 'She's mad. She must be stopped.'

'Well, quite,' Hermitage agreed.

'Oh, I don't know,' the retainer put in. 'As I say, he really is the most dreadful man. I don't think the world will miss him.'

'But the sin?' Hermitage asked.

'It won't be us sinning, will it? It'll be Osgifu.'

'One of her men will do it for her,' Cwen said.

'Good for them both, then,' the retainer concluded.

'And we will commit the sin of omission. The omission of allowing a murder.'

'Sin of omission doesn't sound as bad as murder,' the retainer shrugged his shoulders.

Hermitage knew there were more reasons to worry about this than the sin involved. 'And the Normans? William and his men? Are they likely to be content that Odo was murdered in Kent? You don't think they might, oh, I don't know, come down to Kent and kill everyone?'

The retainer did at least give this some thought.

'And you're his retainer,' Wat pointed out. 'I should think you'll be top of William's list. Doesn't do to be on any list the king has, let alone at the top of it. Still, at least you'll go first and won't have to watch everyone else being murdered horribly.'

The retainer sighed heavily. 'I was looking forward to him being dead. I think about it most nights. Attack, horrible accident, disease, plague, anything would do. I'd wake one morning to find him stiff as a board and that would be that. Now I get the chance to see it happen, I have to save him?'

Hermitage had nothing to offer.

'We could say we didn't know?' the retainer suggested. 'If we agree that we weren't here, William need never find out.'

'We lie?' Cartimandua and Hermitage spoke together.

'Erm, yes?'

The frowns from the abbess and Hermitage made it clear that this would not be acceptable.

The retainer stood from his bench. 'Oh, come on then, if we must, we must.'

'You will get your reward in heaven.' Hermitage smiled.

'And the Normans will probably be quite pleased,' Wat added.

'Heaven is a long way off and having the Normans pleased with you doesn't go down very well in this part of the world.' The retainer was very glum. 'I assume they went that way?' He indicated the door.

'They did,' Cartimandua confirmed.

'Do they want to do him anywhere special?'

'Special?' Hermitage couldn't quite understand what was being asked.

'You know, in front of his men, in a village square, that sort of thing.'

'I rather think they want to do it somewhere quiet and then leave him to be found.'

The retainer nodded appreciatively at that. 'Good plan.'

He led the way out of the door, muttering to himself. 'I can't believe we're going to save a Norman. Any Norman, let alone this one.'

Hermitage had some sympathy with this, but really could not let anyone face death without doing something about it; even though he found people a lot easier to deal with after they died.

Cartimandua made sure that the injured nun was as comfortable as she could be and followed along. 'I am not having Normans murdered in my abbey.'

'Quite right, Mother Abbess,' Hermitage agreed, although he

thought she should probably object to any murder, never mind who the victim was.

'Think of the trouble,' Cartimandua fretted.

Hermitage was rather thinking of the mortal sin.

Out of the refectory, the retainer quickly realised he didn't have the first idea where they were or where to go. He held back and let Cartimandua lead the way.

'Where will they have gone?' he asked.

Cartimandua simply gave him a withering glance. 'I have never had people running off to kill one another before. We don't have a special room for it, you know.'

Shaking her head, she strode on down a dull and gloomy corridor towards a door at the end. Pushing this open she led them back into the courtyard. Where the place had been a chaos of Normans on horses just a few moments ago it was now awash with nuns.

Hermitage supposed that nuns were perfectly entitled to be in their courtyard, he just didn't expect to see so many of them in one place. It looked as if the entire population had come out at this moment. It might be some ritual of the day, or a routine gathering, but the sight of so many nuns in one place gave Hermitage the shakes.

At the appearance of their leader, all the nuns rushed towards Cartimandua.

Hermitage was already having a bad time coping with the quantity of nuns on display; to have them all running in his direction had a very bad effect. As he turned to get away, he bumped into Cwen behind him.

'They're only nuns, for goodness sake.' She pushed him back, which he felt was particularly cruel.

All of the nuns were shouting at once and it was impossible to make any sense of it. Hermitage managed to get behind Cartimandua, which he thought was the safest place.

'One at a time,' Cartimandua bellowed. The nuns fell to habitual silence at the sound of their abbess in command. 'Sister Bedula. What is the meaning of this?'

'Men.' The one who was called Sister Bedula replied. 'In the abbey. In the rooms.' Sister Bedula sounded as if this was the first opportunity she'd ever had to use the word "men". She was unaccustomed to encountering men, in the abbey, in the rooms or anywhere else for that matter. She certainly had no idea what to do with men, so she had run away.

The other nuns confirmed in their own cacophony that there had indeed been men.

'And Sister Osgifu,' one of them piped up.

Cartimandua drew herself up to her full height. This was not significant but every inch of it exuded authority. 'Where did they go?'

The nuns pointed and called that Osgifu had gone towards the chapel. And the men had gone there as well.

Cartimandua ploughed through her flock like a fox through a chicken house. This fox only had its mind on one chicken in particular, and the others had better get out of her way.

They did so, and Hermitage and the others followed in the wake of the abbess as she rolled across the courtyard.

As he passed along, Hermitage caught a few snippets of conversation about men in the abbey and what some of the nuns were planning to do if they caught one. He drew closer to Cartimandua and stayed there.

Pushing a door in the far wall out of her way, the abbess entered her abbey and woe betide anyone who stood in her path. She seemed ignorant of, or at least disinterested in, the small group she had following. Whatever it was she was planning to do, it didn't need any assistants.

Wat caught up with Hermitage and spoke in his ear. 'If she wants to kill Osgifu, do we stop her?'

Hermitage turned his head, hardly able to believe the question.

'She might have done the last nun round here that died. She's probably got into the habit. Oh, I say, got into the habit, get it?'

Hermitage just shook his head that Wat could be so full of nonsense. 'Of course, she won't kill Osgifu.'

'Looks like she wants to.'

'That's as may be, but there are witnesses. Us, the earl's man, and the earl himself if we get there in time.'

'She seems keen on saving Odo,' Cwen added as she drew close.

'Wouldn't you be?' Wat said. 'He is the Earl of Kent and her abbey is in Kent. He's the sort of man to keep on the right side of. And even if he did die, she wouldn't want it happening on her doorstep. William would turn up and spread her all over the doorstep with his biggest sword.'

They had now arrived at the entrance to the chapel where the three of them had spoken to the quiet nun. All of that seemed an age ago to Hermitage. An age ago and in a world that had seemed to make some sort of sense at the time.

Cartimandua wasted no time in throwing the door open and striding inside.

Such a bare room could not hope to hide the presence of a nun, a monk, an earl and another Osred.

The sight of Hermitage's habit in front of him once more was very disconcerting. He wondered if he might ask for it back, before they got into all the "who killed who" and "who was going to kill who" business. He imagined that it wouldn't be a priority for the others.

The Earl of Kent looked fit and well but had his hands tied behind him and a scrap of material was stuffed into his mouth. From his limited experience of the man, Hermitage perfectly well understood why any captor would want to gag him at the first opportunity.

Odo gave his retainer a very specific look; one that said this was all his fault and that he would be paying for it for quite some time to come.

'Sister Osgifu!' Cartimandua spat. 'What do you think you are doing?'

Osgifu regarded them all with blank disappointment. 'What are you all doing here?' she demanded, as if they should have known perfectly well that she wanted the murder of Odo to be a private affair.

'I remind you that I am the abbess of this house,' Cartimandua growled like the stones of her abbey being rubbed together. 'A fact that you seem unable to comprehend.'

'Did you bring them here?' Osgifu demanded of Hermitage. It was clear that the answer "yes" was expected, and that this would be wrong.

'I'm afraid you have brought them yourself,' Hermitage said, as meekly as he could; which, as usual, was very meek indeed. 'You've got the Earl of Kent,' he pointed out. A fact which he was confident she knew anyway. 'And you took him in the middle of the abbey with everyone else around. You even knocked over a nun in the refectory.' Hermitage was expecting her to ask if the damaged nun was all right, but she didn't.

'Very interesting,' Osgifu said. 'Now, if you could all go away again, we'll say no more.'

'Say no more?' Cartimandua didn't seem to know whether to reprimand Osgifu for her impudence in usurping the authority of the abbess, or walk over and give her a slap.

'And what are you going to do now?' Hermitage asked. 'If Earl Odo were to die, we would know who did it.'

'So? None of us is Norman.'

'But the king is,' Hermitage said.

'Again, so?' Osgifu was either pretending not to understand, or really wasn't.

'The king is the authority in the land, by divine right.'

'By right of conquest,' Osgifu said. 'And he can always be un-conquered.'

'Nonetheless, the king will ask who killed his brother, and we will all know.'

Osgifu sighed heavily at Hermitage's stupidity. 'Well, don't tell him.'

'We cannot lie.'

'I'm sure you could if you put your mind to it.'

'He couldn't, you know,' Cwen said.

Grateful for the support, Hermitage went on. 'And what will happen if we don't say? He will come to Kent with his forces and slaughter everyone. That way he knows he'll get the killer.'

'May I interrupt this conversation in my own abbey?' Cartimandua asked, with terrifying stillness. 'The conversation that seems to involve a sister who is planning to murder an earl, a monk who is no longer dressed as one arguing for the king, and the earl in question being tied up and gagged.' By the time she got to the end of her question, her voice was somewhere up in the rafters of the ceiling, and was very loud indeed. 'I want some explanation and I am going to get it.'

'Be silent, woman,' Osgifu ordered.

Well, that was the straw that broke the camel's back because it was a very large straw indeed. It was also made of stone and had fallen on the camel from a very great height; and this particular camel had a bit of back trouble in the first place.

Cartimandua seemed to fly across the space, her habit streaming out behind her. Before either of the Osreds could stop her, she had grabbed Osgifu by the ear and tugged her head down. She then strode back across to the others, Osgifu in tow, screaming her outrage at such treatment.

The abbess released her grip on the prisoner and allowed her to stand upright. As soon as she did so, Cartimandua delivered the slap.

The Osreds now abandoned their earl and leapt to Osgifu's defence. 'Unhand the queen,' the one in Hermitage's habit instructed, placing himself between the two women.

'Unhand the what?' Cartimandua was diverted from the tirade that was lined up ready for delivery.

'The queen,' the man repeated. 'Unhand the queen.'

Cartimandua looked at them as if someone should explain this. Perhaps she suspected that they all knew something she hadn't been told.

'You will have to tell her,' Hermitage told Osgifu. 'If your plan succeeded you would have to let everyone know. And now, there is no choice.'

Osgifu's face was pinched so tight it looked like the next slap would simply bounce off.

The silence was painful as Cartimandua stared hard at Osgifu, who returned the compliment.

'You know,' Wat spoke up. 'It seems such a shame to interrupt what is obviously going to be a fascinating discussion, but I think there's a question we need to answer first.'

Cartimandua's eyes never left Osgifu and she clearly did not welcome the interruption. 'And that is?'

'I was just wondering where Odo and his retainer have gone? You know, the Earl of Kent fellow. He was over there a minute ago. And the retainer was with us. I thought.'

The Osreds and Osgifu spun round and looked back at the empty chapel. 'Where's he gone?' Osgifu almost screamed at her men.

'That's what I asked,' Wat said, mildly. He reached over and tapped Hermitage on the shoulder. 'I asked that,' he repeated.

Hermitage gave him a hard stare that told him to behave.

'He probably left while you were arguing,' Wat explained.

'You saw him leave and said nothing?' Osgifu demanded.

'Not at all. Saw that he'd left and now I've said something.' He smiled at everyone. 'Only trying to help.'

'Get after him,' Osgifu commanded. 'There must be a door at the back.' The Osreds made for the back of the room and started looking for the other way out. They quickly found a small door, more of an opening really, and ducked down through it. Osgifu followed.

'Get after them,' Cartimandua ordered Hermitage, Wat and Cwen.

Hermitage considered the exit that Odo had gone through, and then considered the size of Cartimandua. He doubted that she'd get through it at all, so it did seem to be down to them. He gave a resigned shrug and got two back from Cwen and Wat as they headed for the opening.

'Does she know where Odo's going?' Hermitage asked as they left.

'Anywhere with some more Normans in it, I would think,' Wat said.

Cartimandua shooed them on. 'That passage leads to the courtyard, I will go round and meet you there.'

'Just shout if you come across a dead earl,' Wat said. 'It would be good to know so that we can stay hidden in the walls for the next year or two.'

Earl Save You

he passage through to the courtyard was not long, but there was no sign of Earl Odo or Osgifu as they emerged. The nuns were still milling about, like sheep in a pen with no dog to scare them into a huddle. They were in two groups though, one against each side wall of the courtyard, as if a stick had been run through the middle of them and they had been washed away.

'Have you seen Osgifu?' Hermitage asked the nearest nun. 'Sister Osgifu?'

The nun looked at the floor and blushed. Then she pointed towards the exit from the abbey.

'They went that way?'

The nun nodded.

Hermitage indicated to the others that they should make for the exit.

'If we can't find them,' Wat said, 'why don't we just keep going?'

'Keep going?' Hermitage wondered where they were supposed to keep going to.

'Yes, you know, leave these awful people to it. They deserve one another.'

Cwen seemed to be more in agreement with Wat's idea of a plan now.

'You've got an earl who's generally considered to be dreadful in every possible way. An abbess who kills her own nuns. A woman who lives on a tiny island and thinks she's the Queen of England. And they probably all want to kill one another anyway.

I've said it all along, not our problem.'

'There is a dead nun to consider,' Hermitage pointed out. 'And the king, who's probably expecting more of a report than "we left them to it because they were all awful."'

Wat shrugged that he really wasn't worried about that.

'And one of them's got my habit.'

'We can always get you another habit.'

'We could make a really nice one in the workshop,' Cwen said. 'It could have some lovely touches on it, you know, weave some religious bits into it.'

'Religious bits?'

'A cross, a saint, perhaps your name?'

Hermitage had never heard of anything quite so revolting but didn't like to say. All he really wanted was his old habit back. His plain, modest and humble habit.

'Have you got them?' Cartimandua asked as she appeared around a corner.

'They went that way,' Wat pointed, indicating that the abbess was perfectly welcome to follow them, while they waited here.

'Come on then,' Cartimandua ordered. 'We won't catch them loitering around here.'

'Do we need to?' Wat asked.

Cartimandua looked as if she had heard a noise but didn't know what it was and didn't care.

'I mean, Osgifu wants to kill Odo and, when Odo makes it back to the Normans, he'll want to kill Osgifu. And I know which one I'd put my money on.'

'We have to save the earl.' Cartimandua obviously thought that this was a simple truth.

'Not sure he'll need saving if we get there after he meets up with his men again. In fact, that would probably be an encounter best kept away from.'

'Then I shall go alone,' Cartimandua announced with visible contempt for the lack of courage around her.

They stood and watched her go.

'She really is keen on saving the earl, isn't she?' Cwen said.

Hermitage looked at Cartimandua's retreating back while Cwen's words seeped into his head. 'Keen on saving the earl,' he repeated as some thoughts waved their hands, deep in the recesses of his mind, trying to get his attention.

'Yes,' Cwen said. 'If he's so awful and is going to kill everyone, why worry about saving him?'

'He is her earl,' Wat said. 'Everyone's got one somewhere. And the next one could be worse. And of course, there's the prospect of William coming here to empty the abbey of nuns and abbesses and fill it with dead nuns and abbesses instead.'

'He is her earl.' Hermitage's repetitions were now soft and vague as the thinking in his head took over from everything else.

'Aha,' Wat said.

'Aha?' Cwen asked.

'Look at him.' Wat nodded towards Hermitage. 'He's gone off to his "Aha" place.'

Cwen stepped closer to Hermitage and considered him as if looking for the faults in a piece of tapestry. She waved a hand in front of his face and his eyes followed, but there was no other reaction. 'You could be right.'

'Any minute now we'll get "Aha". We'll have to gather everyone together and Hermitage will explain who did what to whom.'

'I wonder how long we'll have to wait this time.'

'Hopefully, all the people who want to kill one another will still be alive by the time he explains why they want to kill one another.'

'Oh, Lord,' Hermitage said.

'It's a bad one, then,' Cwen noted.

Hermitage joined them once more, his thoughts now clear and his conclusions reached. Unhappy conclusions, as usual. 'We have to get Cartimandua.'

'Aha,' Cwen and Wat nodded to one another.

'I still think we should just go,' Wat said, as they left the abbey. 'Hermitage can explain it to us on the way home. That should do.'

Hermitage was ahead now and was not going to stop. He needed to get to Cartimandua as quickly as possible, certainly before any encounter with Osgifu and Odo.

Fortunately, the abbess was not a fast mover and they soon caught up with the panting woman as she rolled down the hill away from the abbey gate.

Not far off, the Norman horsemen were gathered and there was some movement and rearrangement of the men going on.

Now, Hermitage spotted something coming in the other direction, quite quickly. He couldn't see exactly who it was, but he knew straight away. No monk could see their own habit running towards them and not recognise it.

'Looks like the plan to kill Odo has gone a bit wrong,' Cwen said.

'Do we stop them?' Wat asked Hermitage.

'Either we do, or the horsemen coming after them will do it in a much more permanent manner.' Cwen nodded off towards two Normans on horseback, swords held high, who were riding after Osgifu and the Osreds.

'Oh, dear.' Hermitage ran on. 'We really must stop all this.'

'At least this will be a murder that won't need much investigation,' Cwen observed. 'If the King's Investigator sees someone get their head chopped off, that's probably that.'

With good fortune on their side, they all met up before the Normans could reach anyone. Osgifu and the Osreds coming up the hill and Cartimandua going down, pursued by Hermitage, Wat and Cwen came together at the same spot.

'Stop,' Hermitage called, when it was quite clear that the Ebonites had no intention of doing any such thing.

'This is your fault,' Osgifu shouted as she ran past, her habit hitched up over her knees so that she could move more quickly.

Hermitage was used to things being his fault, so the accusation didn't bother him much.

They stopped and watched as the three passed them by, quickly followed by the Normans on their horses. It wasn't a few moments before the horses caught the people and the Normans laid hands upon them.

The two Osreds were virtually lifted from the ground by strong Norman hands. Osgifu paused as this happened, but then ran on.

'Well, really,' Hermitage complained. 'You'd think she'd stand by her men.'

'Do we need her?' Cwen asked.

'We certainly do,' Hermitage said.

'Right. Wait here.'

Cwen set off up the path after Osgifu. And she did so remarkably quickly. Hermitage had seen some fast runners in his time, usually because they were chasing him and caught him pretty quickly, but Cwen was something else. She put her head down, her arms pumped and legs pounded the ground with considerable speed.

'Well, I never,' Hermitage commented.

'She did used to work with Briston the Weaver,' Wat reminded Hermitage. 'Running away from the customers was probably quite a useful skill.'

Cwen closed the distance to Osgifu in no time at all. The queen was hampered by her habit, but was running for her life, which tended to make people do it faster than normal.

Hermitage expected Cwen to reach out and grab the habit, hauling Osgifu to a halt. Instead, when she was only a couple of paces behind, she threw herself forward and wrapped her arms around Osgifu's legs.

The scream that came from the Ebonite Queen of England was quite something as she crashed to the floor. It was part surprise, part a reaction to the pain that was going to arrive when she landed, and part outrage.

'Now, that is impressive.' Wat nodded appreciatively. 'Next time we have an argument, I must make a note not to run.'

The bundle of people that was Osgifu and Cwen untangled itself and was resolved into two figures. One of them was lying on the floor and the other was standing on her back.

'Get off me,' was the loud comment that reverberated across the field.

'I've got her,' Cwen explained with an alarming smile.

The Norman horsemen, with their dangling Osreds at their stirrups, trotted up, soon to be joined by Earl Odo and a sheepish looking retainer from the other direction. This time they were accompanied by the entire force of Normans and their leader did not look happy.

'That woman.' The earl pointed his club. 'I want her dead.'

The Norman horde looked quite ready to get on with this straight away.

'The one on the floor,' he clarified. 'Not the one standing on her. Although I might want her dead as well, I haven't decided yet.'

'My lord,' Hermitage bowed his head. He had to intervene to stop anyone being killed. Despite knowing the Normans pretty well now, he still couldn't understand why they thought killing people was the best solution.

'Who the devil are you?'

'I am Brother Hermitage my lord. The King's Investigator.' The earl looked blank. 'Sent by King William? We met in Dover a few days ago?'

Odo looked to his retainer, who gave a compliant nod.

'The king's what?' Cartimandua asked.

'Silence,' the earl barked. 'Or I'll want you all dead.'

The abbess lowered her head.

The earl fixed his gaze on Hermitage. 'Are you going to tell me I can't kill the people I want to?'

There was clearly only one answer to this question, and even Hermitage could see what it was. 'Of course not, my lord. But I think I can explain everything that has happened and then you can take your action.'

'Explain what's happened?' Odo was puzzled. 'We won the battle near Hastings and now we're in charge. That's what happened.'

'I mean what happened with the dead nun and the tapestry and Osgifu and Cartimandua and, well, everything. I think.'

'You think?'

'It seems fairly clear to me now. If I can explain to everyone, you can make your mind up about what happens next.'

Earl Odo's face looked more scheming than anything else. He was clearly trying to work out whether he should have anything to do with this, or should just get on and kill everyone now and have done with it.

'The King's Investigator,' his retainer reminded him. 'You remember the king?'

Odo sighed. 'Very well. Give us your explanation, and then I'll kill the woman.'

'Oh, er, well,' was Hermitage's best response. 'Perhaps we could go to the abbey?'

'Why?' Earl Odo seemed quite content to kill people in a field.

'It's where the tapestry is.'

'My tapestry!' Now Odo was interested.

'Exactly. And I think the tapestry is in the middle of all this.'

'The tapestry being done by nuns,' Wat said, not quite to himself. 'I knew it was a bad idea. I think I said so.'

'Very well.' Odo ignored Wat. 'Back to the wretched abbey. I shall bring more men with me this time, in case any other nuns decide to capture their earl.'

'She wasn't my nun,' Cartimandua pleaded. 'I tried to stop her.'

'Not very well,' Odo observed.

With a nod of the head he brought up half a dozen horse-men and they set off at a gallop, leaving everyone else to walk.

The two Normans who had hold of the Osreds followed on a little more slowly and another joined them. This one went up to Cwen and grabbed hold of a squirming and complaining Os-gifu. These three only trotted up to the abbey, slowly but just fast enough to make the journey very uncomfortable for their prisoners.

'As soon as we get there,' Hermitage called after them, 'there's something very important that has to happen before we do any-thing else.'

One Norman turned his head back with little interest.

'I want my habit back.'

Caput XXIV

The Bayeux Tapestry (Or Is It?)

artimandua's study was a little crowded now. Earl Odo was not going anywhere anymore without at least three well-armed Normans at his side. The retainer was there as well, along with the three Ebonites, who were being closely watched by the Normans. Cartimandua stood by the empty fireplace while Hermitage, Wat and Cwen were near the door.

Hermitage at last felt himself again. The Normans hadn't understood why they had to do this, but the exchange of clothes was arranged and the old familiar habit slipped over his head like a welcoming friend. Not that Hermitage had any friends that slipped over his head, but that's what it felt like.

It did cross his mind to think that someone else had been in here recently, and that such sharing was both an invasion of his privacy, and a possible route to disease, but he had his habit back. Such worries soon faded.

The air of anticipation was another presence in the room as the abbess had sent word that the tapestry was to be brought to them.

Hermitage had said it was central to all of this so thought that having a look at it would be a useful step in his explanation. He needed to take people along the path of his conclusion, so that they would agree with it once he got there. It was no good simply announcing his thoughts without the reasons that went along.

Odo had also insisted on seeing how his commission was progressing and Wat had expressed some willingness to give the thing the once over. Not that he had any high hopes, what with nuns trying to do tapestry and all.

It would have been a more straightforward process to go and have a look at the tapestry, rather than have it brought to them. But apparently, this was beneath the abbess's dignity, and she would not have Lord Odo traipsing all over the place, just to see a bit of cloth work. No, the nuns were instructed to bring the tapestry to the study.

The amount of time this was taking indicated that it was quite a task. Hermitage knew how these things worked in Wat's workshop, and that removing a tapestry from the loom before it was finished was a tricky process. Getting it back in again, without ruining the whole thing was doubly hard. All those little threads had to be taken down and put back up again, the tension of the other little threads sorted out and the whole thing left to settle. It also involved much swearing, kicking of things and loud remonstrations to the person who had asked for it to be done in the first place.

He could not imagine that down in the depths of the abbey somewhere there was a group of swearing, kicking nuns, but he thought that even they would be less than pleased to be given the task.

All the reports were that this was a very large tapestry, and so moving it would be even more of a problem. You couldn't really go carting great things like that around the place. If anyone was interested, surely they could come and look.

Even when a customer commissioned a large work, they hung it on their wall and left it there for people to see. If someone said, "can I have a look at your tapestry", they didn't take it down for delivery.

Nonetheless, the abbess had issued her order and her nuns were following it. In the meantime, the uncomfortable group had to stand in the study and wait.

And this was no place for small talk. The Normans were

glaring at the Ebonites, who were glaring at Cartimandua, who was giving as good as she got.

'So,' Wat broke the awkward silence. 'Do much in the way of tapestry then, abbess? Bit of a centre for the weaving nun, is it?'

Cartimandua almost seemed grateful for the interruption so that she could stop trying to bore a hole in Osgifu with her eyes.

'We have some skill in that area. Hence the offer to my Lord Odo.' She gave the earl a little bow.

Osgifu snorted.

'Until the unfortunate loss of the weaving nun in charge of things?' Wat said.

'Quite.'

'What a shame.' Wat clearly wanted to get to the conclusion that this was just what you'd get if you asked nuns to do your tapestry for you, but he was working up to it.

'We did have another who could have progressed the work.' The look at Osgifu was now positively arrow-like. 'But she decided she had better things to do.'

Hermitage could tell that Osgifu very much wanted to say something at this point but was restraining herself. What she wanted to say looked as if it could be quite aggressive and unhelpful; and probably pretty personal about Cartimandua. Instead, she slipped her eyes sideways at Odo and bit her tongue.

'Perhaps now that our earl is here, she could be urged to attend to her duties.'

Osgifu was now biting anything else she could reach.

'Although what she is now doing wandering the country with so-called postulants, attacking people and threatening to kill them, I have not the first idea. I trust our monk here is going to explain.'

Hermitage trusted he was going to explain as well. He had a tale in his head that he felt fitted the facts, but as usual, had the simultaneous feeling that he was completely wrong. One of these days he would tell his tale of murder and wrong-doing to those gathered before him, and someone would say "no, you're completely wrong. It wasn't them at all, you idiot." He looked forward to that day. Perhaps then, King William would stop making him investigate things.

The abbess had nothing more to say, and the mutual staring descended into shared growling and squaring up to one another.

Eventually, after what felt like several days, there was a quiet knock on the door.

'Enter,' Cartimandua called out.

'Can't be much of a tapestry if they got it down this quickly,' Wat muttered.

The door swung silently open and a nun appeared. She had both hands behind her back and was struggling with some great weight being dragged along. Hermitage stepped forward to help with the burden.

The nun gave him a grateful smile and stepped off to one side so that he could take part of the rope that was in her hands. As he did so he looked through the door with some surprise as he saw another two nuns behind this one. They were carrying the other end of a large wooden box and each of them looked very flushed from the effort.

'Very good,' Cartimandua said. 'Set it in the middle of the room.'

The nuns and Hermitage struggled their load into the chamber, those inside stepping out of the way so that it didn't get dropped on their toes.

'What's this?' Wat asked, as if someone had just delivered that load of manure he ordered but had left it in the kitchen by mistake.

'The great tapestry,' Cartimandua said, with some pride.

'In a box?'

'It's where we keep it.'

Wat just shook his head extravagantly, as if this was the final proof anyone needed that you should never ask a nun to do a weaver's job.

Even Cwen was frowning. 'Why did you put it in a box?'

'It's where we keep it,' Cartimandua repeated with some irritation. 'We have invented a marvellous new method for progressing the work.'

'In a box?' Cwen looked at the nuns, as if weighing them up to see if they would fit in the box.

'Just so. As you know, the tapestry in question is very large indeed. I suspect it is the largest that has ever been produced.'

'It better be,' Odo put in.

'We actually use two boxes.'

'Two boxes? That's all right then.' Wat now added a long sigh to his head shaking, the way all craftsmen are trained to do when they want to fundamentally patronise anyone nearby.

Cartimandua was so enthused by the presence of the work that she ignored Wat. 'The nuns work on one section until it is finished and then put it into one box. The next section to be completed is then rolled out of the other box so that they can work on that.'

'Boxes!' Wat actually laughed.

Cwen was looking more thoughtful, as if there might be something in this, but she couldn't see what it was yet.

'Let's have a look, then,' Odo urged. 'See how you've got on.'

Cartimandua moved over to open the box. 'Obviously, sire, progress has been slowed by the loss of our sister, and the fact that Sister Osgifu left before she could take over.'

'Yes, yes.' Odo wasn't interested in excuses, he just wanted to see the tapestry. He'd deal with the excuses later.

Hermitage could not help but feel quite excited as the abbess lifted the lid to reveal the great tapestry that was to tell the tale of the Normans and the Saxons. He had never conceived that history could be recorded in any way other than writing. Perhaps these nuns had simply created words in tapestry and it would be the sort of work you could read. That would be marvellous.

As this thought occurred to him, whole new worlds of possibility opened up. What else could words be put on? It didn't need to be only parchment. He couldn't immediately think of anything else, but parchment and tapestry had doubled the options already.

Odo stepped forward and peered into the box. 'My Bayeux Tapestry,' he said. Even he was awed by its presence.

Wat leaned over, looked in and turned up his nose. 'What's that?' he asked.

Cartimandua said nothing, but reached into the box and took hold of the end of a sheet of what looked like linen.

Hermitage could see that they were caring for their tapestry very carefully, if they had wrapped it in linen.

The abbess drew out the end of the linen and held it up for all to see. The material was nearly two feet wide and stretched back into the box, where Hermitage could now see there was a great roll of it. He looked back to see what Cartimandua was holding and was simply staggered.

A wonder floated before his eyes. A startling scene of colour and life was emblazoned upon the cloth, so vivid that it made him wonder if the figures portrayed were about to move. It was like nothing he had ever seen before. No painting, no drawing, not even a tapestry of Wat's making was anything like this.

Even Earl Odo was sighing in pleasure at what he saw as he and the Normans gathered closer to examine this exquisite production.

Another silence fell upon the room as the dull light from the windows reflected on the marvellous colours and bathed everyone in their beauty.

Wat broke this silence as well. 'What on earth is that?' he said, as if the box contained the abbey's stock of dead dogs. 'Where's the tapestry?' He looked into the box. 'Is it in the other box?'

The spell was broken. 'This is the great tapestry,' Cartiman-dua said, with a bit more of that irritation.

'No, it isn't,' Wat said.

'Yes. It is.'

'No.' Wat was back to his head shaking ways, this time com-menting on the horrible mistake that someone without the proper training and skill has made. 'That's embroidery, that is. That's what you've got there. Embroidery. Not tapestry at all. Who told you this was tapestry?'

No one had anything to say, but they did not look very hap-py with Wat. Even Earl Odo was looking cross and Hermitage thought that Wat would be well advised to take note.

Odo didn't seem angry that his tapestry was, in fact, an em-broidery, rather he was angry with Wat for pointing it out. Even Hermitage could see that this was an embroidery and not a tap-estry, but he thought that the men with all the weapons could call it whatever they wanted.

'Not surprised you got nuns to do it, being embroidery. And it's not very good at that.' Wat dug a few more inches into the bottom of his potential grave. He moved around until he was facing the image the right way up. 'What's that supposed to be?' he pointed at a figure on the cloth.

Hermitage thought it was a remarkable figure. It was obvi-ously a king, as he had a crown and was carrying a sceptre. He sat upon a throne of some sort and there was the outline of a building all around him. Doubtless it was a castle as it had a large keep off to the left and a tower to the right.

There were two other figures to the king's right, one stood in front of the other and was the smaller of the two. They were all dressed in clothes of startling, and very expensive colour, and even had expressive faces.

Hermitage's wonder was only deepened as he read the words "Edward Rex" above the figures. He couldn't understand how Wat could have asked his question. This was clearly King Edward. It said so. How much more evidence did anyone need?

'That,' Cartimandua said, with a solid foundation of anger, 'is King Edward. He is addressing Harold Godwinson. In the next scene Harold departs for Bosham and thence Normandy.'

'Why's his castle crooked?' Wat asked.

Hermitage started making gestures that suggested Wat might like to shut up.

'Crooked?' Cartimandua almost shrieked.

'Yes, crooked. Look, the lines are all crooked. Honestly, First it's not a tapestry at all, it's an embroidery, now it's not even a very good embroidery.' Wat seemed oblivious of the growing threat that was manifesting itself in the room. A threat towards him. 'And what's all this stuff round the edge supposed to be?'

'That is the border,' Cartimandua ground her words out. 'It contains decoration and animals.'

'Animals?' Wat peered closer. 'Are they supposed to be lions?'

'They are lions.'

'Why have they got snakes on them then?'

'I wanted snakes on them.' Earl Odo said this very quietly, but very firmly and very, very close to Wat's ear as he had stepped over and was leaning much too close to the weaver.

'Ah.' Wat almost jumped backwards. He didn't do so quick enough to stop Odo grabbing him by the throat.

'My tapestry is a very good tapestry,' Odo explained, emphasising the word "tapestry". 'The figures are excellent, the buildings are straight and the lions have just the right number of snakes on them. Are we clear?'

Wat nodded that he was very clear. He couldn't confirm it as he was unable to speak; he needed his throat to do that and Odo was using it for gripping practice, just at the moment.

Odo relaxed his hold and Wat choked himself back into the room. 'Excellent tapestry, as you say,' he gasped. 'Wonderful work. Highest quality.'

Cartimandua beamed, seemingly unconcerned that this excellent comment had been throttled from the reviewer.

'Edward sending Harold to Bosham, eh?' Wat nodded. 'Did that actually happen?' He rubbed his throat.

Hermitage took a breath as he could see Wat getting himself into trouble again. If Odo thought that this embroidery was a wonderful tapestry, he was unlikely to welcome criticism of its contents.

'Only, I thought Harold was captured as a young man by William's men, and dragged to Normandy where he was imprisoned.' As he said this, his words got slower and slower as he saw that they were not welcome. 'But that's just what we'd heard.'

Odo's expression was one of clear instruction in the facts of the matter as he spelled the words out very slowly. 'He was sent by Edward.'

'Good to know.'

'Later on, we have a section where he swears fealty to William and promises that he will support the Duke's claim to Edward's throne.'

'Aha.' Wat nodded and shook his head at the same time. 'And that didn't actually happen, did it? I mean, Harold escaped and swore to fight the duke. Well, that's the news we got over here.'

Now Odo looked as if Wat was spouting gibberish.

'You're just going to make things up,' Cwen accused the earl. 'You can't simply put things in a tapestry and say that's what happened.' She looked to the room for support.

Wat gave the answer. 'I rather think he can.'

'But it won't be true.'

Odo's scowl was of the deep and serious variety. 'Edward sent Harold to Normandy where he was treated with great respect,' he explained. 'He then swore to William. It says so in the tapestry, so it must be true. Who are you going to believe, a lot of chattering Saxons or a carefully made tapestry?'

'Believe what you see in the tapestry, eh?'

'Now you're getting the idea,' Odo smiled a horrible smile.

He indicated that Cartimandua should reveal more of the work.

The abbess beckoned to one of the nuns to assist and between them they rolled up the cloth that had been taken from the box and pulled more out in its place.

As each length was shown, Hermitage was even more staggered by what he saw. It was as if the events of the last few years were being played out for real, right in front of him. Where would such marvels end? Would people in years to come gather in rooms such as this to see a tapestry rolled across a screen in front of them? Unbelievable.

The following scenes were just as Cartimandua had reported. Harold was shown leaving for his manor at Bosham. Then he was praying in church before getting on a boat. It was all so realistic that Hermitage started to feel a bit seasick. He was overjoyed to see that the written commentary continued. The picture of the church had the word "church" above it. Well, "Ecclesia", anyway, it wouldn't do to have something like this written in anything other than Latin.

He did note that some of the words seemed to have been squeezed into the image as an afterthought. They were rather crooked and of different sizes. Having seen Odo's reaction to criticism of his work, he decided to keep this to himself.

After Harold had got on his boat and gone to sea, the tapestry/embroidery simply faded away. There were a few threads here and there, some of them still hanging where the work had been interrupted. Instead of the glowing colours, there were rough charcoal lines indicating what was to be put where when the nuns reached that point.

'The whole thing has been drawn out according to Lord Odo's plan,' Cartimandua said proudly. 'It is his work, we are simply applying our skill to his design.' She bowed again to Odo, who waved her away with some fake modesty.

'So, monk,' Odo said. 'Now that you've seen the thing, what do you have to tell us?'

'Hm?' Hermitage asked, absent-mindedly. His attention was still entirely on the tapestry. Now that he had seen all that had been done, and some of what was to come, the sheer scale of the whole thing took his mind away completely. He even knelt at the side of the box to get a closer look.

'You said the tapestry was central to all of this, whatever this is. Well?' Odo was demanding now. 'What do you have to say?'

Hermitage pulled his head out of the box and looked to Odo with half of one eye. 'Oh, yes, erm that.' He couldn't stop himself turning back to the box with the cloth.

'The missing nun,' he said, from inside the box where he was trying to estimate how much more of the cloth there was.

'What about her?'

'What about her?' He was starting to wish people would leave him alone so he could get on with considering this fascinating embroidered tapestry. He responded as if he'd been asked where the milk was. 'Well, Osgifu killed her, obviously.'

Caput XXV

Who Did It, Then?

ermitage dragged his head out of the box at the cacophony of angry and alarmed voices that burst all around him. Was it something he'd said? Oh, dear, yes, it probably was.

He looked round at everyone, but no one was paying him any attention. Osgifu and her people were looking incredibly offended and were protesting to everyone that such an outrageous statement had no basis in fact.

Odo and the Normans had their hands on their weapons and appeared very keen to do something with them.

Cartimandua and the nuns were simply staring at Osgifu. Then they stared at Hermitage, then they did Osgifu again.

Hermitage was completely flustered as he realised he was doing this all wrong. When he announced a killer, he needed to give people all the reasons first, so that they would agree with his conclusion once it was finally announced.

He needed to sit them down comfortably, while he went through the chain of events that led to the inevitable result. That way people would only go "ah, I knew it was him/her/them/it all along".

To blurt it out like this was only going to cause chaos. And it had.

'What do you mean, Osgifu killed her?' Cwen shouted over the noise.

At least Cwen was giving him the opportunity to explain, even if it was too late.

He opened his mouth to speak but the Ebonites were still in

full flow. 'You're the Earl of Kent,' one of them was demanding. 'Can't you take him away and do something horrible to him?' He obviously meant Hermitage.

'Silence,' Odo bellowed into the room. His Normans now drew their swords, just to let everyone know that he really meant it.

Everyone was quiet, although the Osreds kept up a low mumble.

'Monk,' Odo said. 'Explain yourself.'

Explain himself? What did that have to do with anything? Ah, now he had it. 'Well, my lord, erm, if I may go back and start at the beginning.'

'No, you may not. Start at the end.'

'Start at the end?' Confusing him more wasn't going to help anyone.

'Exactly. You've just accused this nun of murder. Start there.'

'Why do you think she killed the nun?' Cwen asked, helpfully.

'It was the habit.'

'The habit?' Cwen made encouraging gestures that he needed to say a bit more than this. No one in the room was going "aha, the habit, of course, now we see".

'Yes.' Hermitage took a deep breath and tried to work out how he was going to explain all this backwards. 'Osgifu has a habit.'

'What sort of habit?' Odo asked, looking at Osgifu as if she was going to do something unpleasant.

'A nun's habit.'

'Oh, yes, right.' Odo relaxed a bit.

'But where did she get it? That was the question.'

'Where do nuns normally get their habits?'

'From an abbey. Or from another nun who no longer needs it, and that's the point.'

'Is it?' If there was a point in the room, Odo couldn't see it.

'Osgifu has been living on an island for years,' Hermitage explained. 'Her and all the Osreds. How would they know what a nun looked like? Particularly a nun who wore the same habit as Cartimandua's abbey.'

Odo was looking very lost now, and Hermitage thought that he should have let him start at the beginning as he'd asked. Perhaps he could slip there now, before anyone noticed.

'You see,' he began. 'In all of the investigations I've had to carry out, I've found that some people lie and others tell the truth. The problem is that you can't tell which is which until right at the end. Something comes up to make you doubt one story and have faith in another.'

'So, who's telling the truth this time?' Cwen asked.

'The quiet sister. The one who said that the missing nun had run away. Escaped from Cartimandua's harsh regime.'

Cartimandua stood more upright at this and bridled a bit. She didn't say anything, just looked as if having a harsh regime was quite right and proper.

'That's why Cartimandua wouldn't let us see the resting place of the nun; there wasn't one. She was too embarrassed to admit that one of her sisters had managed to run away.'

Hermitage looked around to check that everyone was keeping up. They weren't, but he carried on anyway.

'For a while, I thought the killer might have been Cartimandua herself.'

Cartimandua looked mightily offended at that.

'But she is obviously concerned about your welfare, Lord Odo, and your tapestry.'

Now Cartimandua blushed. Hermitage imagined she didn't do that very often.

'And her name is old Celtic. She probably thinks of the Saxons and the Normans as only the latest in a round of invaders. Probably the Romans as well.'

The look on the abbess's face said that she was an entirely

better class of people than any of those listed.

'And the story of the nun escaping rings true when we think about where Osgifu got her habit. We also have the evidence of Cafnoth.'

'Cafnoth?' Cwen sounded as if she'd never heard the name.

'The Saxon in the woods. He said he'd seen nuns going down into the marshes. Nuns from the abbey.'

'Nuns,' Cwen said. 'Meaning more than one.'

'Are we confident that Cafnoth could count?'

'Ah, no, probably not.'

'So, we have the quiet nun and Cafnoth telling us that a nun left the abbey and went into the marshes. We then have Osgifu emerging from those same marshes, wearing the same habit.'

'Doesn't mean she killed her,' Cwen pointed out. 'She could have bought the habit or exchanged it for something.'

'She could,' Hermitage acknowledged. 'And I have no real evidence that the poor sister is dead, but we didn't come across her in our wanderings. And, knowing Osgifu, she would have announced that she was the Queen of England to anyone she met. She was probably dressed in her fine clothes, which would not serve as any sort of sensible disguise. She needed the nun's habit and took it.'

'She thinks she's queen of what?' Odo burst out.

Hermitage waved him to be quiet; which worked, much to his surprise.

'Osgifu had lived on the island and genuinely thought that she was the Queen of England. She meets a nun on the path and says, "hello, I'm the Queen of England, lend me your habit."'

'Well, this nun, having had the tenacity to escape from Cartimandua, probably thought Osgifu was a loon. She'd have told her that William was the King of England. If Osgifu had let her go, she would have been spreading word that there was some mad woman on the road, claiming to be the Queen of England.

'We already know that Osgifu is prepared to have people tied up to keep her secret. She's also come here to kill Odo, so murder is not beyond her. We only assumed that the Osreds would do the deed for her, but she could quite well do it herself.'

Osgifu and the Osreds were saying nothing now.

Wat put his hand up.

'Yes, Wat?'

'What was all that about Osgifu leaving the abbey and saying she knew what Cartimandua had done? And that she'd be back?'

'That, I suspect, was to do with the tapestry.' Hermitage assumed everyone else would see this now. They didn't.

'The nun, the dead one, doubtless told Osgifu about the abbey and the tapestry and, having taken her habit, it was the only place she could go.'

'The dead nun?' Odo asked, looking puzzled about how a dead nun could go anywhere.

'No, not the dead nun,' Hermitage said, with some annoyance. 'She was dead by now. I mean Osgifu.'

'Oh, right.'

'Osgifu arrives here, dressed as a nun of the order and, in conversation, Cartimandua discovers that she is an accomplished seamstress. So, she applies her to work on the tapestry.

'Osgifu sees that this is a glorification of the Norman conquest and a statement that William is the rightful King of England.'

'If you believe a tapestry,' Wat muttered. 'That isn't a tapestry anyway.'

'That's what Osgifu was upset about. Cartimandua was in league with the Normans and the tapestry was a real threat to her claim on the throne.'

'What claim?' Odo sounded dismissive.

'The claim of her grandfather many times over, Osred, who was exiled there from Northumbria around the year seven hundred and ninety.'

Odo gaped. 'That's, that's, years ago.' He quickly gave up trying to work out the actual number.

'Just so,' Hermitage said. He paused momentarily. This might be the only opportunity he got to let another truth out. 'And, sorry to say, when Osred returned from his exile, he only ruled for another year before he was murdered by Aethelred.' He bowed his head at this harsh means of delivering sad news. Sad news that was two hundred and fifty years old, but sad nonetheless.

Osgifu's eyes were wide and the Osreds were looking at her for reassurance.

'And then Aethelred was murdered himself.' Hermitage added, for completeness.

'So, she doesn't even have a claim to the throne at all.' Odo was a happy Odo now.

'It seems not.'

'And where did you say she'd been?'

'On an island in the River Rother. A place called Ebony.'

'Never heard of it. She's been there two hundred and erm,' Odo's retainer whispered in his ear. 'Two hundred and fifty years?'

'Well, not her personally, but her people, yes.'

'Good God. What a bunch of idiots.'

Hermitage could tell that Osgifu wanted to protest this tale, but she was outnumbered.

'What did she want to kill me for then?'

'A route back to the throne. Get rid of you and William and she could put herself forward. She saw the way things were from the tapestry. She knew her reign from Ebony was at an end. It would only be a matter of time before the Normans arrived at her home.'

'The River Rother?' Odo's retainer spoke up. 'Down in the marshes?'

'That's the spot.'

'They always were funny people down that way. Don't think

there were plans to go anywhere near the place.'

Odo was weighing up all this information. He looked from face to face, as if trying to determine where the truth sat, and then what he was going to do about it.

'You say you have no evidence that this missing nun is really dead?'

'Well, no.' Hermitage wasn't sure where Odo was going with this. 'Until we see the body, it's hard to confirm that anyone is dead.'

'So, she could still be out there, walking round dressed as the so-called queen?'

'She could, but she would have been seen. Word would have spread, I am sure of it.'

'Hm.' Odo thought some more. He turned to Cartimandua, 'Is this one any good at the tapestry?' He tipped his head towards Osgifu.

'Erm,' Cartimandua looked very confused. 'She was only here for a very short time, but she did reasonable work, I suppose. She completed one of Harold's boats from Bosham in good time.' She gestured towards the boat in question, which was on display as it hung out of the box.

Odo went over and examined it.

'There we are then,' Odo stood back and spoke as if everything was agreed.

Hermitage had no idea what was going on. There wasn't anything to be agreed about anything, but Odo seemed happy for some reason. He didn't like to dwell on the things that made Normans happy.

'Erm?' he asked.

'The queen who isn't a queen can stay here and get on with my tapestry.'

Osgifu fumed in silent rage at this.

'But she wanted to kill you,' Cwen pointed out. 'You and William.'

Odo shrugged. 'Lots of people want to kill me and William. Shows they've got some spirit, at least. I tell you, she got closer than most.'

Hermitage shook his head that capture and attempted murder was considered some sort of badge of merit.

Osgifu ground out her words. 'I will never...,'

'Yes, you will,' Odo said brightly. Then his words darkened considerably. 'Because if you don't, my men outside will finish off your postulants here and now. Then we'll send a modest troop to this Ebony place of yours, find absolutely everyone still standing and we'll put them to death. Or lying down, come to that.' He cheered again. 'Ask anyone, we're really good at killing large groups of people. We do it quite a lot.'

Osgifu looked around and got reluctant nods from Hermitage, Wat, Cwen and Cartimandua.

'Tell me about it,' the retainer mumbled.

'If you do this, you get to stay alive, your people get to stay alive and we can leave Ebony to its marshes. How's that? It's just the sort of thing queens have to do, sacrifice themselves for their people.' He nodded encouragement. 'Particularly when the alternative is sacrificing all the people.'

Osgifu was obviously boiling inside but couldn't say anything.

'Abbess Cartimandua will look after you.'

'It'll be a pleasure,' Cartimandua said with a smile more like the lion than the Christian.

'Good.' Odo clapped and rubbed his hands, satisfied that everything was settled now. 'You can go and let your people know they can go home now. Say goodbye forever, that sort of thing. I'll lend you a few men to make sure they get back safely. And stay there.

'We'll head back to Dover and the monk can go and tell William that the tapestry is underway once more. And he can tell Stigand that his nun might not be dead at all, and if she is, it's nothing to do with me. Everything worked out fine in the end. '

'Unless you're a dead nun,' Hermitage pointed out.

'Who we don't know is really dead anyway,' Odo responded.

Osgifu was clearly incapable of moving, so Odo gave a nod to his men, who stepped forward, lifted her from the floor by her elbows and marched her from the room.

The Osreds followed, complaining that their queen should not be handled in this manner, or in any other manner, come to that.

'Off you go then,' Odo now indicated that Hermitage and the others should leave. 'Don't keep the king waiting. You know what he's like.'

Hermitage did know, and was wondering whether he could send word that the tapestry was underway once more, rather than have to tell William in person. He looked to Wat and Cwen with a mixture of relief that they could go, and worry about where they were going.

'I'll catch up,' Wat said. 'I just want to have another look at this embroidery.'

Odo gave him a very suspicious look.

'Purely from the point of view of a master weaver,' Wat explained, looking very honest; which Hermitage knew he could do when he was being very dishonest. 'Your retainer can stay and make sure I don't do anything.'

Odo reluctantly accepted this and left them to it. He bundled Hermitage, Cwen and Cartimandua in front of him. 'I've had a wonderful idea for another scene with me in it,' he said to the abbess as they left.

'Now then,' Wat said to the retainer when they were alone with the tapestry. 'What are we going to do about this thing?'

Caput XXVI

Do Not Adjust Your Tapestry

hat did you do?' Cwen asked pointedly as they walked on the road out of Lyminge.

Hermitage was grateful that they weren't having to go back to Dover with Odo and the others, having been dispatched to get straight back to William as quickly as they could, in case he decided to come and see how things were going personally.

This also meant that they could avoid the Archbishop of Canterbury, who would doubtless be disappointed that they hadn't managed to accuse Odo of murder. As there was still some doubt that anyone was dead at all, Hermitage thought that he would be able to argue his case on that point.

'What do you mean?' Wat was the picture of innocence. A picture Hermitage knew to be only a picture of a picture of innocence.

'You didn't stay behind to have a look at the lovely embroidery. What did you do?' Cwen repeated the question.

'Nothing.'

'Nothing?'

'I swear that I did not touch the embroidery. I made no alterations or changes to it in any way.'

Cwen frowned in a very thoughtful way. 'What about the sketches then?'

'Sketches?' Wat's voice had gone very high.

'Yes,' Cwen was narrowing down her own investigation. 'If you didn't touch the embroidery itself, what about the sketches?

The charcoal drawings that showed the nuns what they had to do next?'

'Oh, those sketches.'

'Those are the ones.'

'Nothing of note, really.'

'You are going to tell me,' Cwen said quite plainly. 'You know that you're going to tell me sooner or later. You might as well get it over with.'

Wat shrugged as if he was only explaining how he'd packed the thing away in its box again. 'We just added some clarification that's all.'

'We?'

'Me and Odo's retainer. He really doesn't like his master, you know.'

'I think we picked up on that,' Cwen said. 'What clarifications?'

'Well, not so much clarifications as pointers.'

'Pointers? If you don't get to the point soon, I'll find a point and stick it in you.'

'You didn't change any of the scenes?' Hermitage asked with some worry. 'Odo said what they should be. He'll know if anything's altered.'

'No, no, nothing so blatant.' Wat sighed heavily. 'Look, all we did was add a few details. A few details that will tell anyone who looks at the thing in the future that the tale it tells isn't true.'

'And what details will tell people that?'

'We just added some features, some things. Ninety-three of them to be precise.' Wat gave his broadest grin.

'Ninety-three?' Hermitage knew the tapestry was large, but even so. Ninety-three was a lot of anything to add.

'It will just send the message down the years.'

'I'm not sure that this Bayeux Tapestry will go down many years,' Hermitage said. 'It's a rather fragile thing after all. And if Osgifu has anything to do with it, it'll probably be destroyed before it even gets finished.'

'Well, this is just to make sure no one gets the wrong idea. They'll see our little additions and know that the scenes in the thing are a load of coc..,' he looked at Hermitage and stopped himself. 'I mean a load of rubbish.'

'You didn't,' Cwen snorted.

'Had to make it as plain as we could. 'When people look at it, they'll see the, erm, features, and realise that what's displayed is not to be taken seriously. If you've got a tapestry with ninety-three whatnots in it, it can't be true.'

'And you think an abbey full of nuns will embroider things like that?' Cwen was grinning herself.

'I'm sure they will, particularly if Osgifu is in charge of the work. Be a bit of illicit entertainment for them.'

'What?' Hermitage asked. 'What did you put in the sketches? What are these features? These pointers? These thingies?'

'Thingies,' said Wat the Weaver as he slapped Hermitage on the back. 'Exactly.'

FINIS

Brother Hermitage will return in The Chester Chasuble. *The first chapter can be found overleaf. (Consider it a free gift, or perhaps some sort of compensation.)*

Don't forget to inflict Brother Hermitage's other twelve investigations on yourself, if you haven't already. (Or pick a friend…)

Sign up for exciting news at **howardofwarwick.com**
(Terms and conditions: not all news will be exciting)

The Chester Chasuble

by

Howard of Warwick

Being the umpteen and two-th
Chronicle of Brother Hermitage

Caput I

Monks will be Monks

I just don't want to go.'

The other three monks stopped their forward progress, again, and turned to face their young companion.

'Brother Hengard,' the leader implored with a weight of despair and some barely contained impatience. 'We have been over this. We did agree.'

'I know we did, Brother Paul, I know we did. But now we're here, I find second thoughts disturb me.'

'The time for that was before you volunteered.' Another monk spoke. This was Brother Brede, who never had any problem hiding his impatience with others; nor his irritation, anger or frustration. He frequently let them out, usually through slapping the palm of his hand against the other's head. And he was a big monk with a big palm. 'It's too late now. What's the matter with you, for goodness sake? We've not traipsed half way across the known world for you to change your mind.'

'It all sounded reasonable when we were discussing it, but that was miles away. And days ago. Now the prospect is close at hand, I have worries that we are taking a dangerous step.'

'Dangerous?' Brother Brede retorted. 'You know perfectly well what's dangerous.' He gave a good hard glare. 'Pah. If your courage fails you, so be it. Wait here while we go ahead.'

'We support one another,' Brother Paul said gently. 'It must be all of us. You know the reasons.'

Brother Hengard remained hesitant. 'It's just, well, him.'

'We knew he would be here,' Brede explained with a rubbing

of his palms to get them warmed up. 'We went over it, and people were asked if they wanted to come or not. Some said they didn't. Some said they would rather do penance in the animal yard and clean the privy with their bare hands. You were not one of them.'

'I know, I know.' Hengard wrung his hands and rocked backwards and forwards under the force of his dilemma.

'It is our duty, Brother.' The final monk, Brother Girunde spoke. A pious and devout fellow, his words were few but were thoughtful and were always taken seriously by his brothers.

Brother Hengard sagged further.

'Come, Brother,' Paul encouraged. 'We have travelled far on our mission. Farther than many have ever been. To fall at this late stage would be to let down those who have put their trust in us.'

'The sin may be too great. Our eternal souls are in peril.'

Brede was ready for action. He stepped over and delivered his slap. 'Pull yourself together.'

'Brother!' Paul complained.

'Well. He needs more than a slap. Useless whelp. How do you get to determine where your duty lies?' He turned on his brother and was now pointing a finger. 'You have the instruction of your abbot and you decide to disobey. Is that it? You know better than the abbot? A man appointed by the bishop, who was himself appointed by the Pope, who is God's own representative on earth. There we are then. You know better than God.'

'No, no.' Hengard now buried his face in his hands.

'Come on.' Brede took his companion by the elbow and dragged him along the road. 'We are seeing this through whether you like it or not.'

Brother Paul looked as if he wanted to do something about this, but as they were all moving again, he held off. He was pretty confident that there would be at least one more crisis before they reached their destination, but bridges could only be crossed once you stepped on them; or something like that.

The approach to the town brought even more fretful noises from Hengard. He started slowing his pace until Brede had to walk behind him and push.

The crossing of the boundary into the town proper was a struggle. The stroll up the main street was a challenge, and by the time Brother Paul had got directions for their final destination, and they were moving on, Hengard had come to a complete stop.

'If you don't move, I shall pick you up and carry you,' his herder warned.

Unsurprisingly, perhaps, the people of the town started to notice that there were four monks walking along their street, one of whom looked like he wanted to go in the other direction.

The sight of four monks together was unusual enough, to see them squabbling and pushing was quite entertaining.

'I should carry him, if I were you,' one fellow at the tavern called out.

'Brother, you are making a scene, and a fool of yourself.' Paul now instructed obedience.

'I don't want to go,' Hengard now wailed. 'You can't make me. Help. Help.' He called to the townsfolk to rescue him from his awful plight.

The townsfolk looked on with folded arms, all of them genuinely intrigued about what was going to happen next. No one rushed forward to the rescue. There hadn't been this much entertainment in town since that old mummer came by, and dropped dead in the middle of his play.

As the narrative had called for the death of the character he was playing at the time, it was several moments before anyone realised the man wasn't getting up again.

That had provided weeks of lively conversation.

Brother Brede now took matters, and Brother Hengard, into his own hands. He simply grabbed his fellow round the waist and hoisted him up onto his high and strong shoulder, carrying him like a sack of bones.

Hengard's head hung over Brede's back and his feet swung out in front.

'Help me,' he called pleadingly to the now significant gathering of folk.

The significant gathering gave Brede a round of applause. They even started to wager whether the tall monk could pick one of the others up as well. He could even juggle them, perhaps? That would be good, juggling monks. One of their number claimed to have met a monk who could juggle once, but never one who could be juggled.

'Quickly now,' Brother Paul called. This was all getting completely out of hand and the sooner they got away from the public gaze, the better. There was no way their mission was going to have any privacy about it now.

Just when he thought they might escape the edge of the town without interruption, Brother Paul was brought up short by a large fellow standing in the middle of the road.

'What's going on here then?' the large one asked. It sounded as if he asked with a fair degree of authority.

'Oh, nothing, nothing,' Brother Paul tried.

'Nothing?' The man was clearly not persuaded that the scene before him was nothing. 'I am the head man of this town, and we don't have monks carrying one another through the streets.'

Both men considered one another and the sense that this statement made. At least the head man had the decency to frown at his own words, it being clear that monks carrying one another through town was not actually quite such a regular nuisance.

'I assure you that it is nothing to be concerned about. We are simply on a long journey and the brother here has reached the end of his strength.'

'Get me down,' Hengard called, quite strongly.

'His moral strength,' Paul specified.

'Where you taking him, then?' The head man clearly thought that the destination was the most important question whenever you came across a monk carrying another one.

'Where are we taking him?'

'That's right, where you taking him?'

Brother Paul looked up and down the lane and beckoned the head man to draw close, so that a great confidence could be imparted.

'I cannot say,' he whispered in a low voice. He also nodded significantly, making it clear that this was not the sort of information that would be handed out to anyone. Not even someone as important as a head man would be privy to secrets like this.

The head man frowned some more. 'You'd better make your mind up soon, can't go on just carrying him all day.'

'No, no.' Paul let his impatience sharpen his words. 'I know where we're going, I just can't tell everyone. Or anyone.'

'Oh, right,' the head man nodded that he understood the words, but shook his head that they made no sense.

'I don't want to go,' Hengard added.

'He doesn't want to go,' the head man let Paul know.

'Moral courage,' Paul shook his head sadly. 'There are many trials in life that we would rather not face, but our duty and our courage must make us do so.'

The head man sombrely agreed with this. 'And you have to carry him to this trial then?'

'It's not a real trial for heaven's sake. It is just something that we have all sworn to do, and this brother's courage is failing him as the end draws near.'

'I see.' The head man gave this some consideration. 'And this end is in these parts, then?'

'I cannot..,'

'I know, you cannot say.'

They were at an impasse.

'Perhaps you could whisper?'

269

'Whisper?'

'Yes. If you can't say, you could whisper. Whispering's not the same as saying at all.'

Paul wasn't ready to split that particular hair.

'And I am the head man,' the head man pointed out. 'I can be trusted. You wouldn't believe the sorts of things I could tell you about some of the folk around here. But would I? No, of course I wouldn't. It's like your duty. It goes with the role of head man, keeping confidences.' He leaned in closer so that Paul would find whispering a bit easier.

Paul reluctantly shook his head. 'I would tell you if I could, but it really is the most awful secret, one that even I am sworn to keep.'

The head man looked disappointed and resigned. 'The lock up it is, then.'

'The lock up?'

'That's right. It's not what I would choose to do at all. Not me personally. But me as head man, I have to protect the community.'

'From four monks?'

'One of whom wants to go home,' Hengard threw in.

'I don't know what you're up to, that's the problem.' The head man folded his arms. 'I don't even know you're real monks.'

Paul was feeling quite out of his depth. 'What else would we be?' He held his arms out to point out that they were all dressed as monks.

'I don't know, do I. That's the point. You could be Normans.'

'Normans?' This really was getting ridiculous.

'That's right. Normans disguised as monks the better to take us unaware.'

'When have you ever heard of a Norman wanting to take anyone unaware. They ride in at full speed with swords swinging, that's how you tell that they're Normans.'

'You could be an advance party.'

'An advance party of Normans dressed as monks? What are we going to do, trick you all into prayer?'

'Not going to do anything now, are you. You'll all be in the lock up. We'll take stinking Gerald out first. It's not nice with him in there.'

'And then what?' Paul was getting a little worried now.

'We'll have to call the town moot to decide what to do with you.'

'How long will that take?'

'Oh, not long. Next moot is in a month. It's a pity you didn't come yesterday, we only just had one.'

'A month? We can't wait a month.'

'Might be longer than a month. Moot might decide to keep you longer if you don't tell them what you're up to.'

Paul's shoulders dropped. He took a deep breath. 'And you can keep a confidence?'

'That I can.' The head man sensed his victory.

'You're not the sort of head man who goes blabbing everything he knows in the tavern of an evening then?'

'Absolutely not.' The head man was mightily offended that such a thing could even be suggested. He also looked a bit worried that this monk might have been spying on him in the tavern.

'And you're the sort of head man who can carry this confidence to his grave.'

Talk of graves seemed to prompt some wariness on the part of the head man.

'Because it is the sort of confidence that kings would tremble to reveal.'

Now Paul beckoned the head man to draw near, which he suddenly seemed a bit reluctant to do. Taking the man firmly by the shoulder, the monk whispered their destination into his ear.

The head man stepped back sharply. 'Oh, right,' he said, looking a touch pale. 'Off you go then, on your way. Let's have no loitering. Move along please.' The head man shooed the monks along his road, very keen on getting them out of town as quickly as possible.

All of this delay had done nothing to calm Brother Hengard. As expected, his complaints and struggles only got stronger the closer they drew to their goal. Even Brede, big and strong as he was, was having trouble controlling the wriggling load on his shoulder.

Finally, with a cunning combination of a roll to the right, a push with a hand and a kick, Hengard fell to the floor, Brother Brede staggering in the other direction.

'Stop him,' Brede called from the floor.

Brothers Paul and Girunde, who were far less used to this sort of thing, managed to grab handfuls of Hengard's habit, before the younger monk could get to his feet and start the process of running away.

Unfortunately, their grips were not strong, only really being used to turning the pages of books, even if some of them had quite heavy pages.

Hengard pulled away from the restraining hands and looked around to see where was best to go. There was a large building to his left and the path went on past this and off into the country-side. He obviously decided that the countryside was for him and hitched the skirt of his habit to free his legs for a nice long run.

He'd only taken a few steps before the arms of Brother Brede wrapped themselves around his calves and brought him crashing to floor.

His shout of complaint was only drowned out by Brede's holler of attack. He had obviously disposed of the last of his patience and was now ready to deal with Brother Hengard the way he really needed dealing with.

Spotting that this was getting out of hand, Paul stepped forward and beckoned to Girunde that he was going to need some assistance. Girunde gave a sigh at the frailties of the human spirit and followed.

Paul took hold of Hengard's shoulders while Girunde did Brede. They both heaved but had little success separating the two monks.

Brede was now growling in a very worrying manner, while Hengard's screams were reaching a higher and higher pitch. They were soon accompanied by cries of "get him off me" and "murder, murder".

The two senior brothers did have a firm grip, which was no help at all when the two fighters rolled over in the dirt. They took Paul and Girunde down with them and all four monks created a much bigger mound of monks of the floor.

Each had their own task. Paul and Girunde simply wanted to stand up again, Hengard wanted to get away and Brede's aims appeared to be very unchristian, judging from the threats he was issuing.

'Stop it, stop it,' Paul cried, to absolutely no effect at all. 'In the name of our abbot and God almighty, stop this outrageous behaviour.' He managed to get himself back to his feet and considered the tangle of monks below him as he thought what to do next.

He didn't have to think long as a flailing leg caught him right on the back of the knee and down he went once more.

Girunde was on his knees and crawled over to try and assist Paul. He only got half way before the tumbling figures of Hengard and Brede rolled into him and knocked him onto his back.

By this time, the tangle of monks had managed to roll itself off the path and was trampling the tops of the turnips that were planted in neat rows nearby.

Paul managed to right himself now and offered a hand to Girunde, pulling him back to his feet. They both went over to Hengard and Brede, who were effectively one monk in two habits just at the moment, such was their confusion.

Brede appeared to be trying to strangle Hengard, while the young monk was just lashing out at random, perhaps hoping that he could manage to hit something vital and so stop the assault.

Paul and Girunde now stood on either side of the conflict and simply slapped their hands, completely ineffectively on the backs of the combatants insisting that they should stop this minute and behave themselves.

From an upper window in the building by the side of the road, the very slight figure of a young woman looked out at the display before her. For reasons best known to herself, her reaction was mild interest, rather than shock or horror or outrage.

As there was no sign of this conflict coming to a halt at any moment soon, she thought that perhaps she'd better do something about it. Her voice was part puzzlement, part curiosity but mostly resignation that this sort of thing was happening quite regularly now.

'Brother Hermitage,' Mistress Cwen shouted down from the upper room of Wat the Weaver's workshop, using the word "brother" as a mother would use her child's full name when she wanted to make it clear that such child was now in serious trouble. 'Why are there are some monks fighting in the vegetable patch?'

Watch out for the whole book coming soon;
it might catch you by surprise.